PRAISE I

The Reece Malcolm List

"I loved getting lost
friendships, prolonged k
Malcolm List is moving

—SARA ZARR,

"Funny and poignant.

—HEATHER COCKS and JESSICA MORGAN,
authors of *Spoiled* and *Messy*

"Brilliant! With *The Reece Malcolm List*, Amy Spalding takes you into the heart and mind of her musical-theater-obsessed, fiercely intelligent, achingly funny heroine, Devan. And you will quite literally never want to leave. Ms. Spalding achieved a feat I never would have thought possible—she made me deeply miss being a teenager. Her love and enthusiasm for the theater are thoroughly contagious. Her understanding of the intricacies and heartaches within parent/teenager relationships is spot-on. And her voice as a writer is unique, honest, and quite often flat-out hysterically funny. I laughed, I cried, it was way, WAY better than *Cats*! Brava Amy Spalding! I just wanted this show to go on and on . . ."

—MIRIAM SHOR, star of *Hedwig and the Angry Inch* (Original Cast) and *Merrily We Roll Along* (Kennedy Center's Sondheim Celebration)

"Amy Spalding deftly explores family and identity in this charming, heartwarming, and thoughtful debut. Devan is a laugh-out-loud funny and beautifully honest protagonist navigating life as the not-so-nerdy-anymore New Girl with a cast of characters just as memorable as she is. *The Reece Malcolm List* sings!"

—COURTNEY SUMMERS,
author of *Cracked up to Be* and *Some Girls Are*

"I really enjoyed *The Reece Malcolm List*. It isn't often I come across books with just the right mix of humor and emotion. Amy Spalding has a knack for characterization and dialogue. I very much related to the main character, and I feel like lots of teen girls who are scared to trust others will open up after reading this book. Heartbreaking in the best way, this book is excellent YA contemporary."

—MIRANDA KENNEALLY,
author of *Catching Jordan* and *Stealing Parker*

"I read *The Reece Malcolm List* in a bad month and didn't want to leave sixteen-year-old Devan's new world of sunny L.A. skies, cool choir classes, sexy but sensitive performing arts school boys, and an enigmatic thirty-two-year-old mother that she's only getting to know for the first time. This book has so much warmth and charm that you'll find yourself wanting a second helping."

—CK KELLY MARTIN, author of *I Know It's Over* and *The Lighter Side of Life and Death*

The Reece Malcolm List

A NOVEL

AMY SPALDING

This book is a work of fiction. Names, characters, places, and incidents are the product of the author's imagination or are used fictitiously. Any resemblance to actual events, locales, or persons, living or dead, is coincidental.

Entangled Publishing, LLC
2614 South Timberline Road
Suite 109
Fort Collins, CO 80525

Visit our website at www.entangledpublishing.com.

Edited by Stacy Abrams and Alycia Tornetta
Cover design by Emmett Kenny
Cover photograph by Jessie Weinberg

Print ISBN: 978-1-62061-240-8
Ebook ISBN: 978-1-62061-241-5

Manufactured in the United States of America

First Edition February 2013

The author acknowledges the copyrighted or trademarked status and trademark owners of the following wordmarks mentioned in this work of fiction: Google, BlackBerry, BMW, Converse Chuck Taylors, U-Haul, Facebook, Best Buy, MacBook, Starbucks, Frappuccino, Cheez-It, Altoids

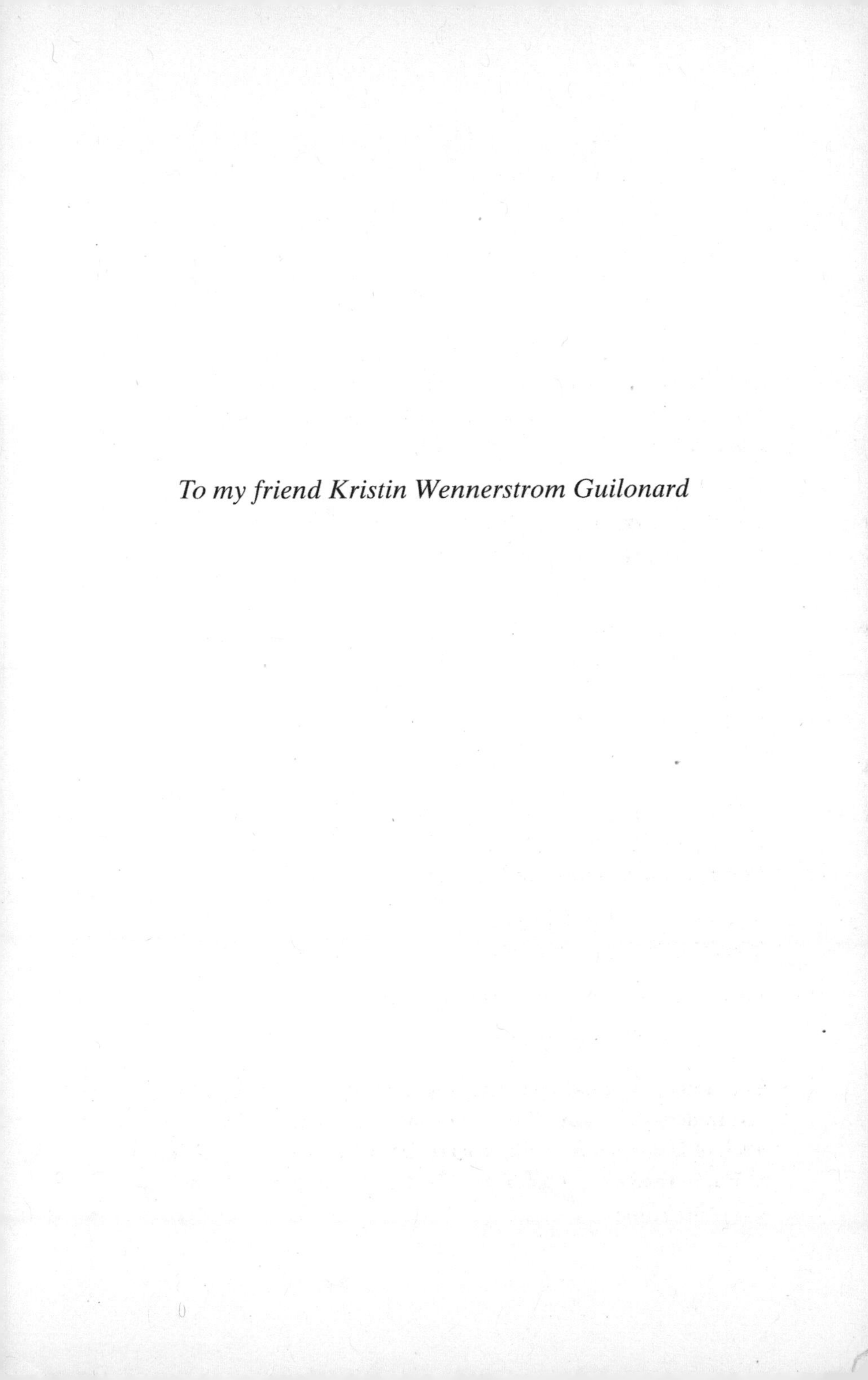

To my friend Kristin Wennerstrom Guilonard

At the end of the day, she thought, there was no difference in choices you made and choices made for you. One would define you no less than the other.

—Reece Malcolm, *Destruction*

Chapter One

Things I know about Reece Malcolm:

1. She graduated from New York University.
2. She lives in or near Los Angeles (even the Internet can't confirm).
3. Since her first novel (Destruction) was released nine years ago she's always had at least one book on the New York Times bestseller list.
4. She likes strong coffee and bourbon, the only personal details she gave in a rare interview with The Daily Beast.
5. She's my mother.

I was in show choir the day I found out Dad died in a car accident. We were singing "Aquarius" right before, which means I'll always associate Dad being gone with the moon being in the seventh house and Jupiter aligning with Mars.

Dad and I weren't close, not lately at least. Maybe really never. I tell myself it's because Dad wasn't the kind of guy who seemed to get close to people, but honestly I'm afraid I inherited that from him, too. Sometimes days would blur by and it would hit me that Dad and I hadn't talked at all. So I know it's dumb that I cried for about three days straight after it happened, if you can even keep track of time during something like that. Mourning should be for kids who have a billion happy memories, like Disneyland and learning to ride a bike and whatever else dads are supposed to do.

Still, I don't think I'll ever be able to listen to the cast recording of *Hair* again. Or go to a planetarium.

Now it's three months later, and I'm on a plane to L.A. Technically Burbank, but thanks to Google Maps I learned that Burbank might as well be Los Angeles. It's very close. That probably sounds like a good thing, but I'm more than a little convinced L.A. is the epicenter of everything superficial and overly tanned.

My mother's lawyer is next to me. Until the plane went up up up into the blue(ish) St. Louis morning sky, he'd been tapping out messages on his BlackBerry. Now that it's off, he fidgets with it, and occasionally he picks up the pamphlet about safety. Since this is my first flight, I'd read it with way more interest. But after trying to imagine myself zipping down an inflatable slide into the depths of the ocean, I figured maybe it was okay to limit my knowledge as far as disastrous possibilities were concerned.

With regard to the airplane, at least.

"Your mom tells me you're a junior in high school," the lawyer says pretty much out of nowhere. I guess he's finally bored with his powerless device.

"Stepmom," I correct. Knee-jerk reaction by now. People always mean Tracie.

He takes a sip of coffee. "No, your mom."

I realize he *is* talking about my actual mother. It washes over me that he actually *knows her.* As her lawyer he probably knows a lot about her. Unlike me, he doesn't only know her as a name on a book cover, a name I plug into Google on a regular basis. "Didn't speak much to your stepmom."

"Don't feel special," I say without thinking, though he chuckles.

"It'll be good," he says. "To be with family at a time like this."

I shrug. No one said anything about me right after Dad died. Not just, specifically, who had custody of me and where I would live, but hardly anything about me at all. Kids in musicals without parents always ended up okay—Annie got Daddy Warbucks, Cosette got Jean Valjean, Christine got stalked by the Phantom, though she did get to make out with Raoul—but I doubted anyone would show up and rescue me. (Or make out with me.) People swooped in around Tracie. But even though I didn't know how to function without a dad any more than she knew how to function without a husband, no one offered to help me figure it out. So when all the legal stuff finally got sorted and the lawyer showed up, that much didn't seem like a surprise. Or even a bad thing.

Until I heard where I was going.

"Must have been tough on you," he continues. "Dad here, mom in L.A. I felt bad enough when my wife and I divorced and I left the Valley for the Westside."

I nod to him as politely as I can manage given what's going on and how early it is. I guess he figures out I'm not up to talking because he turns his attention to the catalogue of bizarre items available to purchase while in the air.

After what I figure is a respectable wait, I get out the iPod my best friend Justine gave me as a good-bye gift. It's loaded with musical theatre cast recordings (the only music I ever listen to, which, okay, is ~~maybe a little~~ totally geeky, but it counts that I know that, right?). I scroll to *Little Shop of Horrors*, which we performed in together back in April. Only about three notes in I'm barely managing not to cry, so I switch it off.

"Did you have to come because you're a lawyer?" I ask. His name is Roger Berman but I don't know if I'm supposed to call him Mr. Berman or Roger so I just don't call him anything. "Or did my— Did she just not—"

"Want to leave the house this month?" Roger Berman laughs. "That's always a safe bet with Reece, isn't it? I guess if you write like that, you're allowed to be a hermit sometimes."

6. She is a hermit sometimes.

"Well, yeah," I say, as if I'm some expert on Reece Malcolm. Her talent probably *does* allow her a lot. I wonder if my talent will ever allow me anything. So far it kind of feels like the opposite.

"You know how she is," he says in a conspiratorial tone, us bonding about what a kooky recluse my mother is or whatever. "I wouldn't make anything out of it."

I have this fantasy of responding that since she ignored me my entire life and *then* didn't even bother to leave the house, there's probably a *lot* to be made out of it. But I never say things like that.

And, anyway, Reece Malcolm has clearly explained things to her lawyer in a way that makes us seem like a perfectly normal mother-daughter combo that just happens to live half the country away from each other. I'm not going to ruin her planned illusion.

I've thought about meeting her. Of course. It's not just that I had the clichéd evil stepmother who couldn't stand me. It's not just that a lot of times—well, most of the time—Dad acted like I didn't exist. Okay, sometimes I thought about nothing but leaving them for my mother. But I never wanted Dad to die. No hypothetical versions happened this way. I wanted a real reunion, not being forced on her. That was the worst part of this. Maybe. It's almost amazing how many bad parts one thing could have.

When the plane lands at Burbank Airport (the only other slightly scary part of flying besides a tiny bit of turbulence is touching down, but, really, it was just a little bump and then we're back on the ground like we never left), I guess I did hope she'd be waiting for us the second we passed through security. But I just follow Roger Berman into the bright sunshine to the baggage carousel like this is exactly what I expect.

I seriously can't even explain how clear and crisp the sky is, the bluest blue I've ever seen. I feel like Dorothy waking up and walking into the colorized Oz, though it's not a witch who's dead, it's someone who shouldn't have been, and it wasn't a tornado-induced falling house, it was a thunderstorm-induced five-car pile-up.

And, anyway, I'm not a blue skies and sunshine person. Life is just life, no matter the weather.

I realize the lawyer is on his BlackBerry, and a woman's voice rings out of the speaker just enough that if I were a dog my ears would prick up. I bite my lip to keep from asking if it's her. A normal kid would recognize her own mother's voice.

"Where are you? No, we'll wait; it's fine, Reece. Great, we'll see you then." He clicks off the phone and smiles at me. "I'm sure you're not shocked she's running late."

"Oh, um." I nod. "Right. You don't have to stay with me or anything."

"Actually, legally, I do," he says. "And it's no problem. She'll be here soon."

My heart shoots into my throat at that full realization.

"So, um, like, what happens if this doesn't work?" I ask. If I wasn't wanted there, and I'm not wanted here, I should at least know what's next.

"You being in L.A. full-time?" he asks. "We can cross that bridge if we come to it. I know Reece is . . . well, Reece.

And L.A. probably seems overwhelming to you, I get that. But I'm sure it'll be fine."

> 7. *Reece is Reece, which never really describes someone likable.*

We're quiet for a little while. I keep scanning the crowd, even though if she were here I'd know it. Not like I'd get some Mother Detection Spider Sense, just that she'd find Roger Berman.

It's weird how different people are here. I've never really left Missouri (driving over the river to a concert choir showcase in Illinois doesn't, in my opinion, count), so maybe this kind of thing is obvious once you've traveled. But the crowd around the outdoor baggage claim is more tanned, and definitely better dressed, and everyone looks younger. Not like I'm going around asking ages, but it's the kind of thing you can just tell.

"You a writer, too?" he asks. He's a very random person for a lawyer. "That kind of thing hereditary?"

"Definitely not. I mean, *I wish*."

"Don't we all." He looks out to the line of cars stopped at the light across from us. "Speaking of."

I follow his gaze, but I don't really know what I'm looking for. A black BMW pulls right up to the stretch of curb lined with cars making drop-offs or pickups, and she jumps out of it. I've only seen one fuzzy little picture (Reece Malcolm is practically unGoogleable), but there's no doubt this is her. I tell myself to really suck down this moment, get every detail because I'll want to remember it forever. So it's weird that she's just this person, one out of lots and lots at the airport.

"Thanks, Roger," she says, no eye contact with me at all. "Sorry I'm—"

"Ten minutes late is practically on-time for you," he says. "Early, even." He hands over a folder to her, the one my birth certificate is in. I saw it when we went through security and I had to show ID. "Give me a call if you need anything."

"I always do," she says in this voice that's, somehow, halfway between monotone and perky. I've imagined my first conversation with my mother many times, but she never sounded like that in my head.

"Devan, good luck." He shakes my hand and gives me a warm smile. "L.A.'s not so bad, I promise."

"Thanks." I try to return the smile. Really he only had to bring me here, but he's been nice the whole time.

She sort of barely turns to me as Roger Berman walks away, which is my first chance to actually look at her, even if it's a lot like staring into the sun. She's taller than me, though not by much—which I guess I didn't expect—and her hair's much better: glossy and chestnut brown, not the mousy shade mine is, hanging to her shoulders. I guess we're built the same, sort of curvy, thin-not-skinny.

And, very depressingly, she's wearing faded jeans, a fitted T-shirt, and fairly grungy Converse Chuck Taylors, while I'm in cropped jeans, a red and white shirt with tiny pearly buttons, and white flats. Up until this moment we haven't been able to share my life, but can't we at least share a duty to style?

She gestures to my suitcase as well as my backpack that I rested on top of it. "Are those all your bags?"

"Um, yeah, I—"

She grabs them both and deposits them in her car's trunk. "They take the no-waiting or -parking rule pretty seriously. Come on."

I get into the car's passenger side and buckle myself in, wondering if I'm being dumb to expect maybe not a hug but at least a hi?

My mother hops into the driver's seat and squeals off from the curb. "Sorry I was late. I'm sure Roger filled you in that it's not exactly an uncommon occurrence."

"Yeah. Um, thanks," I manage to squeak out. "For picking me up."

"Oh." She adjusts her sunglasses as she merges across a few lanes of traffic. "Yeah, of course."

I look out the window as L.A.—or Burbank?—flies past us. I expected the palm trees and sunshine, but I thought everything would be blanketed in smog and way more glamorous than a bunch of strip malls and car dealerships.

A cell phone rings as my mother pulls onto the freeway, and she sighs loudly and gestures to her bag, which I realize is at my feet. Also: soft black leather, amazing detailing, very enviable. Immediately I put a lot of hope into that bag.

"Can you grab that?" she asks. "Sorry."

I reach into her purse tentatively but luckily locate the ringing phone right away. She doesn't take it when I hold it out, though.

"Who?" she sort of barks. I feel like I might never get used to her tone.

I check the screen: BRAD CALLING , and let her know.

She holds out her hand to take the phone, clicks to accept the call, and holds the phone to her ear. "Yes, I got up in time. I can't imagine you're calling for any other reason. Yes, she's here, and— No, I haven't. Your priorities are very strange." The last one is the only thing she's said so far that doesn't sound rushed and vaguely annoyed. I wonder who Brad is to earn a nice moment from Reece Malcolm. "I'm hanging up, all right? I'm completely breaking the law right now— If I knew where it was I'd be using it. No, don't— *Brad*. I'll take care of— Fine, fine. Right, you, too."

She clicks off the phone and tosses it onto my lap. "I don't know about the laws in Missouri, but here you can't hold your phone to your ear while driving," she says. "Not that I follow it. Are you hungry? Are you even up for food? I hate flying."

"Flying's okay," I say, while I try to gauge if I'm hungry or not. My stomach makes interesting decisions when I'm stressed out. "I guess I'm hungry. If you are."

"I don't think it works that way," she says. "But, yeah. Let's stop."

This is beyond weird. Long-lost mother finally sitting next to me, and we're discussing cell phone laws and lunch.

Once we're off the freeway, my mother parks behind a hamburger place she claims is both "a-*ma*-zing" and the closest to her house. I follow her inside, wondering how hamburgers can be a-*ma*-zing, but this place is actually super fancy with red vinyl chairs and shiny chandeliers and a bar displaying—for whatever reason—a stuffed swan. But the only thing I'm trying not to stare at like some kind of stalker is my mother now that she's taken off her sunglasses. Her eyes are brown, just like mine. I wonder if she already noticed, or if it even means anything to her.

Luckily, once we're seated, her attention is on her menu, so I can survey her. No jewelry on her hands and no watch, either, but she is wearing tiny diamond earrings that are way too boring for my taste but obviously really nice. The most striking thing about her, though—well, besides the fact that in most ways she looks like an older version of me—is that she's more like a not-that-much-older version of me. Dad said once that she was young, but he hadn't made it sound like a big deal. But Reece Malcolm is *young.* And for some reason I never imagined that, either.

"Are you sure you're feeling all right?" She looks up at me. "We can take this to go, if you'd rather."

"No, I'm fine, sorry." I force myself to look at the menu, in case her concern stems from me gawking at her. "Just tired." It's sort of a lie, but a plausible one at least.

"I hear that," she says. "How early did you have to get up?"

"Four thirty."

"Two thirty my time," she says. "I wasn't even in bed yet. God, poor you."

I can't think of anything to say to that.

"Though I'd assume you keep more reasonable hours than I do," she says. "School and all. Mine didn't get out of hand until after college."

I nod as a waiter walks up to get our drink order. Two Diet Cokes. I know it's lame to get excited, but I like having it in common with her. Also, when you're a self-identifying choir and musical theatre nerd, you pretty much accept that ~~some~~ a lot of things that excite you are going to be lame.

"Speaking of school, you can wait a few weeks," Reece Malcolm says. "I can't imagine you're anxious to start."

"Well," I say, in no way able to control what's about to come out of me, "the thing is that it's already the second week of school—I mean, it was for me in Missouri at least—and the longer you wait, the harder it is to get into the good choirs. Even now it might be hard, but I'll have a better shot at Honors and Show and whatever else they have if I go right away. Plus depending on when they hold auditions for the Fall show . . . "

By now she's staring at me like the freak I am.

"I mean, we used to move a lot." I decide not to go into how I'd never figured out if Dad was actually convinced a better opportunity was ahead of him or he just got bored with things really easily. "So I just kind of learned that."

"All right then." She takes a leather-bound organizer out of her purse and jots something down. "I take it you're an actor."

"Well, not really, I'm only sixteen, it's just been for school, but . . . "

"You have to start somewhere." It's the nicest thing she could say to my geeksplosion. "I'll make some calls when we get back to the house."

"If it's not a big deal or anything."

"Definitely not." She shuts her organizer with a slam and tosses it back into her bag. "And, God, I meant to say something sooner. I'm so sorry about your father."

I shrug, shoving one of my hands into my pocket, clutching

my fingers around the key I slipped there this morning. (I had to take it out to walk through security but besides that it hasn't left me.) Its teeth dig into my fingers and the metal's warmer than I expected. For a split second, I feel the glow of using it to sneak into the choir room with Justine and take advantage of the acoustics as well as the piano. That had been my first time at breaking the rules, ever.

I'd only hesitated a little when Justine handed over her iPod, but the key? I never thought she'd part with it. If Ms. Stanford realized she'd never asked for it back after granting us access to the choir room the night before state competitions, we would have returned it as if we'd just forgotten. But not voluntarily. To most people a grimy old key to a choir room wouldn't sound like that big of a deal. But to us it was.

"It's fine," I finally say. I figure I should say something. "I mean—now. It's been . . . a while." Three months and a day and a couple hours.

"Right," Reece Malcolm says, though carefully, the way people spoke at Dad's funeral. I don't remember much of that day—because I don't want to—but that tone I can't get out of my head.

By the time the waiter brings our drinks, I still have no idea what I want, so I just let Reece Malcolm order two things for us to split. You know you're desperate to bond when fancy hamburgers are your best plan.

It's quiet again while we wait for the food, and the silence continues once we're served, outside of Reece Malcolm saying, "See? A-*ma*-zing."

To be fair, she's right.

Chapter Two

Things I know about Reece Malcolm:

8. *She always runs late, even to pick up her long-lost daughter.*
9. *She is ~~bizarrely~~ really enthusiastic about hamburgers.*

After lunch I follow Reece Malcolm outside to her car, and she makes a few turns until we end up, just minutes later, on a hilly, winding street where houses jut out from every conceivable angle. She drives up to a big oak house with lots of glass and right angles, kind of modern but in the way I bet people in the past imagined modern would be someday. I'm not sure what I thought houses would be like here—pink and stucco and mansion-sized?—but this is definitely not it.

Since we did move so much, it's normal to pull up to a place I've never seen before with the understanding it would be my home—at least until Dad changed jobs again. With Reece Malcolm's house I don't feel that understanding settling in my gut.

Still, even though L.A. is one of the last places I should be—New York has to be where my future is—I do like this house. If it were Dad and Tracie pulling up to it, something in me would click into place, I'm sure of it.

I wait near the door as she takes my bags out of the trunk (she refused my help). "Your house is amazing."

"Thanks." She lugs the bags behind her and steps past me to unlock the door. "I apologize for what a mess it is right now. By the time the weekend's over I promise it'll be in better shape."

I walk in and glance around, preparing for a disaster but instead notice a few open boxes in the midst of a huge living room. The floors are dark wood, and all the furniture is sleek and streamlined and shiny shiny shiny leather. The glass everywhere ensures you can see blue skies and green trees from every angle. Bookcases line one wall, and there's a fireplace where a TV would go in most living rooms. (Why does someone in L.A. need a fireplace?) There's artwork that looks like original paintings, but no photos at all. Total designer house.

"Oh." I notice the U-Haul logo on the boxes that don't exactly disasterize the room. "Did you just move? I'm sorry, this is like the worst timing ever—"

"For your father to die?" She raises an eyebrow. "Anyway, no, I didn't just move. My, uh, my boyfriend—I guess that's what I'm calling him—just moved in with me."

Somehow I know that's so much worse. Here she is, starting a life with someone, and here I am, messing it up. Not like I know anything about living with boyfriends—or, well, about boyfriends at all—but I'll guess the best start would not include your long-lost daughter getting dropped in.

Plus now I don't just have to deal with her, but some guy as well.

"Seriously, I'm so sorry—"

"Why are you apologizing?" She sighs and drops her purse on the little table near the side door. "None of this was within your control."

That's so different than something actually being okay.

"No, but—" I cut myself off because I'd definitely start crying otherwise. "I'm sorry anyway."

"Oh, God, stop apologizing." She slides my backpack's straps over her arms and rolls my suitcase toward the stairs. "Come on, I'll show you your room."

I follow her up the staircase, down a narrow hallway that overlooks the whole open living room downstairs, and to the very last door. The room's seriously amazing, not all sleek and scary-modern like downstairs, just a normal room with a huge bed, bookshelves, and an entertainment center with a TV bigger than the one in Dad and Tracie's living room—just Tracie's living room now. The rug and bedspread are both striped in shades of blue, and the walls are a nice creamy tan. And, wait— "My room?"

"No, I thought you'd sleep outside," she says. "Yes, your room. I know it's a little dull, and I'm not entirely sure I'm sold on the blue—"

"The blue's nice," I say. "Thank you, really, it's like a perfect room."

"I wouldn't go that far," she says. "But I'm glad you approve. Bathroom's through that door. I envy you for having your own."

"Is, um, your boyfriend, is he mad about this?" It's not any of my business, not exactly, but I should know what I'm getting into.

"I'm not entirely sure my boyfriend's capable of being mad." She sets my backpack on the bed. "But, no, God, don't worry about him."

I nod even though of course I can't just shut off my worry. Tracie had my whole life to get used to the idea of me—and never had—while this guy only had a couple of days.

"Why don't you unpack or take a nap or something? You must be exhausted. I'm going to make some calls to figure out the school situation."

I nod, and she walks out of the room. It's way too weird to even think about unpacking my things into this room that doesn't feel like mine no matter what Reece Malcolm says. Back home my room was only about half the size of this one, but I taped up theatre posters and programs and photos all over, and I framed my mirror with pictures from plays and musicals I was in. It's the kind of stuff I wish I had with me to trick myself into feeling like this room is mine. In the rush and weirdness of the last few days I haven't thought about it until now, and I seriously can't believe I left all of it behind.

I don't feel like thinking of it any more, so instead I curl up on the bed and do my best to doze off. Normally even a little bit of stress keeps me up, but it's like all at once the last three months catch up with me. One minute I'm lying down, and the next Reece Malcolm is calling me.

"Sorry." I try to feel more human and less like a nap. They're supposed to rest and invigorate you, but it never goes like that for me. "Has it been, like, hours?"

"It has been, like, hours," she says. I don't miss her voice really landing on that *like*, just a little bit of mockery to make me notice she notices I talk like an idiot. "Brad's home and he wants to make dinner. I want to go out. What do you think?"

I'm not sure whose side is safer to be on. "Either's okay with me."

"You're no help. Come on downstairs."

I get up, slip my shoes back on, and follow her to the living room where this guy with shaggy hair, hipstery black glasses, and a scruffy face like he hasn't shaved in days is waiting at the foot of the stairs. My brain can't handle the fact that this guy who doesn't look much older than me and is dressed in a faded concert T-shirt and jeans more worn than my mother's can be the person in question. I mean, Reece Malcolm has bestsellers and probably a ton of money and a freaking Pulitzer.

Does not compute.

"Hello, Devan," he says, waving to me. It's a geeky move, but his posh British accent makes up for that. (Well, almost.) "Welcome, it's wonderful to meet you."

"Take it easy there." Reece Malcolm pushes him back from the staircase. "She just woke up, and you don't need to be the welcome wagon."

He shakes my hand really enthusiastically, despite her warning. Up close he still looks young, but at least closer to my mother's age than mine. Cute, too, not that I'm judging my mother's boyfriend's attractiveness on any level, just that I guess after closer examination he seems acceptable enough for her.

"Nice to meet you," I say.

"Brad Harper," he says. "I apologize for any welcome wagoning."

"Shut up," my mother says, but she laughs. She's much less terrifying when she laughs. "Let's go out for dinner. I've had a long day, and Devan an even longer one—"

"Which means it does make more sense to stay in." Brad glances at me. "We've literally had this argument every night since I moved in."

"I usually let him win," my mother says. "But only because he's an amazing cook."

I can feel that they're not really talking to me, so I just kind of stand there hoping I can go back upstairs soon. This whole day has been some kind of exercise in awkwardness.

"Sit down," my mother tells me. Commands, really. "We'll stay in. Sadly, I think Brad has a point."

I walk past them and gingerly sit on the sofa. It's surprisingly comfortable considering how angular it is. One of the moving boxes is close enough to look into, and so chockfull of CDs I have to resist the urge to dig through.

"Devan, what's your favorite meal?" Brad asks. "I'll do my best to accommodate."

No one has ever asked me that before. I like Brad already. "Whatever's fine."

"You'll have to tell him something," my mother says. "He's relentless."

"Um, I guess pasta's good." It feels like a safe choice. "If that's okay."

"Pasta's always fine," says my mother, as Brad says, "I can definitely accommodate pasta." He leaves the room, and my mother sits down across from me in the big leather chair.

"See?" She folds her legs under her. "Try to imagine Brad angry about anything."

"Well, right," I say, because she has a point. Though I can imagine *her* angry pretty easily, and just because Brad is the welcome wagon doesn't mean she's okay with any of this.

"So." She stretches her arms above her head. "After some research, it turns out the school down the street has a great performing arts program, and it's not too late to have you audition for a couple open slots in the advanced choirs, since I guess some kids have moved away and left them. Hardly shocking in L.A. You'd have to audition first thing next week, though."

"Oh my God, seriously?"

"Yeah, Monday, nine o'clock sharp."

"No, I meant . . . performing arts program. For serious? In a high school?"

"For serious." The ease with which she can turn a phrase into an insult is strangely impressive. Dad could be distant but I never felt like he was *trying* to make me feel like crap. "And you probably don't care, but their academic standards are fairly high, too."

"I do care," I say, even though I don't.

She leans forward to pick up a laptop from the floor, and moves over to sit next to me. "Here's their website. I should probably offer to assist Brad in the kitchen, so, you know, do whatever else you need to, email, Facebook, I have no idea what else relevant people do online."

"Thanks," I say, to the MacBook resting on my legs as well as to the insinuation that I'm relevant.

New City School actually looks, as Reece Malcolm might say, a-*ma*-zing. It's a private school with tons of acting and choir classes, and the alumni page features bright shiny headshots of people apparently actually on Broadway and television and in national tours of musicals. In case she asks, I look at the academics page and memorize class size (no more than twenty), destination colleges of recent graduates (all the best performing arts programs plus all the Ivy League ones, too), and historical information (founded in 1979). Finally I click on the tuition link. My heart figuratively sinks and my mouth literally falls open.

Just because I went all geektastic about choir and fall musicals doesn't mean I want her to do . . . well, this. If she's already annoyed about the total intrusion I must be on her life, I can't imagine what she's thinking now.

Okay, technically, *right now* music is blasting from the kitchen, and she and Brad are laughing loudly. So I tell myself to relax for a second and at least drop an email to Justine to fill her in.

My mother's email is still logged in when I go to pull up mine, and I tell myself ~~a little~~ really sternly to log out right away. But I don't. Of course I click on the most recent exchange between her and Brad, though I find nothing bitching about or even mentioning me, just an argument about putting a TV in the living room (Brad is pro, my mother is con). The next email is from her agent, Vaughn Sinclair, and he's sending a snarky fake congratulations on *letting the English invade*. It's kind of weird to see, because even though it wasn't helpful in learning about Reece Malcolm, I would read Vaughn's agency's blog all the time, hoping eventually he'd drop some little tidbits.

Hopefully that makes me smart and enterprising vs. creepy and stalkery.

The email after that is dated a couple days before we even heard from Dad and Tracie's lawyer and then my mother's with the news, so of course it'll have nothing to do with me. I read it anyway. Spying is kind of hard to stop once you start. It's from Kate Logan, who I know is Vaughn's wife—he blogs about her *a lot*—as well as a Tony and Emmy Award winner. I guess she's one person in Hollywood I wouldn't call a sell-out. Kate's just checking that my mother hasn't killed Brad in their first few days of living together.

Clearly, my instincts about my mother's nature are to be trusted.

Finally I log in to my own account, but I can't make myself email Justine. Putting this day into actual words doesn't seem possible. Plus, I'm not sure I've had one truly honest conversation with her since Dad died or she went to choir camp at the beginning of the summer. So instead of trying, I log myself off and set the computer on the coffee table. I feel only a little guilty for snooping in my mother's email; isn't it fair to know what I'm getting into?

"Hey." My mother walks into the room, hands on her hips. I have this sudden horrible fear she knows exactly what I've been doing. "Come on, Brad needs help. Can you handle chopping?"

"Sure," I say, even though knives kind of freak me out, being so shiny and sharp and pointy and all. (Except for the times I've brandished them while singing selections from *Sweeney Todd*.) Being helpful can only ingratiate me to them, though. Right?

The kitchen is large and airy with stainless steel appliances and a nearly black wood table. How am I supposed to lead a normal life when every inch of this place is straight from a magazine? Although, to be fair, my chances of leading a normal life are already way gone.

"Devan, could you grate this for me?" Brad holds out a wedge of Parmesan and a cheese grater. I can handle that. It's nice being in here anyway, with garlic sizzling on the stove, music playing, and Brad hustling between the counter and the table and the stove like someone on a cooking show. My mother is tossing greens in a bowl and asking Brad for clarifications every minute or so ("What now?" "How much?" "I do *what* with the goat cheese?"), which leads me to believe her cooking skills aren't far ahead of mine.

We sit at the table to eat, which is something totally not normal for Dad and Tracie, and not at Justine's house, either, thanks to her parents' weird hours as doctors. So if this whole situation isn't scary enough, now I have to worry about table manners and conversation and all of that.

"So, Devan, Reece tells me you're an actor," Brad says once he makes sure I get the first servings of the salad, pasta, and steamed green beans. I can't believe this amazing meal is for me. "Have you been in any shows lately?"

"Last spring I was in *Little Shop of Horrors*," I say. "But I couldn't do anything over the summer because we were living in this little town without any local theatre, and no bus or anything to get into the city at all."

"How dreadful," he says, as my mother says, "That sounds like hell."

"Well," I say, "yeah. It was."

"This will be a nice change for you, then," Brad says, then sort of yelps as my mother very obviously kicks him under the table. "I apologize; given the circumstances of your father's death, I can't imagine why I'd say such a—"

"It's okay, I say dumb things all the time. I mean—not that it was dumb, just—"

My mother laughs really hard at that, which makes me feel bad for Brad, though he laughs, too. Eventually. And I realize I'm smiling a little.

"I should tell you," my mother says, "this whole using the kitchen table thing is entirely Brad's idea. He feels the need to live like adults, which is something I'm only occasionally on board with. So we'll see how long it lasts."

I nod, using my fork to wind a wide ribbon of pasta around a perfectly crisp piece of chicken. "By the way, this is like the best thing I've eaten in forever."

"Thank you," Brad says.

"Yeah, he's fucking amazing," my mother says in a tone I can tell is holding back a mushy one. Despite the f-bomb just dropped. "Did you check out the website for New City, Devan?"

"Yeah, um, it looks great and all, but . . ."

She reaches across the table to pour more wine into her glass. "But?"

"Just, the tuition? It's kind of crazy. And you totally don't have to do that, and—"

"Don't," she says. "If you like it, that's what matters."

"No, but—"

"But what?" she asks, which is a dumb thing to interrupt with. *Maybe I was just about to tell you.* "This is the type of school you need to attend. Discussion closed."

I don't don't don't *need* to. But now I feel like maybe I'm doing something wrong, and I'll blow it. My place here isn't exactly safe. "Okay. Sorry, I just—"

"Oh, God," she says. "Not the apologizing again."

I'm pretty good at acting, which is the only reason I manage not to cry. I get through dinner and help load the dishwasher even though Reece Malcolm and Brad say I don't have to, and then it feels like it's hopefully late enough I can politely excuse myself upstairs. From their reactions it seems I'm right about that much.

The room's so perfect I feel weird messing it up with my stuff. So even though I'm not really ready to accept this is where I live now, I unpack my suitcase into the closet and the chest of drawers, and then stow the suitcase under the bed.

It doesn't take very long, unfortunately, which just gives my brain more time to think about everything going on. And that's the last thing I want it to do, because I hate the stuff it's dwelling on. I hate how sure I am that my mother thinks of me as an imposition, that she hasn't been waiting for me to arrive for sixteen years, that she hasn't said anything about that at all, and that she seemingly has no excuse for just pretending I didn't exist this whole time.

But most of all I hate that I've spent my whole stupid life dreaming about this and waiting for it to happen, and here it is and it isn't at all what I'd hoped for. It's ~~definitely~~ probably stupid to still think about Dad as much as I do, considering he spent so much of my life ignoring me, but somehow it feels stupider yet to want more from someone who's done way less for me.

All books are filled with words, obviously, but Reece Malcolm's aren't just there on the page. It's as if something living is captured, and reading her novels releases it: emotions and an understanding of how life works. Or maybe it's more like this admission that you can't understand how life works but instead, like, a devotion to trying to figure it out.

When I read and reread Reece Malcolm's books I imagined the person who wrote them. She wouldn't be like Tracie, who thought anything to do with the arts was a waste of time, and she wouldn't be like Dad, who kept the world at arm's length so what did it matter what he thought about life and passion if he'd never tell anyone anyway? But my mother must constantly overflow with creativity and passion and art, I thought. She would understand life and its endless weirdnesses and complications.

But it turns out that isn't Reece Malcolm at all.

"Devan?"

I jump to my feet as Brad steps into the doorway. "Sorry, I—"

"Sorry for what?" He holds out a little plate with a piece of pie on it. Some kind of custard with a crispy crust.

Probably a British thing. "I wanted to bring you dessert, if you're up for it."

"Thanks," I say. "You didn't have to but—"

"It's no problem," he says.

It's weird how I just automatically know he means that.

"Well, I'll leave you to your pie. Enjoy." He leaves the room and closes the door behind him. Maybe the dinner and the dessert and the accent just easily sway me, but I trust Brad. So I assume he's leaving to give me privacy. Still, it feels an awful lot like being shut into a room so no one will have to deal with me.

Which feels a lot like the past three months.

But I shrug it off and curl up in bed with the pie, Justine's iPod, and my notebook. Even just last week the thought of being in Reece Malcolm's house would have sounded like science fiction, so it's funny how this feels so much like falling asleep any other day.

Chapter Three

Things I know about Reece Malcolm:

10. *She interrupts a lot.*
11. *Her boyfriend's way nicer than she is.*

I sleep okay in the big, soft bed in Reece Malcolm's house, and end up awake early thanks to the time difference. I kill most of the morning with a long shower (the bathroom is stocked with some amazing stuff that smells citrusy and lathers up luxuriously like in a commercial) and then a handwritten letter to Justine detailing every reason L.A. is a terrible idea. I end up shredding it into pieces and tossing it, though, because it gives away way too much.

"Hey there." My mother leans into the room, wearing a

ragged tank top and plaid pajama pants. "You're not a terrifying morning person, are you?"

"It's later in Missouri," I say. "So not really."

"Let me get showered and dressed, and we'll run errands, all right? You should head downstairs, though; we've instituted Pancake Saturdays until we get sick of them."

I decide not to ask about errands, and instead walk to the stairs, where the scent of maple syrup hits me about halfway down. Brad is at the stove, flipping pancakes in the air like a fancy chef. "Um, she said I should come down to eat, so . . ."

"Absolutely." He flips a pancake with a spatula once more before depositing it on top of a stack and handing me the plate. "I hope you like these; I did some experimenting with leftover berries."

"They smell amazing." I sit down at the table and reach for the butter and syrup. "Are you like a chef or something?"

He laughs, but not in a way that makes me feel stupid. "Not at all. I just like cooking, especially in this kitchen. In my apartment, I had about this much space." He holds his arms out at his sides and then in front and back of him to indicate a space maybe a sixth of the room. "I'm not sure why people make such a deal of it. Most cooking is rather easy."

"Maybe just to you," I say, which makes him laugh. I think about adding that I didn't think British people were supposed to cook very well but it doesn't seem polite.

"Reece says the same. Oh, and I feel the need to warn you that I've seen the shopping list she's made, and it's quite lengthy. You should load up on breakfast; you'll need the energy."

I have no idea what to make of that, but I would have pancake-overloaded regardless, because these are the best I've ever had, and I tell him so as my mother walks into the room, wearing almost exactly the same clothes as the day before: T-shirt, jeans, Chuck Taylors.

"Blackberries?" She leans over Brad's shoulder to look at his plate. "You're a genius. Where's my order?"

"Coming right up," he says, jumping to his feet. I wonder if he's a little scared of her, too. How could he not be? "Devan, more while I'm making them?"

I've somehow cleaned my plate already. "Um, yeah, if you have extra."

"Are you going to keep this up, or are you on good behavior since you just moved in?" my mother asks.

I feel like throwing up until I realize she's referring to Brad and his chef mode and not me at all.

By now I'm pretty good at being invisible. That's all I really was to Tracie, except for when she yelled at me. And even though I used to feel like the brightest part of Dad's universe, everything kept shifting the older I got, like I betrayed him for not staying a little kid. And, anyway, being invisible was useful. You can't be a weird new girl or a choir geek if you slip right under everyone's radar. So if Reece Malcolm and Brad Harper want to speak to each other like I'm not even here, that's just fine.

"We'll see." Brad sets a plate in front of my mother and kisses the top of her head before going back to the stove. Knowing they're in, like, True Love is a weird thing to comprehend. I feel a weird surge of happiness for them, along with a lame zap of jealousy that I could have made it to sixteen without any boys even wanting to kiss me.

Also, ugh, really? Dad is dead and my long-lost mother would have totally preferred to stay long-lost, and I'm feeling sorry for myself *about boys*?

"What are you doing today?" my mother asks Brad. "You'll have time to unpack those boxes in the living room, yeah? I'm sick of it looking like squatters live here."

"I can't unpack those until we get another shelf," he says. "But if you'd like, I could take care of that."

"*Fan*-tastic," she says before turning to me. "We'll get everything you need, all right? And we can grab dinner tonight so you can see more of L.A."

"Um, sure. Seriously, though, I don't need much."

"You didn't bring much," she says very matter-of-factly, which is true, though I still feel like I messed up.

Brad sits down with his own plate of pancakes, as my mother and I are finishing. "Reece, before you leave, did you see I bought you another headset for your phone?"

"I did see, and I'll deal with it later," she says, jumping to her feet. "Thanks, though. I think we'll be out all day. You can keep yourself occupied?"

"I'll manage. Give me five minutes and I'll fix your phone before you go."

My mother rolls her eyes but sits back down as Brad dashes out of the room. "Have you been to L.A. before?"

I shake my head.

"So no requests on where we shop or eat?"

I shake my head again, as Brad walks back into the

room with my mother's phone and a bag from Best Buy. "I hope you don't lose this one."

"Well, so do I." She gets up to pour coffee into a travel mug. "How bad will the Grove be on a Saturday?"

"Pretty bad," Brad says, while configuring the phone with the tiny earpiece headset. "Can you wait until Monday? Considering your hatred of both shopping and other people . . . "

"I really don't want to wait. Devan's audition is first thing Monday, and I'd like to have her more settled before then. My coffee will keep me sane."

Brad laughs at that and hands her the phone. "Here you are, love. Devan, please steer her away from large crowds if you can."

I laugh like I'm part of their inside-jokes, but I probably just look a little crazy.

My mother and I walk silently out to the garage to her car. She pulls out onto the winding road and then back to the busy street we were on yesterday.

"Coffee before we attempt this?" she asks.

"Don't you already have coffee?"

"Oh, please." She gestures to her travel mug. "I'll be done with this by the time the stoplight changes to green. Some might say I have a bit of a problem."

"Like caffeine addiction?"

"Brad says there should be a twelve-step program." She pulls over and parks by the curb off the busy street. I can't wrap my brain around how many shops and restaurants and cars and people there are everywhere. "He has a point."

I walk with her down the block to a tiny, dimly lit coffee

shop. Way more my mother's style, I can tell, than some happy and bright coffee chain. And, to be fair, it smells amazing, and they make my mother's coffee without her even having to order it (something with four shots of espresso and foam only, while I stick with something frosty and chocolaty).

"So this is my list so far." My mother takes a folded-up piece of paper out of her purse and hands it over to me. "You're only allowed two vetoes."

Okay, this is the thing: I know that I don't want my mother spending much money on me, especially after finding out about school tuition. But? I really really really like shopping. Yes, there is more to life, like love and art and creativity and passion and a lot of big things I hope I'll eventually experience, but there's also the promise of being a newer, better you once you discover the perfect article of clothing or random accessory that suddenly perks up the way everyone sees you. I hope that isn't superficial because I feel it deeper than it sounds.

It's very rock and a hard place. Guilt and a shopping spree. Fear and the new Fall lines. If I were a character in a musical, there would totally be a song devoted to my current inner conflict.

"It, um, I guess it all looks okay to me," I say. "If that's fine with you."

"Well." She holds open the coffee shop door for me so we can walk back to her car. "You need it."

In less than twenty-four hours I've really begun to hate the word *need*.

The Grove turns out to be a mall that's all outside in the

warm sunshine. I want to hate it for being so ridiculously L.A., especially since my mother clearly does, given her cursing about the crowded parking garage and the swarms of people. It's nice, though.

I figure my mother won't be thrilled about shopping, but she stays with me, carries all my possibilities to the dressing room, and even offers up opinions when I'm not sure ("too weird" and "a-fucking-dorable" are my favorites). She doesn't flinch at all at prices even though I do, a lot. Obviously Reece Malcolm does okay, money-wise.

Not like that automatically makes it okay. It would be different if she wanted to instead of feeling like she has to. Yeah, I'm staring at my reflection in the fitting room mirror, looking better than usual in clothes I love that I haven't had to seek out on the clearance rack. Yeah, my mother—of all people—is offering up opinions like we're in on this together. But it's like a pretend good day, since I have to block everything else out of my mind just to sort of enjoy it (okay, to totally enjoy it).

We carry the shopping bags to her car but walk back so we can eat lunch at the Farmer's Market, which looks more like a regular food court to me, just outdoors. We both get Mexican and manage to find an open table in the crowd.

"Thank you, seriously, so much for everything," I say, munching on some chips *sans* salsa. Spicy things worry me. "You totally didn't have to do so much."

She shrugs as she takes a huge bite of an enchilada. "You needed things."

Of course I'm baiting her to get the response I want. *I'm happy to do this for you* or *You deserve all of this* or even *I have a lot to make up for.* I want to be mad at her for not saying any of that, but obviously I know she *isn't* happy to be doing this and that I *don't* deserve so much and maybe she has a lot to make up for but mothers who only show up when they're legally required to won't see it that way.

"Do you need to do anything to prepare for your audition on Monday?" she asks.

"I guess it'd be nice to do some vocal warm-ups," I say. "But you don't have a piano, so I'll be fine."

"Hmmm." She digs her phone out of her bag. "I do have friends with pianos, though. Let me see what I can do."

"You don't have to—"

She's already calling. "Hey, it's me. Are you free tomorrow? No, I wondered if Devan could use your music room. Auditions Monday for school. Right. I'm aware. *Fan*-tastic, we'll see you then."

She clicks her phone off and tosses it back into her bag. "You're set."

"It's really okay?"

"I hate to put any pressure on you, but competition seems pretty cutthroat at New City. You should have every possible advantage."

I shrug, trying to look modest. "I usually do pretty well in auditions. It's, like, my one skill."

"And, *like*, a good one to have," she says. "Whereas I make terrible first impressions, and am therefore lucky to have a career where they don't matter."

It's the first thing she's said even *sort of* about her books. I guess I could take it as an opening, but I'm not quite ready to mention the dedication. My dedication. We're only twenty-four hours in, after all.

"So I feel like we should go out tonight," she says. "You should see more of L.A., and despite my love of Brad's cooking, all the domesticity is starting to get to me."

"Um, okay, if you want."

"It's a *lot* of togetherness," she says, and I'm worried for a moment she means me. "He's there when I go to sleep and he's there when I wake up, and we eat almost every dinner together, and—" She kind of cuts herself off and chugs a bunch of soda. "God, sorry. I doubt you want to hear the minutiae of my relationship."

"It's fine," I say, like we're on *Sex and the City* or something. "Brad's nice, though."

"Oh, God, yeah. I'm dating a Boy Scout. I feel like handing him badges when he takes care of things so eagerly." She laughs really loudly at that. "Seriously, let me shut up about this. I promise I'm not one of those people who wants to sit around and *dish* about her damn boyfriend. Anyway. I can always kick him out if it gets to be too much."

I'm going to be around all the time, too, so does that mean she'll kick *me* out if *I* get to be too much?

"I really am sorry about timing," I say, softly. "Since he just moved in and all. I know it must be pretty crappy."

"Don't look at it like that," she says. "You have enough on your plate."

In other words, it must be pretty crappy indeed.

After we finish eating, we knock out the rest of the list and head back to her car. I thank her when it doesn't feel awkward and stay quiet the rest of the time. Lunch must have been some kind of anomaly. As surreal as it is listening to my mother at all, much less regarding her Boy Scout of a boyfriend, now I kind of miss it. You know things aren't great when an awkward moment is what you're longing for.

"This is it, right?" I ask as we head to her car again. "I feel like this is a lot."

The air seems thick with silence, which is why I decide to tack on another "Right?"

"For now, sure," she says as we get into the car and she begins navigating out of the garage. "Let's go home so you can organize all of this. Hopefully Brad—"

She stops as her phone rings. I automatically dig it and her headset out of her bag without asking, which hopefully isn't overstepping any boundaries. Or just plain weird.

"Thanks," she tells me, clicking on the phone. "Hey, I was just theorizing to Devan about how nice it would be if you'd already gotten those shelves and unpacked your—*fan*-tastic. No, we're heading back now, no, I didn't kill anyone, yes, we had lunch already, and yes, I'm using my damn headset. Oh? No, it's perfect; Devan and I are going out tonight anyway. See you in a while."

She tosses everything back at me. "He gets a merit badge in shelf-purchasing."

"And headset-programming."

She laughs. "Right."

"Is it, like, a rude question to ask how you met?" I hardly understand how anyone meets anyone. How are you just a person going about things in your life when suddenly another person becomes more to you? I never look at boys like possibilities that way.

"My friends had a party, we were both there, I thought nothing of it, but he somehow commandeered my number from someone and called me the next day. We sort of ended up going out every night for a couple of weeks, so it was Instant Relationship. Not my style, but sometimes life falls into place and you just have to accept it."

For someone like Reece Malcolm, who has everything a person could want, life probably works like that all the time. For someone like me, I'm pretty sure it'll never be that easy.

Chapter Four

Things I know about Reece Malcolm:

12. Even though she has no personal style, she's pretty good at shopping.

I get up early again on Sunday and get dressed in one of my new outfits—perfectly cut jeans and a strappy but super-casual sleeveless top—before sitting down with the laptop my mother insisted I needed for school. It's exhausting deciding what's worse: accepting all the money she spent on me or arguing against it. Okay, I never actually argued. If I'm stuck here against my mother's wishes, an amazing wardrobe at least cheers me up and hopefully looks like I'm learning to stop apologizing.

"Good morning, Devan." Brad knocks on the doorframe

and stands a very respectful distance from the actual doorway. “Breakfast?”

“If you’re making it anyway,” I say.

“Always on the weekends.” He nods at the MacBook. “How’s the computer?”

“I can’t get the Internet to work, but good otherwise.”

“May I?” He gestures to the doorway like he’s a vampire who has to be invited in.

“Yeah, of course.”

He sits down on the floor and takes the laptop from me. “How was your night?”

“Really good; the restaurant was so nice.” I don’t mention that my mother and I didn’t talk much, especially because I’m sure it’s my fault as much as hers. It would just be better if one of us was good at conversation, period. Justine is so far the only person I’ve ever communicated well with, and even that didn’t totally last.

“Here you are.” Brad hands the computer back to me. “I know at some point today you’re going with Reece to Kate and Vaughn’s so that you can prepare for your audition—”

Wait, *that’s* where I’m going?

“—but if you need anything for your room or to settle in otherwise, let one of us know. I’m happy to take you to pick up anything remaining.”

“Oh, um, sure.” I doubt I’ll ask my long-lost mother’s boyfriend to take me shopping, but the offer’s nice.

“We may be able to drag along Reece as well, but you may have noticed her patience is a bit lacking when it comes to shopping.”

"She was totally fine yesterday," I say. "I can't believe how much she got me. It's kind of crazy."

"For such a restrained person, she does go a bit overboard at times," he says. "For her birthday I bought her a new coffeemaker, and then for mine she had my car stereo upgraded quite dramatically. I, understandably, felt a bit lacking in comparison."

"Yeah, but she seems to take coffee really, really seriously," I say. "So probably it totally evened out."

"You've a point. I'll call you when breakfast is ready." He leaves the room, and I pull up my email, praying that Justine has written.

TO: its_our_time@email.com
FROM: defying_gravity@email.com
SUBJECT: L.A.!!
Hi Devan,
What's L.A. like? Amazing?
You won't believe it but Noah called and wants to meet up soon. Details to follow . . . Call me if you can!
Love, Justine

I wonder if I'm a bad friend for being pretty much over Justine's drama with The Tenor she met at camp. Justine was the best friend I've ever had, but something shifted when Dad died and I didn't know how to talk about it. "You'll feel better if you *talk to me*," she said, and often. And probably she was right.

But I didn't know how to explain the tangled mess of emotions heavy in my heart, and even worse I couldn't find the words to define what was the hardest for me, the idea of peeling back my outsides and letting people *just know* what I feel. That stuff is all easy for Justine; she cries over greeting cards and freaking pet food commercials, and she tells me everything. It took five minutes alone for her to detail what she thought the first moment she saw The Tenor. I probably can't even fill five minutes with explanations of what and how I feel. Dreams of New York and Tony Awards are one thing. The deeper stuff is another story I seriously don't know how to tell.

So it's pretty easy to guess things shifted even further from wherever it was they started—best friends forever?—over the three weeks she was away at camp. Then again, if even one boy had ever so much as breathed on me, maybe I would be more understanding.

After breakfast I help with dishes again and then sort of assist Brad organizing the CDs and records from the remaining boxes onto the new shelf. He clearly doesn't actually need my help but is nice enough not to state the obvious.

My mother sits near us in her leather chair with her laptop, glaring at the screen and occasionally typing. At some point it hits me that I'm probably witnessing her at work on a future bestselling novel, which feels pretty special.

Back in freshman English for extra credit we could write an essay about a modern classic. I already had an A, but extra credit always seemed stupid to turn down, plus the shelf of books to choose from looked way more interesting than slogging through *The Odyssey*. I picked a book, *Destruction*, completely at random (okay, not *completely* at random—I liked the cover) but once I opened it, I wondered if a higher power—Fate? God? . . . My English teacher?—was at work.

To Devan, the dedication read. *While our paths may never cross, be sure you've never left my mind.*

Back then—and my whole life leading up to it—I basically assumed every woman of a certain age was my mother. I didn't know her name or have any photos, so I did a lot of guessing. If she had mousy brown hair or brown eyes, total mom contender. All that and a little younger than Dad and Tracie? Bonus points. I never knew when I'd turn a corner and smack right into her. And we would know, and it would be amazing.

I'm aware that sounds more than a little crazy, but when no one tells you anything, what are you supposed to think? There never was a big talk; I just always knew Tracie wasn't my mother. As I got older and overheard things and figured out the timeline of events, there was enough to put together: Dad cheated on Tracie when he was away at college, and it resulted in me. Lucky us. Maybe without my existence Tracie could have gotten over Dad's mistake, but instead she had to see me every single day.

It was probably even worse that she couldn't have her own kids. When I was little I kept expecting to eventually get a younger brother or sister, and I asked Tracie about it once. Of course it was a super invasive question but at the time I didn't know that. Little kids think super invasive questions are just part of conversation. It was a long time ago but I still remember how she completely froze.

"You think that's funny?" she asked. "You think you'd be here if I could?"

I mean, *of course* she hates me.

So, okay, maybe it was jumping to conclusions to assume Reece Malcolm, who wrote this book, was my mother. But on the other hand, my name isn't exactly common. Plus the only other thing Dad ever said about my mother, besides that she was younger, was that she liked to write. It was a big leap from liking to write to writing an award-winning bestseller, but my brain makes big jumps all the time. And Dad had gone to college in New York, and Reece Malcolm's bio in the back of the book confirmed she went to college in New York, too.

So I tested out this theory. I took *Destruction* out at home where Tracie could see me. Honestly, I was prepared for her not to react at all. By then I was used to having crazy thoughts about who might or might not be my mother.

So I literally jumped when she swiped the book from my hands.

"I can't believe you'd read this in front of me," she said. Like I knew for sure and planned it. Sometimes Tracie gave me way too much credit.

But also—I realized that meant it was true. For once I hadn't put way too much stock in my imagination. That book was written by *my mother.* My mother was an actual person who actually existed and I finally had tangible proof of that. My mother dedicated a book—a *modern classic* to me.

"What, you have nothing to say about this?" Tracie asked.

I hadn't meant to say nothing. I just couldn't stop

thinking about Reece Malcolm. "I didn't— No one told me—"

"Right," she said. "Did your dad brag or something?"

"Dad's never said anything."

"I don't want to see you with that again," Tracie said. But the next time we went shopping I slipped into Barnes & Noble to buy my own copy.

I never said a word to anyone about it, most especially to Dad. I promised myself that eventually I would. I wouldn't stay silent and I wouldn't hint around and I wouldn't change the subject if I got nervous. Just because he didn't want to tell me didn't mean he didn't have to. Except now Dad's gone and I'm here and it's way way way too late.

❀ ❀ ❀

We're all supposed to go to Vaughn and Kate's that evening—which is why I switch out my jeans for a skirt that matches my new shirt—but as we're getting ready to leave Brad suddenly remembers some work he has to finish before Monday morning. From my mother's raised eyebrows I know she thinks he's lying, but she says nothing except that she'll meet me in the garage. I take that as a hint and head out ahead of her.

My mother walks in behind me a couple minutes later and points to the passenger side. "Get in; it's just us."

"Is that okay?" I ask, only because her eyebrows aren't quite in place and she's stomping a little.

"Of course." She gets into the car and slams the door. "It's just—"

"Just what?"

"Just that you are not my sounding board for all things Brad-annoyance-related," she says. "I apologize. Moving on."

Except neither of us says anything else.

This time we turn off one winding road onto another one even more winding (and another one I recognize from pop culture or whatever, Mulholland), and then progressively hillier ones like we're in the middle of nowhere until we pull up to this house straight out of a fancy Hollywood party—or at least how they look in movies, absolute cliché. Walls in earth tones, like a makeup palette and not at all what houses are normally colored like, a flat roof like a warehouse, and giant windows all over.

"Right?" My mother catches my gaze. "I call it the Logan-Sinclair Compound. It's ridiculous."

"I'm glad you have a normal house."

"God, me, too. Come on." She jumps out of the car and walks up the driveway, me right on her heels. "I should warn you . . ."

"What?"

"They're a lot to take. Separately, together, in groups, one-on-one. They're my best friends, but I won't act like that isn't true. So." She rings the doorbell.

The door opens so quickly it's like someone was waiting on the other side. A woman at least a few years older than my mother with very artfully messy light brown hair and huge green eyes who all at once looks just like Kate Logan and yet smaller and different, somehow, rushes out and throws her arms around my mother. Up until then I truly couldn't imagine *anyone* hugging Reece Malcolm. Maybe when you're famous you can get away with more?

Actually I guess to most people, Kate Logan isn't super famous. She's been in, seriously, dozens of Broadway shows (if you count the ones that only lasted a few performances) and sung on a ton of cast recordings. Now she lives here, obviously, and acts in TV shows and sometimes little parts in movies. Probably a lot of people won't know who you're talking about if you mention Kate Logan, but to me she's a huge star.

"Hey, sweetie, you look great," she says to my mother. "I presume cohabitation is treating you well."

"It's feeding me well, at least. This is Devan. Devan, this is my friend Kate."

"Devan, it's so wonderful to meet you." Kate grasps both my hands in hers. "Come on in, dinner's very nearly ready. Brad couldn't make it?"

"Don't ask," my mother says.

"I'm not asking right now." She giggles at her own joke, when a man I recognize as Vaughn—thank you, Google—walks into the room. He's also shorter than I expected. His brown hair is thinning a little, which you can't tell in photos, but his smile is one of those mega-watt ones I'd kill for, and he moves with ease, like nothing in life is uncomfortable.

I'd kill for that, too.

"Malcolm, good to see ya." He crosses the room to join us and leans in to kiss my mother's cheek. "Where's your English schoolboy?"

"Shut up, Vaughn. This is Devan. Devan, this is Vaughn Sinclair, who I'm ashamed to tell you is also my agent."

I pretend like that's news to me and shake his hand. "Nice to meet you."

"You too, kid. How's L.A. treating you? You see anything besides the Valley yet? A shame your mom settled herself there, but if I could figure out the weird stuff people do, I'd go be a shrink. Drinks, cocktails, wine? Full bar as always."

"She's *sixteen*," my mother says.

"Right, you never drank at sixteen." Vaughn makes his way to the bar at the back of the living room. And when I say "living room" I mean giant space decorated entirely in an Art Deco style, with the kind of light fixtures and divans and whatever else I've never seen in a real house before. Compared to this, my mother's house is down-to-earth and homey, though weirdly enough this feels way more my style. If you're going to keep your house like a magazine spread, at least make it one you'd want to read, right?

"It's weird, huh?" Vaughn says to Kate once he gets a drink for my mother and a Diet Coke for me.

"Be nice," my mother snaps.

"It's just that she's a total mini-Reece," he says. "That's all I'm saying. You looked just like this at sixteen, didn't you?"

Very slowly, my mother nods. "Yeah."

"Bad news, kid," Vaughn says. "That's definitely you at thirty-two."

Thirty-two? Holy crap. I don't like that math at all. It's one thing knowing she's young; it's another to actually pin this number onto it.

"Bad news? Reece looks amazing," Kate says, which I

guess is true, not that I know exactly what a thirty-two-year-old should look like. I only know that a thirty-two-year-old is not what I expected to get as a mother. "Devan's very lucky with those genes. And Reece's mom looks amazing for her age."

"Please, my mom's had a lot of work done," my mother says. "There's nothing we can gauge from her except a different set of priorities."

I wonder what this plastic surgery–getting person is like. *My grandmother*. Dad's parents lived far away, on the other side of the state, so we didn't see them very often, only once a year at Christmas. Dad clearly inherited his ways from them because I could never figure out how to get close to them, either.

Kate, Vaughn, my mother, and I eat dinner in a huge dining room off fancy square plates with heavy brushed-silver forks and knives. The longer I'm here, the less ridiculous it seems. Where and how else *would* Kate and Vaughn eat? Afterward, my mother and Vaughn promise to clean up, so Kate and I are free to head to the music room. I'm not sure what I'm expecting, considering the rest of the house, but this is just a simple room holding a piano and a shelf's worth of sheet music.

"I'm good at warm-ups." Kate sits down at the piano. "Actual music, less so. Isn't that unfair? Five years of piano lessons, but I finally had to accept the truth."

"I'm not any good at it, either," I say. "But doing scales is totally all I need."

So she launches right into some, and my voice just sort of flies out of me, like it always does. I feel the past days' events rise off of me like steam on a cold day. Nothing feels wrong or bad or hopeless when I'm singing. The whole world is just music.

"Oh my God," Kate kind of squeals when we've gone through a few different warm-ups. "*Your range.* I'd kill for it."

"Yours is amazing, though," I say, my first acknowledgment that I know who she is. "Mine's no better."

"Oh, sweetie, trust me, it is. Maybe not better than when I was your age, but now, yes. It's hard maintaining it, since I can't even remember the last musical I did."

I can, but decide it would be creepy to mention.

"So." She grins up at me from the piano bench. "You must have nosy questions for me about Reece, right?"

"Um." I find myself grinning against my will. (Okay, my will isn't *that* strong.) "Um, I don't know. Not really."

Kate snorts. "Devan. You either need to think harder or stop being so restrained."

Obviously I have a lot of questions, but they aren't for Kate. And I'm not sure how much I want to hear the answers anyway.

But I guess I have to ask something. "Is it weird I'm here?"

"Oh, Devan, I've lived through a lot weirder stuff."

It's a yes, but a nice one at least.

"She's as tough as you think," Kate tells me. "But a person can be so many things at once. You know?"

I don't, not really. It sounds encouraging, though.

She pats the piano bench, and I sit down next to her. Three inches from a fairly famous person. "I'm here if there's more you want to talk about later, okay? So if you need anything at all, you just have to let me know."

"Um, thanks." I can't exactly imagine dialing up Kate Logan for random advice. Still, celebrity or not, it's a nice thing to hear.

My mother and I go home not long after, since my audition is early and all. It's another quiet drive, but obviously I'm already used to it. And the weird thing is—okay, I'm still terrified of Reece Malcolm, but this silence doesn't feel the same as sitting in a silent car with Dad or Tracie.

And because of that, I feel safe enough to speak up as she pulls the car into the garage. "Thanks for taking me tonight. I think I'm way more ready for my audition now."

"Good," she says.

A lot of things are flooding my brain, but for the moment, I make myself smile at her before I head inside.

Chapter Five

Things I know about Reece Malcolm:

13. *She's thirty-two.*
14. *Therefore, she was sixteen when I was born.*
15. *Her friends are also nicer than she is.*

My first "real" audition was in seventh grade for *Bye Bye Birdie*, which is one of those shows I think everyone has to perform in school at some point. Teachers had been telling me I had a beautiful voice in any class where singing was involved (like up to and including dumb stuff like "The Star-Spangled Banner") so I didn't even realize I *should* be nervous. And even though (like every girl there) I tried out for Kim (the lead role), I got cast as Rosie. And like every girl who didn't get cast as Kim, I started off a little disappointed. But I realized how much of a better fit Rosie was for my voice, and I started thinking about that, who I'd be best at, not who'd get the most songs to sing. After that I always landed the role I went in for.

Of course, I've never stood near the cutest guy on the planet pre-audition before.

"Hey!" He jumps up from his chair as I walk into the music department waiting room at New City School. His hair is nearly black and kind of swooped forward, somewhere between really preppy and a little punk. It is Very Serious Hair. I think about how it would feel to run my fingers through it. (Good, obviously.) "You're auditioning too? Not just me?"

Now I'm face-to-face with his chest, since 1) the room is pretty small and 2) he's several inches taller than me. (When you're 5'3" a lot of people are several inches taller than you.) It's a nice chest. He's wearing a totally normal T-shirt from the mall or whatever, but it hangs on him like the shirt has fulfilled its sole mission in life.

The guy is staring expectantly with his dark blue eyes, and I realize he's probably *not* a hallucination and definitely talking to me. And it's ~~possible~~ ~~likely~~ true I'm just staring at him.

"Oh, um, yeah, auditioning, I am." To be fair, it's more than I've ever said to a cute boy in my entire life, so I'm not entirely disappointed in my performance.

"You go here yet?" he asks. "I just started this morning. It's crazy, compared to my old school. Maybe not in California, I don't know. What about you?"

"I, um, no. I don't." I sit down in one of the folding chairs and hope he'll stop talking soon. That's right, I wish silence and lack of communication on Hot Boy. When a hot boy has never even spoken to me before, much less with so much enthusiasm. Auditions are that serious.

"Anyway, I'm Sai, S-A-I, it's an Indian name, if you didn't know. My mom's half Indian and half Chinese. She named me after her great uncle, for some reason." He pauses. "My mom's weird."

I nod until I realize I'm probably supposed to say something back to S-A-I Sai. "Devan." I think about spelling my name, too, but I'm afraid it won't sound cute, just weird. If Justine were here she'd tell me how to be cute on purpose, but she's not.

"Awesome to meet you." He's pacing the length of the room, which doesn't exactly help me maintain my usual pre-audition cool, but does at least give me a chance to watch him from multiple angles. "When do you start?"

"I don't know yet for sure," I say. "I just moved."

"Me, too. St. Louis," he says, blowing my freaking mind.

"Seriously? Me, too," I say, then feel dumb because Pacific is not exactly St. Louis, and also maybe I'm talking too much and the laws of nature will do something dramatic to maintain the world where hot boys and Devan do not mix.

"No way." He pauses from pacing and rocks back on his heels. "Where'd you go to school?"

A woman leans into the room with a clipboard. "Say Lawrence?"

"It's Sai," he says with a smile. He probably corrects it a lot. "Hey, Devan from St. Louis, let's talk later, okay?"

"Sure!" I say wayyyy too enthusiastically, and watch him leave the room. My heart pounds and I feel vaguely crazy, and I guess lots of people go through this pre-auditions all the time. If only I had such a good reason.

Sai is back only a few minutes later. "Fastest audition ever. No clue what to think. Anyway, here's my email. I have to get back to class, but we should talk."

"Um, yeah." I take the scrap of paper from him. If it still exists later I can prove he does, too. "I'll—"

"Devan Malcolm?" The lady is back, and now my heart is racing and my breath is all shallow and I feel cold sweat on the back of my neck. Because in addition to this cute boy *handing over his email address*, New City School has mangled my name in a horrible, amazing way. New City School doesn't know who Devan Mitchell is. New City School thinks I'm a Malcolm.

"See ya, Devan Malcolm," Sai says before heading out of the room. (Does that count as flirting?) I follow the woman down the hallway to a choir room. A man probably no older than my mother, wearing a button-down shirt, sweater vest, jeans, and Adidas, sits at the piano. I had no idea teachers could dress like that.

"Hi, Devan," he says, and directs me to a spot next to the piano. He goes through my range first, then hands me a piece of music to sight-read *a cappella*, and finally lets me choose from a few pieces of music to sing four bars of. (I pick some weird folk song just because I've sang it in a previous class, I figure no one else would go for it, and there's this section I can belt the heck out of.) The teacher doesn't give any indication of how I did and dismisses me without a positive or negative word.

I make my way back to the admin building, pausing for a moment at the little pond where goldfish are swimming. In Missouri my school was one big brick building, but New City School is broken up into lots of little white buildings, bright against the blue sky, with lots of tiled walkways connecting everything. What a weird school. What a weird *day*, and it's only nine thirty in the morning.

My mother's waiting in the hallway when I get back, reading a big promotional New City booklet. "How'd it go?"

"No idea. Do we need to do anything else?"

"Not yet. They'll let us know if you're accepted into any choir classes by this evening, and they'll schedule you for classes according to that."

We walk outside to the parking lot. Sunshine and blue skies. Again. I open my mouth to let her know about the name mistake, except that I really like the thought of being Devan Malcolm. And if I tell her, she'll call up New City, get it fixed, and I'll have to go back to being Devan Mitchell.

And suddenly she's the last person I want to be.

❀ ❀ ❀

When I get the call from New City letting me know I've been placed in Honors Choir, Women's Choir, and the New City Nation (most pretentious name for a show choir ever?),

I feel good enough to get up the nerve to take out that piece of paper from my purse.

```
TO: sai_of_tj_eckleberg@email.com
FROM: its_our_time@email.com
SUBJECT: Choir Auditions
Hi Sai,
I'm the one who auditioned right after
you today. Did you find out where you're
placed yet?
```

I type in the list of choirs I'll be in but then delete them, considering it feels a lot like bragging. And, anyway, what are the chances Sai is gorgeous, from St. Louis, *and* an amazing singer on top of that? So I just sign my name and hit send. Whatever.

(Not *whatever* at all, really. I check my email *a lot* after that.)

According to school policy, I have to start the next morning so I won't delay the choir classes any more, which is fine. Being new is so normal to me that I can't get too worked up over it. At least here I have a ton of clothes that Missouri Me would have killed for, and—when I check first thing after I get up in the morning—an email from a cute boy letting me know he's in Honors, Men's, and Show choirs. He even sounds *excited* about all of that as well as about talking to me. If it were a musical we would totally be kissing soon, but I'll probably find out that, despite my instincts, he's gay.

Brad drives me to school because, as he puts it, *seven*

a.m. seems a bit dangerous to let Reece out into the world, which is okay because he has a muffin and cocoa waiting for me, and he chatters on all the way to school in a manner that's somehow distracting in a good way, not an annoying one. I wave good-bye when he pulls up to New City and walk inside like I have any idea at all what I'm doing. First day survival strategy.

It's probably dumb to hope Sai will find me, but I do—and he doesn't—so I head off from the Junior Cottage (seriously, that's what my locker assignment sheet calls it) to the Music Hall for Women's Choir.

Women's Choir has never been my favorite of choir classes, since it's just tons of girls, and I prefer the variety of having more of a mix of voices. (Also, not to sound snotty, but since it's usually such a large group, it's not as competitive as the other choirs and therefore not everyone is as skilled as in my other choir classes.) Plus Women's Choir generally only sings pretty traditional songs. Honors Choir is much better, since there are boys, and it's way more selective. Still, in Honors Choir we generally sing pretty standard and classical songs in precise arrangements. But they're good for my voice, great for learning to sing well with others, and it isn't as if I mind any time spent singing, period.

In show choir, though, at least there is a performance aspect, too, since the whole point is performing showier numbers with movement and choreography. I actually think it's ~~kind of~~ ~~a little~~ pretty cheesy. People say the same thing about musical theatre, but I don't think that's true at all. It's one thing to burst into song in character because there's such an overflow of emotion it can't be contained. It's another entirely to randomly sing and dance, apropos of nothing. I mean, I *love* it, but I can't deny its cheesiness. (Musical theatre, on the other hand, I'll defend to its—and my—death.) Still, show choir is a small group of talented people, and you occasionally even get to sing songs from this century. It's the best of all of them.

I make my way through the crowd of girls to the piano, where the man from yesterday sits. "Devan, hi," he says. "Killer audition yesterday."

"Oh, thanks." I look down at my schedule because I'm pretty sure that *Deans comma M* is listed for all three of my choirs. "Do you teach every choir class here?"

"Just the advanced ones." He hands over a folder of music. "Here's everything you need for this period. We'll take care of the others when you get to them. There's one other person beginning today in the Nation and Honors, too, so you won't be the only newbie."

I don't tell him that I know that last bit already.

"So you'll be in good company," he says. "If you don't mind waiting off to the side, once everyone's seated we'll find you a spot. Cool?"

"Cool," I say, and step back to survey the room. It's a lot less like being out in Hollywood this weekend and way more like most choir classes I've had before. (Though to be fair, being out in Hollywood isn't actually scary; people are just dressed either super nice or super casual or somehow both.)

Once I'm seated with the altos, things feel even more familiar, and of course once I'm singing I couldn't be convinced my life is weird in the least.

Plus here I'm definitely not Missouri Me. My schedule is for Devan Malcolm, and that's how Mr. Deans introduces me to the class. It sounds really good, and I like how it looks in my handwriting, and when I practice my autograph during second-period chemistry class it definitely improves upon my standard one. Here at New City, I'll be Devan Malcolm. I'm not some girl missing part of who she is with a weird secret unknown mom. Maybe here I can try being normal.

On my way from the Science Building (no fancy name for this one) back to the Music Hall, I spot Sai and force myself not to wave until he does. But at last he does.

"Hey." He stops walking until I catch up with him. "Did you get my email?"

"Yeah, this morning." Is it weird that I check my email in the morning? "We have two choirs together."

"That's awesome. Also awesome I got to transfer out of sociology to take this class. My dad made me start right away instead of waiting to see what choirs I got into. Let me see your schedule."

I hand it over, and hope that people walking by take note that the mousy new girl is in the presence of the hot new guy.

"We have English lit together, too," he says. "Best class after choir for sure. And Acting I."

I feel like I owe New City School a thank-you letter.

Obviously, the New City Nation is a small class, only sixteen people, eight girls and eight boys. It's usually kind of weird being the new person in a show choir class, especially in schools where it's pretty competitive, but then again I've done this more than once. At least this time I'm new with someone else.

"Hey, Devan, Sai," Mr. Deans says. "Go ahead and take a seat. We'll introduce you once everyone's here."

That's the other thing about show choir: it's a lot closer-knit group than other classes. It's not like I ever had good friends in any of them, besides Justine of course, but you still know everyone by name.

The kids next to Sai and me do not exactly look thrilled to see us, which happens sometimes. I guess it can seem unfair if it takes you years to get into a class, and some new kids make it their first day. I just don't think you earn spots by waiting it out. The good stuff should be earned by being the right one, period. This part of my life comes so naturally to me—unlike pretty much the rest of it, besides knowing how to scour the clearance racks and vintage shops for the best pieces—that it's easy to know this is what I should be doing.

We go through warm-ups and run through a couple songs before Mr. Deans asks Sai and me to each sing a recent solo to give the rest of the Nation an idea of our voices and styles. I let Sai go first (he sings "Being Alive" from *Company*, which just further closes the case on his perfection, especially because he nails it), and then I sing "Now You Know" from *Merrily We Roll Along* because it's kind of big and fast and showy but not as much as, like, "Getting Married Today" from *Company*, another song I love singing to strangers who aren't expecting anything. (Also it's clichéd enough for us both to sing Sondheim, even if he's the greatest musical theatre composer of all time, but both singing from the same show on top of that would be pretty ridiculous.)

People here obviously act pretty cool about things (barely raising an eyebrow when Sai hit this seriously impressive note) but there is a little murmur of appreciation for me, and so everything feels okay.

"Interesting choice, Devan," Mr. Deans says as I sit back down. "This can't leave the classroom yet, but the fall musical's going to be *Merrily We Roll Along*."

Oh my God, I love this place.

Merrily We Roll Along is only one of my favorite shows ever. My freaking email address is even a reference to it. Justine pointed out (post-Tenor, of course) that it's a show about friendship and not love, and maybe that's why I love it so much, with me not having experienced True Love yet. (I haven't experienced much True Friendship, either, but I didn't leap to point that out.) There's a lot about life I don't get yet, but I don't want people actually telling me so.

It's a pretty ambitious show for a high school to perform, especially since I'm used to performing in the seemingly obligatory shows most schools do. *Merrily We Roll Along* is about this composer, Franklin Shepard, who starts off as a great guy who dreams of writing musicals with his best friend, Charley. But as he gets older, instead of staying true to his ideals, he falls for the Hollywood thing and abandons everything he once believed in. Totally, of course, losing Charley along the way because Charley actually holds on to his beliefs in the face of money and fame. The role I've been dying to play since I first watched a shaky video of this amazing production at the Kennedy Center is their other good friend, Mary, who doesn't abandon Frank—mostly because she's in total hopeless love with him—but does go from a successful writer to a washed-up alcoholic. (Which, okay, sounds pretty bad, but she gets amazing songs and scenes.)

Oh, and the whole crazy thing about the show is it goes backwards. When it starts, everyone's old and jaded, and by the time the show ends, everyone's young and sure they can make all their dreams come true. I guess that's actually ~~completely~~ a little depressing, but I think you understand everyone's relationships and loyalties better that way. Also the truth about life is sometimes it's pretty depressing, and I'm pretty sure art should tell the truth about life.

"That should count as her audition, then," says a blond guy wearing a preppy shirt with a little alligator on it and jeans that probably cost twice as much as even my nicest pair paid for by Reece Malcolm. "That was amazing, New Girl."

The murmur of approval turns into something less positive upon that utterance. I guess I don't blame them, but honestly I'm used to walking into new schools and almost immediately scoring roles kids who'd been there for years thought they deserved. If I hadn't gotten used to how that felt I would have given up a long time ago.

"New Girl!" the preppy guy calls after class. I'm sort of walking with Sai, though we aren't talking, really; he's just trying to help me figure out where my next class is. "Hey, New Girl, wait up."

"She probably has an actual name," says a girl with black hair styled into something of a fauxhawk who I saw earlier in Women's Choir, and who is also in the Nation.

"It's Devan," Sai volunteers, like he knows me so well. *Go right ahead and spread that rumor, everyone.* "I'm Sai."

"You are to *die* for," the guy says to me. He's not much taller than I am, and he's built kind of athletic, kind of small, like musical theatre chorus dancers often are. "Have you had voice lessons? I told my mom if she'd let me take actual lessons I'd be so much better."

I'm way more comfortable with attention from a gay guy than I am figuring out how Sai can be so nice to me.

"I haven't." I shrug and try to seem modest. "Thanks, though."

"I'm Travis Kennedy," he says. "This is Mira Sato. What class do you have next?"

"Acting One."

He wrinkles his nose. "I'm already in Acting Three. But don't worry. There are a lot of crappy freshmen in there but other people, too. Oh, crap, you aren't a freshman, are you? You don't look like one, and they hardly ever let them into Nation."

I learn that Travis and Mira are juniors as well, and that I have English lit with Mira and both world history and algebra II with Travis. And choir, of course. Part of me is pretty weirded out that barely into my first day, there are people who seem eager to talk to me, but then again my wardrobe has received a full upgrade, and I'm being seen in the presence of Sai-ness. When I walk into the cafeteria to get lunch (it seems most kids actually eat outside in the courtyard so I haven't quite figured out where kids without friends sit), Travis waves me over to the line for sandwiches, where Sai is also standing, like we're all friends already.

After we get through the line, Travis leads us outside, where I hear a little voice in my head think, *Yay, the weather's so nice today*, which is kind of terrifying. No way am I going to start loving L.A. weather. The Midwest is my past and New York is my future, and this is just for now.

"Hey, Sai." This girl appears, like, out of nowhere, the kind of girl who makes me feel like I'm some other species, tall and thin and with every blond hair in place. The kind of girl who *should* be talking to Sai. "You were going to eat with us, right?"

"Right, Nicole," he says. "Hey, guys, you know Nicole?"

I wonder if there's something wrong with Sai that he thinks we should be associating with Nicole at all. We're in *show choir.* He just gets an exemption for looking like some gift from a God who's spent too much time looking through my dreams for specific examples of what boys should be like.

"I promised Nicole I'd have lunch with her, meet some people," Sai says to us. "But I'll see you in Honors, yeah?"

This is the thing: he isn't being a jerk. I want him to be a jerk because then I could hate him. But, no, he looks like he genuinely wants to honor Nicole's offer of table location, not get away from us.

"I can't believe it." Travis pouts as he sits down across from Mira. "I thought we snagged the fresh meat. Then Nicole Ediss happened to walk by. It's almost a cliché."

"It *is* a cliché," Mira tells him. "It's probably for the best, though. I don't know if I want someone like that sitting at our table. He looks too Disney."

"What, like too Disney Channel?" Travis makes a face

at the sandwich he just special-ordered. "New Girl, did they mix ours up?"

"No, too Disney," Mira says. "He looks like Aladdin or something. It freaks me out. I feel like his teeth should sparkle."

I can't help laughing at that. "Thanks for letting me sit with you guys."

"Where else were you gonna sit?" Travis asks. "There's no other option. There're choir nerds, that's not you. There're kids who think performing a lot's gonna get them seen by an agent or casting director, that is *definitely* not you. There're the few who rise to—well, Sai—and then there's the rest of us. Geeks but, you know, not in a geeky way."

For some weird reason, that makes me feel a lot better about Sai sitting anywhere but here.

"He spends a lot of time on this," Mira says. "So don't think he came up with that on the spot."

"What?" A red-haired girl sits down next to Mira. She's wearing a Ramones T-shirt with cuffed jeans, and her pale skin seems impossible in this setting. "Is Travis explaining social order again?"

"Of course." Mira grins at her, and it's the nicest she's seemed since we met.

"This is Devan Malcolm," Travis says. My heart pounds a little extra at my new name. "Devan, this is Lissa Anderson."

"Hi," she says, and smiles at me, and then her smile widens as she looks up beyond us. "Hey."

A guy who you could probably find in the dictionary

under Tall and Handsome and Brooding drops into the seat next to Lissa. He isn't my type at all, all in black with eyeliner and black nail polish, but I get it. I'm sure he's Lissa's type, and the way they glance at each other makes me think they're either something or they will be soon.

"Hey," he says, not just to her but to the whole table. For some dumb reason the way he says that one word makes me think he must be nice.

"This is Devan Malcolm." Travis is back in introducing mode. "This is Elijah Cross."

"Hi," he says with a wave. "Nation? I could salute instead."

I laugh and nod. "Yeah. I mean, to the Nation part. Please don't salute."

"We almost got a hot guy for the table," Travis says to no one in particular. "Laws of nature took him away."

"Liss thinks we already *have* a hot guy," Mira says like her whole tone is an eye-roll. If I were Lissa I'd curl up and die with embarrassment, but she laughs Mira off and it's like it never happened. I've never been able to let stuff just go like that.

Travis tells Lissa about the close call regarding Sai and the lunch table, while I wonder if Justine is sitting alone at our old table. I mean, not *alone* alone, but we weren't exactly the center of attention in the group of other girls from choir we sat with. Back there she's probably being left out of conversations and here I am meeting people eager to hang out with me. Well, sort of eager at least? Travis seems eager, and no one else looks at me funny.

I walk to English lit with Mira, Lissa, and Elijah. It's honestly nice to walk into an unknown classroom with a group, especially when Sai drops into the open desk behind me.

"This class is pretty awesome," he says.

"English lit?" I have no idea what he's talking about or why he suddenly seems like the hottest nerd in the world, so I just smile and shrug a little.

"We should hang out soon," he tells me. "Exchange war stories."

"War?"

He grins at me and I really really really hope I don't visibly melt. Inside my brain it sounds like *slosh slosh slosh*. "St. Louis, war, whatever. We'll talk."

❋ ❋ ❋

My mother is on time picking me up after school, which shocks me at least a little, and she has a blended mocha waiting for me in the second cup holder. "You don't look traumatized. I take that as a good sign."

"It was actually a totally good day. People are really nice," I say. "How was your day?" It feels polite to ask, though I have no idea if that's my business or not.

"Good," she says. "Productive."

"That's good," I say, as if I know what I'm talking about.

"I think Brad's working late, so we should definitely go out tonight. And isn't that what you're supposed to do on first days of school? My mom always took me out."

Something about her mentioning her mom in the

context of us hits me weirdly. Maybe it does for her, too, because she's quiet until we're home. I have homework to get through, so I sit down in my room with it until I can't take it anymore and pull up my email.

Of course, I don't have a message from Sai waiting for me. What do I expect, that he'll run home to immediately email me, when there's now a tall, skinny blonde in the picture? (Honestly, Nicole or no Nicole, who runs home to email anyway? ~~Besides me.~~)

My mother knocks on my doorway a little after six, and waits until I respond to lean into the room. Living with her isn't like living with Tracie at all. "Dinner?"

"Sure." I close my laptop and pick up my copy of *Beowulf* like I've been reading that and not looking up everyone from school on Facebook. (I don't add anyone but I change out my last name for my middle name, which is a thing some people do for privacy but I'm doing it so I don't have to explain to New City people why I'm listed as Mitchell or to Justine why it's now Malcolm.)

"Oh, God," she says. "English lit. I suddenly feel incredibly old."

"It wasn't that long ago," I say for some idiotic reason. Feast or famine with what comes out of my mouth.

"I guess not, when you include college, too," she says. "Trust me, it feels like a very long time ago."

"What was your major in college?" Safe question, which means the filter is working again. Good brain.

"English. I minored in creative writing," she says. "There were probably programs better-suited for me, but back then I was convinced I'd never leave New York."

"I can't believe anyone *would* leave New York," I say. "Ever."

"I needed a change," she says. "L.A. was definitely that."

I shrug, following her downstairs and out to her car. "I guess."

"Dubious, I can tell." She grins at me. "Just wait."

No idea what to make of that, but I feel safer when she's smiling.

"So I'm craving sushi tonight," she says. "And you're lucky—we live in one of the sushi capitals of L.A."

"I've, um, I've never had it." I restrain from adding that the very thought terrifies me.

"I wouldn't dare lead you astray."

I guess I'm dubious about this, too, but I keep it to myself. Plus the restaurant she drives to is beautiful, decorated in dark colors and bamboo, and just dimly lit enough to create ambiance or whatever on a bright day.

"God, sorry." My mother digs her phone out of her bag and clicks it to answer. "Hey, what? No, Devan and I just got to Teru Sushi. Hang on." She covers the phone with her hand. "Brad's out earlier than expected. Should we send his codependent ass on his way or tell him to join us?"

The thing is, I do want one-on-one time with my mother. But the other thing is that one-on-one time is the quietest time ever. At least when Brad's around, we talk.

"It's fine if he comes," I say. "Right?"

"Sure." She uncovers the receiver. "Hey, yeah, meet us here. Right, I know. Yeah, yeah, you, too."

She throws the phone back into her purse. "What do you think? Normal that he ends every damn call with *I love you*?"

I shrug because what do I know about that from experience or observation? "It seems nice."

"It's like talking to an elderly relative." She places her hands on her hips and sighs very dramatically. "What about you?"

"What *about* me?"

"I don't know. Guy back in St. Louis? Guy here, magically, already? Are you one of those people?"

"No way, definitely not. And not in Missouri, either."

"Yeah, I find dating very much overrated. Despite everything, I kind of liked that Brad was just Instant Boyfriend. Cut right through the crap." She leans against the wall and fiddles with her hands. "For all that he annoys me, I shouldn't complain so much. He could be making pancakes for someone much nicer than me."

I don't know what to say, because I know exactly what she means.

We're still waiting for Brad when we're seated at a back corner booth and opening up our menus. Probably based on my blank stare when my mother asks me a few obviously basic questions, she leans in next to me and nicely explains what the different sections mean and what some of the Japanese words are in English. I'm still fairly terrified of raw fish as well as her, but—weirdly enough—she makes everything sound less worrisome.

Brad shows up a few minutes later, and he slides into the booth next to my mother right before kissing her.

"Not in public," she says, and I can tell Brad is sort of riding it out to see if she's kidding or not. "How was work?"

"Fine," he says in a way that I know it was totally *not*. "How was your day?"

"Productive," she says. "Devan claims her day wasn't awful, but I'm not sure that's even possible on a first day of school."

"It does seem unlikely." He grins at me. "That's great, if it is in fact true. Does everyone sing and dance constantly?"

"Oh, God, I meant to ask that!" My mother laughs as she flags down a waiter to place our drink order. I notice that her arm slips around Brad's shoulder. It's weird she has this other side, the one that explains unagi (eel, no way) and tamago (egg, not raw, so not scary), and tries to take away Brad's less-than-fine day. I can't connect that with the person she seems to be most of the time.

Plus, seriously, how do either one of those people go sixteen years without bothering with me at all?

After we eat, my mother and Brad bicker over who should pay for dinner. By now I'm used to the way they argue, always two steps or less away from laughing. No, I'm not included in their little routine, but the very fact that it's routine already is somehow comforting.

"Seriously," my mother says. "I'm paying. First of all, I'm positive you paid last time we went out, and there's also the fact that you shouldn't have to pay for her."

I'm sitting right here, I think but do not say.

"Reece—"

Then they whisper back and forth while I focus all my strength on not bursting into tears.

It doesn't make sense. One minute she could be so kind only to end up here the next. I have to figure it out, because if in her lurks the person who could ignore me for sixteen years, she has to be capable of ignoring me for sixteen more. Right?

And if there's anything I'm good at—well, besides auditioning and singing and hopefully acting and, okay, shopping (if shopping counts?)—it's researching Reece Malcolm. Doing it from her house has to be the easiest task yet, right? Life will have to make more sense once she does.

Chapter Six

Things I know about Reece Malcolm:

16. *She made a possibly not-great college decision based on not leaving a city she'd leave four years later.*
17. *Sometimes she can actually be a nice person.*

My Reece Malcolm investigation starts off pretty small the next day. My mother runs out for errands once I'm back from school, and after at least starting homework for all my classes—and adding Travis on Facebook because he pestered me about it earlier today—I walk downstairs with my notebook.

School was fine, almost just like the day before, though

today Sai sat with us at lunch. I don't think anyone knew what to make of him, so at least I'm not alone there.

I guess right that my mother's office door won't be locked, so I slip in and glance around like something huge will be revealed immediately. Okay, it's just an office. Desk, filing cabinets, shelves, printer, bulletin board. The only thing amazing about this room is that the desk is old and beat-up, the walls are a totally normal white, and the shelves don't even match one another.

I open the top desk drawer and flip through, even though there are only index cards and tubes of lip balm inside. The next down is just as hopeless: some boxes of ink pens and what looks like a very old bag of chips. The third isn't nearly as boring. It's jam-packed with promo stuff for her books, some old review clippings—I guess before the Internet this is what people used—and copies of postcard-sized author photos she obviously never used. (I stare at them for a while, because she's even younger in them, and there's a lot of me looking back from the drawer.)

Nothing at all leads me to understand her, though.

Her laptop is just lying there, so I open it and pull up her email. Only one new in her inbox, from Brad. Considering it seems to be a response to more arguing about the TV issue, it isn't too exciting. (It isn't exciting at all, really, except that he calls her *a biased snob*, which makes me giggle aloud.)

But buried in the chain of emails back and forth is a sentence I don't know how to feel about. Does it make last night better or even worse? Brad wrote, *You need to stop apologizing regarding Devan.* I keep staring at it, but I can't make myself scroll down farther in the email chain to see the apology in the first place. I click the right buttons so the email will still show up as new before dashing out of the office.

It isn't fair that you can never go back to not seeing something.

❊ ❊ ❊

By Thursday morning, Travis is waiting by my locker like it's routine. "New Girl, what are you doing this weekend? There's some production of *Into the Woods* that should either be fun or fun to laugh at. You in?"

"Um, yeah, I should ask my mother, but, maybe?"

"Good." He links his arm through mine. "I'll walk you to your class."

I fall right into step with him. We pass Sai, who's hanging out with Nicole near her locker. They're talking and laughing, but he still waves to us.

"Ugh, it's so predictable," Travis says.

"Yeah, I think it's dumb to believe guys like that would look at anyone else." I don't go on to say that believing the contrary is a pretty immature line of thought. Just because you know people in your actual life doesn't mean you're any better than a kid dreaming a celebrity could be his or hers someday.

"Ooh, a pessimist," Travis says. "Interesting. I would have called you as more glass-half-full, with your whole flouncy skirt thing you've got going on."

"I'm not a pessimist." I pause at my Women's Choir classroom. "Just a realist. Also, I just really like fashion."

"Well, duh." He takes off in the opposite direction. "See you later, Devvie."

I walk in and take my spot. Mira isn't far behind me, but we don't really talk unless Travis or someone else from our lunch table is around, too. I've tried—as much as I'm capable of, at least—but I still don't take it personally or anything. Travis's fast friendship is kind of a miracle; I don't expect that from ~~anyone~~ everyone.

Sai practically rushes me when we walk into show choir later. It must mean something that he's around Nicole so much, like that they're falling in love or at least making out with each other, but I still like his attention.

"Kennedy just invited me to a show this weekend. Are you coming?" Sai asks.

I wonder if there's some kind of Secret Boy Handbook with rules like #87: Only refer to other boys by their last names.

"Um, yeah, he invited me, too. I think I can go. I just have to check with my mother." I'm excited and embarrassed at once. Despite everything I said earlier, Sai and I might be socializing this weekend. But then there's me needing permission. Do popular people ever need to ask their parents to do anything?

He grins at me like that answer made his day. "Awesome, I don't know everyone else as well as you, so it'll be good if you're there."

I wish that meant more than it actually does. "What about Nicole?" Of course I don't want him to invite her, but I'm testing to see what he says about her. Hopefully that's not awful of me.

"She's not into the whole musicals thing," he says.

"Why does she go to this school, then?" I actually am curious about the New City students who don't participate in everything that makes this school what it is.

"It has the best academic standards in the Valley," Sai says. "Which I only know because that's how I convinced my dad to enroll me here."

I think of ten other things I suddenly want to ask Sai, like why he moved here, if he hates that his dad had to be convinced, and does he ever feel guilty loving a thing his dad probably wishes he didn't? (Because I did, sometimes.) And if theatre and music are so important to Sai, is it weird spending so much time with a girl who doesn't feel the same?

I mean, despite his hair and his chest and his eyes and the way jeans hang on him, I'm definitely into Sai because of his voice and the way those eyes flash when he talks about the same things I care about. The rest is pure bonus. (Well, it would be, if I were naïve enough to believe I could ever have a boyfriend like him.) Guys—well, straight guys—never seem like that to me. Of course I believe there are things they do care about but at school it's like there's a secret boy contest to see who can act the most *whatever* about everything. Sai would lose that contest immediately, and I ~~love~~ like that about him.

And I don't mind how I feel around him. Even when I'm thinking about his hair or whatever, conversation is easy. For me that's pretty amazing, hotness or no hotness. Thanks to him and Travis being so friendly, I don't feel words piling up in my throat, bursting forth at the worst times. I think New City is good for me.

I'm the last to head over to the table at lunch, since I ended up in another conversation with Sai while in line for sandwiches, until Nicole walked up and he very nicely waved good-bye to me.

That's how I overhear them talking. ". . . just don't know her very well," Mira is saying. "Her *or* Aladdin. You can't just invite everyone who's ever been nice to you to everything."

"God, Mir," Lissa says to her, laughing. "You're making a really big deal out of seeing a show that might suck."

"I just like knowing people before I start hanging out with them," she says. "So tell them we changed our minds about going, okay, Travis?"

I manage to back away without anyone spotting me—I guess I'm still good at being invisible—and sit down with my tray at one of the tables in the very unoccupied cafeteria. Travis told me people really only use it when it rains or gets cold. I don't know if that was a joke or not, since those are two things I didn't think happened in L.A.

"Hey."

I look up from my Acting monologue to see Elijah standing at the table. "Oh, hi."

"Everything cool?" He digs through his pockets, pulling out a few coins. "You have eighty cents? I think it's gonna be a two-sandwich day."

I pull out my wallet and hand him a dollar. He presses two dimes into my hand.

"Everything's fine. I just thought I could concentrate better in here."

"Yeah?" He gestures to the line for sandwiches. "You want anything?"

"You had to borrow eighty cents just so *you* can get something."

He laughs. "I'm not offering free food. I'm offering free service."

"I'm okay." I think about how he said *free service*. Elijah isn't really the kind of boy I'm into, and, anyways, he's clearly earmarked for Lissa, but it's still *something* to feel anything extra from a boy's words. "Thanks, though."

He gives a salute before walking off. I get back to my monologue and think how much easier things are now that life has been put into place. Those few days of having a regular lunch table and people who could be friends were, clearly, pretty nice, but I should be at this empty table. Social order.

In English lit I do my best to ignore everyone—and Mira seems happy to go with that—though Elijah makes a big deal of paying the eighty cents back to me, and Lissa talks to me like all is normal. I don't know how to handle any of this, so I try not to.

After my mother picks me up from school, she takes me to get a cell phone because she claims it'll make life easier. I don't know about that, but everyone else I know at school takes out their phones at lunch and checks their texts and Facebook and who knows what else. So at least I'll look more normal. It's almost as good as invisible.

"Everything all right?" she asks on the drive home, while I tap my phone, figuring it out as best I can, after programming in the only number that matters, Justine's. (Also obviously the only one I know.) "You seem . . ."

"I'm fine," I say because I'm sure to Reece Malcolm,

getting snubbed out of seeing a musical interpretation of fairy tales isn't exactly up there for bad days. "Thanks again for the phone."

"You're welcome," she says, almost like a question. "Seriously, you're allowed to have a crap day. I myself have tons."

I hope I'm not to blame for any of those crap days. "It's nothing."

"Hmm." She leans over and taps my phone. "Seriously?"

"Sorry, I was just figuring out where everything is." I drop it into my purse. "And I'm really fine. Sorry if I acted like I wasn't."

"Between you and Brad, I'm getting a little tired of people acting as if they're perfect for my benefit." This is the thing: it sounds mean. Except she says it in a nice way, and then leans over and puts one of her hands on top of mine. "Trust me, it's entirely unnecessary."

"Thanks," I say. "But, really, it's just dumb school stuff. Totally not worth it."

"That's fair."

Her hand is still on mine, which gives me time to realize it looks exactly the same as mine does, except my cuticles and nails are in way better shape. A nice discovery today. (The similarity thing, not the cuticles.)

"We could go do something," she says. "Unless you have a ton of homework. Or even if you do, and you want to live dangerously."

I grin at that. It's a relief that after a bad day she's the right blend of understanding and funny. When she's not being scary, I actually like Reece Malcolm a lot. "I don't have much, which is good. I don't think I'm cut out for living dangerously."

"Somehow not surprising." She turns the car to merge onto the freeway, which is clogged with cars already, even though back in St. Louis four p.m. wouldn't exactly be rush hour yet. "It's a really clear day. We can go to Griffith Observatory and see the whole city."

"Sure." I reach toward the car stereo, reconsidering living dangerously. "Is it okay if I turn on the radio? If there's nothing good I'll turn it off, I promise."

"Oh, sure, it's fine. Brad signed me up for satellite radio, so I'm sure you'll find something. I myself have to wonder about someone's music addiction when he finds the need to outfit his girlfriend's car with this much music, on top of his own."

I zip through the stations, pausing when I find one that plays Broadway hits. Adam Pascal is whining about his hypothetical one song glory. "Is this okay?"

"Sure," she says right away, like anything else would be, too. I guess it's nice of her. Still, I'm not going to lie and say it isn't more than a little disappointing she doesn't love music like I do. I keep waiting for something we share, besides our eyes and hands and build and preference for Diet Coke.

Griffith Observatory is up high, requiring my mother to drive curvy roads surrounded by green. I totally didn't expect there would be anything lush or green in L.A., except maybe money, but I don't say anything because maybe I should have known it could be so pretty. We walk around the outside of the building (my mother declares the inside is a science museum, something neither of us is exactly dying to explore), and I take a picture with my new phone of the bust of James Dean. Finally we climb the stairs to the roof of the Observatory itself, where seemingly all of L.A. stretches beneath us, out to the ocean.

"Do you know my favorite thing about being up here?" My mother leans over the railing, stretching her arms out into the sunshine. "For me, at least, when everything is actually going well and I'm succeeding in whatever I'm doing—and let's face it, that's always writing, because that's the only thing I'm good at—that figurative feeling of being on top of the world? This comes close to literally recreating it."

I think about being onstage with my voice filling the air around me, around everyone, before leaning out to mirror my mother. "I know what you mean."

"See that apartment complex?" She points to a near-ish tall building, tucked into the hills and trees. "Brad just moved out of it."

I try to imagine that. Even to total no-relationship-experience me it's obvious they're stumbling around new in the living-together arena, but it's also hard to imagine them so separate.

"We hiked up here once," she says. "And I hate hiking, but I did it for him, and then we got up here and I thought I'd pass out, considering normally my idea of exercise is walking from the couch to the refrigerator, and I noticed he'd gone red and huffy and was probably closer to fainting than I was. He said he only suggested going because he thought I would enjoy the view, so we stood here and promised to be honest, since clearly not speaking up could have led to our deaths." She laughs her usual brusque laugh at that. "So while we were still being honest, I told him he should move in with me. I think he almost cried."

I love the way Reece Malcolm talks about her life.

"What's your favorite—" She cuts herself off. "I was about to ask what your favorite thing about L.A. was so far, but I should probably ask if you can even stand it enough to have a favorite thing."

"Is it dumb if I say the weather? It's totally a cliché, right?"

"It's a cliché for a reason," she says. "It's generally glorious here. I won't deduct points for lack of originality."

"What's your favorite thing about L.A.?" Right now feels like a safe time to ask.

"Oh, God, don't repeat it, but probably that most of the people I care about are here." She raises an eyebrow at me. "But I'd hate to lose my rep of not giving a shit."

"So the weather?"

"Right," she says with a smile. "The weather."

Chapter Seven

Things I know about Reece Malcolm:

18 *She apologized to Brad about me.*

19. *Her hands are the same as mine.*

20. *Most of the people she cares about are in L.A.*

Travis is at my locker again the next morning, which is a relief. I have no idea how stuff works in groups of friends, but at least Mira not wanting me around doesn't necessarily translate to Travis feeling the same. "So did you talk to your mom?"

It's still pretty weird being asked that question.

"About what?" I ask, even though of course I know about what.

"About *Into the Woods*, duh. So did you? Can you go?"

"I, um, I thought you guys weren't going."

"Oh, please." He rolls his eyes with such flourish it's like he thinks I'm watching him from the back of a theatre. Actors! Sometimes we're ridiculous.

"Did you talk to Mira or something?" he asks. "Mira!" Of course she happens to be walking by us, and I can't get Travis to shut up. "Did you tell Devan we weren't going on Saturday?"

Mira slams to a stop in front of us. "I didn't tell Devan anything."

"I didn't say you did," I tell her really quickly. "Travis just—"

"I have to get to class," she says before taking off.

"Ig*nore* her," Travis says. "Also I don't have your number."

I memorized it the night before so I wouldn't look weird in case anyone asked. "It's really okay if I come?"

"Why wouldn't it be?" He gives me his number, so now I have two programmed in my phone. "See you in Nation."

At lunch I'm ~~terrified~~ ~~scared of~~ nervous about Mira, but I still follow Travis from the sandwich line outside. (Honestly, Travis is hard to escape.) I sneak a glance at Mira as I sit down, and she meets my eyes. I feel like it's a challenge, and I'm too much of a wimp to rise up to meet it—whatever that would be—so I look away and quietly eat my chicken and avocado sandwich. Lissa and Elijah show up, and Mira seems to forget about glaring at me at least temporarily, so I turn my attention to my monologues book again while they talk about some movie they saw last weekend.

Sai stops by a little bit later and squeezes in next to me. His thigh is pressed right against mine, which feels a little R-rated. I mean, in my head at least.

"What's up for tomorrow?" he asks. "Who's driving? I would but my car only seats two."

"There're six of us," Travis says.

"Good work counting," Mira says. "No wonder you get A's in math."

I guess I can take everything less personally if Mira seems to hate everyone at least once in a while.

"I, uh, don't think we're coming." Lissa glances at Elijah, who sort of shrugs. "There's an all-ages show at The Satellite we're going to."

Mira narrows her eyes. Now no one has escaped her death glare. "You didn't tell me that."

"I'm telling you now," Lissa says in this really light tone, even though I ~~know~~ think Mira is completely serious. Her eyes are still narrowed, after all.

"If there're only four of us, we can take my car," Travis says, like nothing as high-stakes as a hostage situation is going on. "Devan and Sai, you have to give me your addresses."

I'm trying to figure out a non-weird way to say I don't know mine yet, when Sai just pipes up that he doesn't know his yet. Also, yes, his leg is still next to mine.

"Me neither," I say. "I only moved a week ago. It's really close, though, only like five minutes away."

"I'm not much farther," Sai says. "But I'll call you with the actual address later, okay, Kennedy?"

"Definitely," Travis says, giving Sai his number. I try to

imagine giving a (straight) boy my number with such ease. (I can't. Even in my daydreams I get tongue-tied and can't remember the digits or how to write or also my own name.)

"So does anyone have a curfew besides Mira? Because we should go out after, not before."

"I'm good," Sai says, as I say, "I can check," and Mira says, "My curfew's not *that* early."

I ask my mother for permission to go to the musical practically as soon as she picks me up, and I guess I'm not that surprised that it's fine with her. Tonight we're apparently going out with Kate for dinner, so the weekend is off to a good start.

At the house I wait what feels like an appropriate length of time before calling Travis. He answers on the first ring. "New Girl, hi, you'd better be calling to tell me you can come or I'll be devastatingly heartbroken."

"Not just normal heartbroken? No, I can come, it's fine. And I live on Reklaw at Laurelwood." I'm proud I thought to, you know, read some street signs. "The second house on the left."

"I have no idea where that is but I'll Google Map it," he says. "So, New Girl, what do you think of school so far? All you ever wanted? Or are you a tough sell?"

"No, it's . . . I know this makes me a nerd, but I think it's kind of amazing. Like *Fame* but with normal kids, too."

"You couldn't be a nerd if you tried," Travis says, which is one of the nicest things anyone's ever said to me. "Everyone who's into it loves it, too. And you're so freaking *good*, if you were one of those bitches who acted like she was above all of it, I'd hate you forever."

I think about asking Travis about Mira. Maybe there's something I can do to make her not hate me. Maybe there's a reason she does. Maybe this stupid thing that makes lunch totally tense can be fixed.

But I don't ask. After all, I'm the new girl; Mira's been here. I don't want to risk loyalties having to come down on one side or the other because there's no way I can win it. And, anyway, I should be grateful for what I have already.

"What are you doing tonight?" Travis asks. "We could hang out if you want."

"I'm going out with my mother and her friend," I say. Probably I should worry about it sounding at least vaguely nerdy, but hanging out with Reece Malcolm and Kate Logan definitely doesn't qualify as nerdy. So even though Travis has no way of knowing that, it makes me feel decidedly less lame. "So another time?"

"Of course, Devvie. See you tomorrow."

My mother leans into my room a few moments later. "Hey, can you help me with something? It's kind of embarrassing."

I have no idea what help I could offer Reece Malcolm on anything. "Um, sure."

She leads me down the hallway to her and Brad's room, which I haven't been in yet, despite my commitment to figuring her out. The email had thrown me for a loop.

It's just a little bigger than my room, with one wall painted a gorgeous eggplant color and the others kind of a parchment-y tan. Their bed is huge, and it has a beautiful dark wood headboard with all these cutouts, and above it hangs a giant painting that stretches wider than the bed, all splashes of bright colors that somehow works with this very classy room. But what catches my eye right away is the nightstand on the side of the bed—well, there's one on each side, but only this one is packed with framed photos.

"I have to go with Brad to this event tomorrow." My mother crosses the room to the closet and opens the door. "And I have no idea what I should wear."

"What kind of event?" I ask, like I'm a big expert on any kind of event.

"A party for some TV show Brad used to write for." She shrugs. "It's their hundredth episode celebration, and I get the feeling from Brad calling earlier and dropping in *love, what exactly* are *you wearing tomorrow evening?* that I should probably steer clear of my usuals."

I laugh at her amazing Brad impression. "Is Brad a TV writer or something? For what show?"

"Yeah, now for *The Gamers*," she says.

It's surprising to me because *The Gamers* is a show most people have heard of, and it's weird my mother's boyfriend is a part of something big like that. Actually, on second thought, I guess it isn't weird at all.

"My best friend—back in Missouri, I mean—loves *The Gamers*." Justine never misses an episode of the show, which is about hipstery people who work for a big video game company but are secretly bringing down evil corporations and stuff. Also—at least in the episodes I've seen—they seem to spend a lot of time relaying witty banter and making out with each other. "I don't watch a lot of TV or I'm sure I would, too."

"I only watch it now out of girlfriend duty," she says. "But it's not bad. Tell me what to wear."

"It's not like I know what people wear to events like that."

"You always look nice," she says. "Trust me, you'll have a better idea than I would. Just advise, all right?"

I flip through her closet, though seriously almost everything in there is a T-shirt or a pair of jeans. When I get to the back—clearly the stuff she never wears that gets cast aside for her favorites—it's almost as hopeless. A couple of pairs of black pants, a formal dress that's probably from a wedding or something. I pull out anything that's even a vague possibility: a sleeveless black shirt, a black cocktail dress, the pair of black pants that doesn't look outdated and smooshed, and a dress shirt that's kind of a man's style but cut low in front.

"I hate dresses," she says. "So that's out. I don't even know why I own it."

"It's nice, though," I say.

"It's yours, then. Keep it. The pants are fine, but I'm afraid if I wear the white shirt I'll look like one of the waiters. Because it's happened before."

I laugh and consider for a few moments before speaking. "I have some stuff you could look at, if you want. Is that weird?"

"No, you're going to save me from getting drink orders all night." She dashes ahead of me down the hallway, so I take a spare second to glance at the framed photos, even though it's dumb dumb dumb to think any of them will be of me.

In my room we settle on my deep green knit shirt, which

actually looks even better on her because she has much better hair than I do. I feel so good about helping her out that I even mention it.

"Oh, please," she says. "My hair guy is just really good. Should I make you an appointment? I would have offered but you look fine to me."

"Would it be okay, seriously?" I imagine the one remaining piece of mousy me gone, even if it might make my chances of invisibility smaller. Less safety, but better hair and therefore style. It would be a tougher call if style didn't always win out.

"Seriously," she says. "I'll call later." She examines herself in the mirror. "Brad's ex is going to be there. I should shut up about all of my ridiculous relationship drama but it's as if I literally can't. I've become a crazy person who is actually concerned her boyfriend's ex will pick a more appropriate outfit for an event."

"The shirt looks good," I say, because it's the only thing I can think that might help at all.

"You're too kind." She switches it out for her T-shirt. "Thanks for putting up with my unhinged rantings."

I shrug and consider telling her the contents of my brain are pretty much always crazier than the things she says. But then my phone beeps with a text message.

I don't know the number, which is weird, but my heart bangs like a percussion section when I read it, not just because of its contents, but because I can tell from reading it that it's from Sai. *Got your number from Kennedy, was at school late, heard Deans saying auditions for musical next week.*

"Everything all right?" my mother asks, still examining her reflection, even though she's back in her kind of crappy normal clothes.

"Yeah, I, just, this guy, school, auditions." My mouth is dry and I've forgotten enough of the English language to even know how to fix what's wrong with my response.

"Auditions for what?" she asks.

"The fall musical," I say. "It's, like, a really big deal. For me, at least."

She laughs. "I want to hear about the guy who's terrifying to speak of when *really big deal* auditions aren't."

"He's no one," I say. "I mean, just a guy, this guy from school, it doesn't matter, I don't even like him."

"Uh huh," she says with a raised eyebrow. "Definitely sounds like it."

"Shut up," I say without thinking. And then we both laugh really hard, and I tell myself to get how amazing this moment is, my mother and me, at last, cracking up together, even if it's sort of at my own expense.

"For now I will." She turns from the mirror. "All right, I have to get through another chapter today, so I should attempt that before dinner. Thanks for the shirt."

"You bought it for me," I point out.

"Ah, technicalities. See you later, kid."

❀ ❀ ❀

On Saturday night, I'm still settling on accessories and perfecting my outfit for my first official night out with friends in L.A. when my mother knocks on my door. "Come in!"

She does, shutting the door behind her. "Two boys are here for you. One, I should mention, I'm leaving Brad for. *Damn.*"

Oh my God. Sai is here. In my freaking *house*.

Okay, fine, I definitely meant everything I said about there being no point in liking Sai. But I guess I've been lying to myself to think that means I *don't* like him. I have no willpower against the hair, the voice, the chest, the weird nerd qualities lurking just beneath the surface. I mean, he *likes English lit.*

"I think he likes this girl at school," I say for some extremely stupid reason, like my mother is serious about dumping Brad for Sai. "I mean—"

That makes her laugh. "Then hopefully I can restrain myself. Anyway, cash for tonight." She hands me a wad of bills. "And would you call me if you're going to be out late? That seems like the right thing to do, yeah?"

"What's late?" I tuck the bills into my wallet. "Like midnight?"

"One? Sure."

We walk downstairs together, where Travis and Sai are standing in the living room. Sai is at the bookshelves while Travis is in front of one of the paintings.

"Devvie, oh my God," Travis says. A good greeting. "Your hair is amazing."

My mother's stylist was booked for a couple of weeks, but Kate called hers last night and got me in first thing in the morning. My hair now falls just below my chin with a bit of a swing, like I always have a wind machine on me, and instead of mouse brown it's colored auburn. And I'm still just Devan, with a face that's too round and eyes that are boring, but this is maybe the best I've ever looked.

"It looks good," Sai says with a nod. From a straight guy that's a solid hair compliment. "Man, your house is *awesome*."

"Very posh." Travis looks at my mother. "Are you Devan's mom? Is this your posh house?"

"I am and it is," she says. "Thanks, both of you."

"We should go, if we have to pick up everyone else," I say.

"Hang on." Sai leans in closer to the bookshelf he's examining. "Man, this is an awesome collection. I had to leave most of my books behind when I moved."

Oh my God, such a nerd. Unfortunately that just makes him hotter.

"Were you in a hurry?" Travis asks. "Like, running from the law?"

"You're so weird," I say to Travis, which is the kind of thing I said all the time to Justine, and suddenly I miss Justine so much I could puke. She has only emailed to say things are *very very good* with The Tenor, though. It's like we were gone from each other before it was even true.

"Nah, my dad just had limits on how much I could pack, said books take up too much room." He shrugs like it isn't a big deal, but I think maybe it is.

"Okay, you've looked at books enough, this isn't a library," Travis says. "'Bye, Devan's Mom; it was nice to meet you."

"You, too, guys."

I follow Travis and Sai outside to Travis's Beetle. Sai gets into the back so I take the front passenger seat. "Thanks for picking me up."

"Really no prob," Travis says. "So if you moved only a week ago, were you living with someone else then or whatever? Because your house looks way nicer than if you moved in a week ago."

"Yeah, um, before I lived with my dad and stepmom," I say. "In St. Louis."

"With Sai!" he says all excitedly.

"Not exactly," I say, because, okay, St. Louis isn't as big as L.A. or anything, but it's not like everyone there knows one another. People who were born in L.A. probably think all other cities are like teeny tiny towns.

"But you're here for a while?" Travis asks. I wish he'd stop with the questions. I don't want anyone to know how weird my whole situation is. "I mean, you're not gonna, like, land a part in the fall show and then go back, are you?"

"No, I'm not going back."

"I don't blame you," he says. "The Midwest, ugh. But won't your dad mind?"

"He's dead," I say, "so probably not."

"Oh my God, Devan, I'm sorry," he says as Sai leans forward and touches my shoulder, saying, "Man, that sucks."

I hope it isn't a bad sign that he keeps calling me *man*.

"It's okay," I say. "My dad and I weren't close or whatever."

"Still," they both say. A popular reaction.

"Still. I'm okay." That much, I'm nearly positive, is starting to feel true.

"Did you want to stay there?" Travis asks. "Like, does it suck being here?"

I seriously wish he would stop asking me things.

"Man, Kennedy, leave her alone," Sai says. His hand is still on my shoulder. It's probably bad I'm taking a nice, comforting moment and enjoying the weight and warmth of his hand on me when we're talking about my dad. "Would *you* wanna talk about it?"

We pick up Mira next. As she walks up to the car, Travis leans over and elbows me. "You need to get in the back. Mira'll be all carsick unless she rides shotgun."

I wonder if that's true or if Travis just wants me to sit in the backseat next to Sai. Or maybe Mira doesn't want to have to sit by Sai because she hates us both.

Honestly, I'm not complaining. And Mira barely says a word to us, but I'm determined not to let her ruin anything. Plus I'm *in the tiny backseat of a tiny car with Sai.* Travis and Mira are having a big discussion about the filmed production of *Into the Woods*, but I'm not listening very closely because Sai starts this game on his phone and keeps passing it to me to take a turn. If I forget Nicole exists, it feels like a moment out of a montage in a romantic comedy.

The theatre is a tiny building off a dark street, and I hope it isn't just my Midwestern naïveté or whatever telling me we aren't in a great part of town. But people swarm into the little theatre, and seeing the showcards on the walls and the ushers holding programs, I feel like I'm home.

I saw my first musical as a fluke. In seventh grade, our choir class went as a field trip to see the high school's spring show. It was just this average production of *Grease* but watching those kids onstage, something in me shifted. This need surged from my heart, and all I could think was that

I wanted it to be me. I wanted to be up there. I needed to be part of this.

Choir is great because I get to sing, and show choir is better because it has a lot in common with musical theatre. But they're just placeholders and ways to get better, until theatre is in my life all the time. I'm not sure I could go on if I didn't believe eventually I'll have it there constantly.

Which means that this tiny theatre is exactly where I need to be tonight.

During the show I sit between Travis and Sai, which is good for obvious reasons, but also because I'm pretty sure it isn't just my paranoid imagination that Mira is still glaring at me. Also—probably more likely my imagination—Sai has plenty of space in his seat but he's leaned in nice and close to me and I can pretend for at least the sake of the rest of the crowd that we're here *together* together.

The show isn't the most amazing production ever or anything, but I still get wrapped right into it as soon as the curtain goes up, and I feel the pull between the stage and myself. And, even more amazingly, I feel it from everyone else I'm sitting with, too.

Afterward Travis drives into Hollywood to a diner located under the freeway, and we crowd into a booth while Travis tries to spot celebrities (no luck but it doesn't stop him). Sai and Mira both have their phones out, texting, I assume, with Nicole and Lissa, respectively.

Weirdly enough, though, I don't feel left out, or out of place, or any of what I would have worried about. It's enough just sitting here, listening to everyone else, chiming in occasionally.

It's such a great night I don't even freak out when I let myself into the house and walk in on my mother and Brad making out. (Okay, in my head of *course* I freak out. In person I pretend to laugh along with them before making a quick escape to my room.) And I feel—well, actually *happy* as I change into my pajamas and get into bed.

"Hey." My mother leans into the room. "*So sorry.* We lost track of time and— You don't want to hear this. How was the show?"

"Fun," I say because she definitely does not want to hear a bunch of my thoughts about Stephen Sondheim and musical theatre, so I'll leave it at that. "How was the event?"

She walks into the room and sits down on the edge of my bed. I think about the billion times I had trouble falling asleep as a kid and wished my mother were there to read me a story or say the right comforting thing. "It wasn't too boring and no one ordered a drink from me. I'm calling it a victory."

"What did Brad's ex-girlfriend wear?" I ask, because I want to know, but then I realize I've asked something insanely intrusive and I want to disappear. "I'm sorry, that's totally none of my business."

"Oh, please, I brought it up yesterday. Something red and sparkly. She looked beautiful; I looked like me." She shrugs. "But I don't mind looking like me."

I can't explain why but it makes me so happy she feels like that.

"I'll let you get some sleep," she says. "Good night, kid."

Chapter Eight

Things I know about Reece Malcolm:

21. *She has no idea how to dress for anything.*
22. *She actually is insecure about things, like Brad's ex-girlfriend, despite all opposing evidence.*

Next week we have official notice of auditions on Thursday. You can feel this sense of terror and stress in my choir classes and in the hallways of the Music Building, but for me it's like everything is finally happening. This is what I live for. A million things about life might scare me but this will never be one of them.

By lunch on Wednesday all anyone is talking about is

tomorrow's auditions. Sai's not at our table today—it's a popular table day for him—and so that means I feel a lot like the odd person out, because everyone else has been through this before, specifically at this school. Also Mira just has this magical way of directing conversation around but not including me. It's fine, because I'm getting used to it, and it's basically being invisible, which, again, I'm great at.

A foot taps my shin, and I assume it's a mistake until it happens again, *taptap* this time. I glance up and Elijah grins at me with a sideways look to Mira like she's nuts. I don't mean to but I laugh aloud.

"What?" Mira turns to look at me, then Elijah. "What's funny?"

"You're not the comedy police," Travis says, then goes back to whatever he was saying about him being suited for both leads equally. It's funny how I can tell we all think he's crazy for saying that but no one—not even Mira—corrects him.

When the bell rings, I trail everyone inside, but today Elijah does the same. I sort of expect he'll say something about not worrying too much about Mira. But he doesn't say anything, just grins at me.

"You got me in trouble," I say.

"That's me," he says. "Trouble-getter."

"Trouble*maker*," I correct.

He laughs. "Both, really."

We have show choir rehearsal after school that day. A lot of people would obviously rather take a night off to get ready for auditions, but I'm happy to be here. Working to perfect vocals and choreography is probably the best thing we could be doing the day before anyway. Plus I love rehearsal, especially because this is by far the best show choir I've ever been in. Not only is everyone a totally high-caliber singer, but Mr. Deans is smart about picking show tunes the whole world hasn't already sung to death (like we're currently working on "New Music" from *Ragtime*, which isn't super well-known but a really beautiful song) and mixing them up with standards and random stuff, like pop songs from the eighties and nineties.

After rehearsal, even though I'm still not nervous about the imminent auditions, I just kind of want to get out of school and shut myself in my room alone with my sheet music. If I'm totally prepared, I'll have no reason to get nervous even in the moment. And the moment is what matters most. But someone stops me on my way outside. The good news is that it's Sai.

"Hey." He rests his hand on my arm as we walk outside. Too much to hope he's about to declare his love for me? "How are you doing with your monologue for Acting?" Uh, yes. "I've gotta read mine tomorrow and I was gonna see if you wanted to work on it with me. Kinda worried that with auditions and all I won't focus on it enough otherwise."

"Um, totally, yeah." I nod toward the curb in front of the school, where my mother's BMW is parked. "Like, now? My mom's here to pick me up."

"We could go to your house, if that's okay," he says. "Mine sucks anyway, since we just moved in and all."

"Yeah, um, let me ask." I walk up to the car and open the passenger door. "Hey, so, um, Sai and I were going to work on our monologues for acting class; he said he could come over, is that okay? If not it's totally fine, I just—"

"Of course it's fine," she says. "Hey, Sai."

"Hey, Ms. Malcolm," he says. "Can you wait so I can just follow you?" He points across the parking lot, where a blue Audi is parked. "I'm right there."

"I can handle that," my mother says. "Devan, go with him in case he gets cut off from me so he won't be lost."

Considering we only live five minutes away, I'm pretty sure my mother is just trying to get me alone in a car with Sai. Is that a normal mom thing to do? (Okay, who cares if it's a normal mom thing to do? It's an amazing mom thing to do.)

"Your car's really nice," I say, because it is, but also because I figure guys who drive cars like this want to hear it.

"It's blackmail, but it's fine," he says as he opens the passenger door for me. I must look kind of shocked at that, so he laughs really quickly—but in this obviously fake tone. "Just kidding."

I don't say anything to that, just buckle in as he squeals out of his parking space to pull up behind the BMW. Even if it took weird meddling from my mother, it's a highlight of my life to be speeding down Ventura Boulevard in a hot boy's car.

Sai pulls into our driveway. "Your mom seems cool."

"Sure," I say. I still haven't figured out how to talk about her without saying everything. Saying nothing is much safer.

"How was school?" my mother asks as the three of us walk into the house together. As if it's normal to have Sai along with us.

"Fine," I say. "Show choir was mostly for the guys today, but it was still fun."

Sometimes I honestly kind of forget about my classes besides choir and acting when I'm thinking about my day.

"Deans is really good," Sai says. "Ten times better than my last director."

"Oh, you're in the Nation, too?" My mother looks more than a little surprised. *Yeah*, I want to say, *you're not wrong. He's way too hot for show choir.*

"Yeah, it's awesome," he says.

In my head I say, *Show choir is many things, but it's not awesome*, but I'm so bad at trying to be snarky or whatever that I stay silent.

"I'll leave you guys to your monologues," my mother says. And then she sits down in the living room with her computer, which I guess means I'm supposed to take Sai up to my room. So even though that feels wrong for a million reasons? I totally do.

"Awesome room," he says right away, of course, because what *doesn't* Sai think is awesome? "So ya like it here compared to St. Louis? Or is it rough with your dad gone?"

"No, I like it," I say. "I didn't think I would, but L.A.'s not what I thought it would be like."

"So you hadn't been before?" he asks. "Even though your mom lives here?"

"I meant like full-time," I say, which is only sort of a lie. I don't want to lie to him but I don't want him to know the truth, either. So it's my best compromise.

"Oh, yeah, okay," he says. "I came here on vacation,

sort of, when I was a kid, did the whole Disneyland thing. So I didn't know what it was gonna be like."

"Why did you move?" I ask. "I mean, if you don't mind . . . "

He shrugs, sitting down on the edge of my bed, tapping his black Vans on the rug. "My parents are getting divorced. Kind of a long story."

"Sorry, I—"

"No, it's okay. Yours, too, I guess."

I shake my head. "No, they were never . . . Anyway. Sorry about your parents."

"Sorry about your dad," he says.

"Thanks." I sit down next to him and page through my *Fuddy Meers* script to find the monologue I highlighted.

"Were you and your dad close?" he asks, looking very directly at me.

"Totally not," I say, even though that makes me seem like a terrible person. "Not lately, at least."

"Yeah, me neither, with mine," he says. "And now it's just us. *Awesome*."

"That sucks," I say.

"A lot. Yeah." He leans forward to take a well-worn *The Glass Menagerie* script out of his back pocket. "Things good here at least for you? Yeah?"

I nod, because it's true. I want a lot more than I have: answers, explanations, understanding. But there's seriously no denying things are better.

"Okay, you wanna go first? Or should I?"

"You can go first." I pull my feet up and hug my arms

around myself while Sai paces the room a couple times before launching into Tom's monologue about writing poetry on his warehouse shifts. I've watched Sai enough in class to know he's good, but Sai is *good*. He's instantly someone else, fully dedicated to the character, like he isn't in my room with me. It's hard to do that, to completely let go of who you are, even for only a few minutes. I'm not even completely sure of who I am sometimes and I still find myself hanging on to me when I act. It takes this combination of bravery and openness I just don't possess.

"So?" he asks when he finishes, shoving the script back into his pocket.

"It's, like, perfect," I say, then slightly regret my gushy choice of words. Even though it is. "If you can do it like that tomorrow, you'll get an A for sure."

"Man, thanks. You wanna go?"

I would honestly rather stand in front of an auditorium full of strangers than a few inches from Sai in my freaking *bedroom*, but I try my best to put him out of my mind and focus like I always would. And I guess it's okay because I get two *awesome*s and some applause.

"You ready for tomorrow?" he asks, and I guess it's weird we haven't brought it up yet.

"As much as I can be, yeah." I hope I don't sound over-confident or anything. But I know the talent level in The New City Nation—which at our school is the best of the best—and I guess I feel ~~really~~ pretty good about my chances, even here.

Sai gets up and examines my bookshelf, as my mother leans into the room. "Hey, Ms. Malcolm."

"Hey, Sai." She grins at me like we're sharing a joke. (I assume the joke is that for such a hot guy he's also a dorky goofball.) "Are you guys hungry? I thought we could have Brad pick up dinner on his way home."

"Dinner would be awesome," Sai says. "I'm not intruding or anything?"

"Definitely not. Burgers from In-N-Out all right with you?"

"For sure," Sai says. Really enthusiastically. I can tell my mother is fighting back laughing at him.

"I'll place our order with Brad," she says. "And call you guys down when he's here."

Sai thanks her before she leaves the room. "Who's Brad? Your stepdad?"

"Sort of, yeah, her boyfriend. He lives here and everything."

"Is it weird?" he asks. "It's still weird to me my parents don't live together anymore."

I shrug. "I knew my stepmom like my entire life. So it doesn't seem weird. Also Brad's like the nicest person in the world."

Brad is home before long, and we settle at the kitchen table with the burgers and fries, even though my mother proclaims it pointless to eat fast food in such a proper manner. (I kind of agree, even though I like the whole sitting-at-the-table-like-a-real-family thing a lot.) Brad asks lots of questions about show choir and school in general, and I mostly stay quiet because Sai rambles on forever.

I mean, in a charming way.

He has to go after we eat, which I figure has something

to do with the beeps his phone made while we were nearing the end of the meal. And that's fine. If I were Nicole and capable of commanding the attention of a hot guy, I'd use my powers, too.

My mother gives me A Look as I help her clean up once Sai is gone. "The boy couldn't keep his eyes off you all night."

"You're totally wrong," I say.

"Yeah? Trust me, I'm unskilled at many, many things, but I know when one person's into another. Are you going to believe your years of life experience versus mine? Please."

I giggle, partially because she's funny but mostly because it's nice to hear.

"So you're aware about birth control and protection and everything, yeah?" my mother asks, totally casually, while wiping off the kitchen table.

"Um, what?" I mean, *seriously*?

"I don't think sex is anything anyone needs to treat like this big secret. People have it, big deal. I just want to make sure you know how to keep yourself safe."

I just stare at her.

"Don't look at me like that." She laughs. "Take a gorgeous boy up to your room, I'm going to check in. Trust me, it's worth being embarrassed in front of me now. My mother never talked to me about it, and I ended up ruining my goddamn life."

That actually means *I* ended up ruining her goddamn life.

I have to run out of the room because all at once I need to cry, puke, lay down, punch a wall, kick something, anything at all not to feel that sentence over over over. Not that it works. I do cry, and I do feel a little pukey, and I definitely slug the bathroom wall (it seems sturdiest), which *hurts* (because it's sturdiest, I decide, not because I'm a huge wimp who's never punched anything in her life). But I still feel it. Over and over and over and over.

She doesn't come after me, and I'm not sure if that's good or not. Clearly she isn't going to say what I need to feel better (*I didn't mean you, you weren't responsible at all for ruining my life, I'm sorry I spent so much time away from you, I'll spend all my time making it up to you, and you should definitely start calling me Mom*), so it's probably for the best. But the silence is hard, too, and it might be an acknowledgment. Right? I'm crying and punching and feeling pukey because what I feared is absolutely true.

Chapter Nine

Things I know about Reece Malcolm:

23. I ruined her life.

As usual, Brad takes me to school the next morning. He's quieter than normal. It's a lot scarier than my mother's silence, which is at least natural. When someone who normally sounds like the blustery leading man in some indie British romantic comedy goes silent, it's another story completely.

"Do you, um . . . " I time it so no matter what he answers, we'll be pulling up at school the second after he responds. "Think you could pick me up today after auditions?"

"What time?" Brad asks, as if my request isn't weird at all. Maybe it should comfort me, but all I can think is my mother told him enough that he knows neither one of us will want to be around the other.

"Five," I say. "Sorry, I know you probably can't because of your job."

"I think I can manage," he says. "Don't panic if I'm a few minutes late, though."

"I won't," I say as he pulls up to New City. "Thanks, Brad."

"Certainly," he says.

I start to open the car door, but I can tell Brad's about to say something.

"I know she isn't always the easiest person to talk to," he says. "But you should try."

I nod, even if I don't know if that translates over to me or not. Boyfriends are one thing, long-intentionally-lost daughters are another.

"Have a good day, Devan."

"You, too," I mumble, and then feel rude, so I clear my throat. "Thanks for the ride."

Elijah is walking in as I am, and he holds out a bag of Cheetos to me. "Breakfast of champions?"

"It's too early for anything that orange," I say. "But thanks."

"You don't know what you're missing." He kind of cocks his head at me, making his longish spiky blond hair flip around. "You okay? Rough night?"

I shrug. "I guess. Not really."

"Bad night, you gotta have a Cheeto." He shoves the bag at me again, and this time I take a handful. Artificial cheesiness is not necessarily a bad way to start the day. "You need to talk?"

I shake my head, imagine saying it to him or anyone else. *Hey, I ruined my mother's entire life.* "Thanks, though."

"Oh, hey." He unzips his backpack, takes out a piece of bright orange paper. It matches the Cheetos. "My band is playing a gig next weekend, and you should definitely come. It's all ages. And I can put you on the list so you won't have to pay or anything."

"Thanks, I'll see if I can go." I look over the flyer. "Which one's your band?"

"Killington Hill," he says with a note of pride in his voice. Something about New City that's so different than back home is how much everyone seems to care about things. "We go on at nine. Definitely you should go, if you're into music and everything. We finally don't completely suck."

I laugh. "I'll try, yeah."

"Also I hear Kennedy is organizing some karaoke thing this weekend, which you should definitely come to," he says.

I am truly truly truly not an expert in anything having to do with boys, but I do see how they act around girls they're into, and there is something about Elijah's tone, and the way he leans in when he talks to me, and how he is adamant about his gig and the karaoke. And *obviously* I like Sai the Lost Cause, and *obviously* Elijah and Lissa are an item or almost one or something.

But I still like it.

My phone beeps as I'm dashing to Women's Choir, and having no idea who it might be, I grab it out of my purse and check the screen. *NEW TEXT FROM: REECE MALCOLM.* I programmed her name that way, obviously, but it still feels like a kick while I'm down, just another reminder that I'll never have a normal relationship with my mother.

Still. *Sorry I'm a bitch. xo*

Okay, it doesn't change the fact that she *does* think I ruined her life. It doesn't make me feel better about her mentioning sex and Sai like that's ever going to be a possibility. It definitely doesn't make up for her ignoring me all of last night. Or, you know, my whole life before that.

But it's good she reached out. Right? Maybe I should want an actual apology. Not an apology for the fact that she feels the way she does about me, because that much is fair.

Lissa bumps into me as we walk into the choir room together, and she gives me a little shrug. "Everything okay?"

"I'm fine," I say quickly. "Actually—I thought today would suck and I guess it won't completely."

"Aw, that's cause for celebration." She grins as she tucks her long red hair behind her ears. "So I don't know if you heard from anyone yet, but Travis wants us all to go out for karaoke this weekend, one of those places in Little Osaka where we'll have our own room. I hope you're coming."

"What's Little Osaka?" I ask, because—unlike Mira—Lissa isn't someone I worry about looking stupid in front of.

"Oh, right, you're new to L.A. It's a Japanese part of town on the Westside, but it's smaller and newer than Little Tokyo, which is downtown. You should come."

"I'll ask my mother, but I'll try. I've never actually gone to karaoke before."

"You'll love it, I'm sure. Especially when you have a private room, you can be an idiot and not worry what anyone thinks." She waves to Mira as she walks into the room. "Hey, I was filling in Devan on karaoke."

"Oh," Mira says. "You're coming?"

I notice Lissa elbow her. "Yeah, probably," I say.

"Oh, good, E gave you one of his flyers?" Lissa points to the neon orange paper sticking out of my folder. "Are you going? We can ride together."

"I just have to ask my mother," I say.

"Is your mom really strict?" Lissa asks.

"Totally not at all, I should just ask before agreeing. She never says I can't do anything, though." I shrug. I don't want to talk about my mother. "It'll probably be okay."

"Must be nice," Mira says before walking to her chair. I start to walk to mine, but Lissa grabs my purse strap. Of course Mira is watching us intently.

"She's been weird lately," Lissa says quietly. "I wouldn't take it personally."

I wonder if it's actually amazing that people here—besides Mira, of course—are so nice to me. Back in Missouri, yeah, no one went out of their way, but I also now keep thinking of times I could have talked to people more, been less invisible, not been so afraid. It's possible my instincts are ~~kind of~~ ~~almost~~ completely backward.

Unlike the last auditions I went through—last February in Missouri—when we waited to audition sitting on the floor of the hallway outside of the choir room, today I'm in a chair in the room where I first met Sai. I can't believe how much has changed since February. Seriously, I can't believe how much has changed just since I first met Sai. Today in this room every chair is full, to the point that some kids are sitting on the floor while others pace as well as they can. I'm between Sai and Travis; all three of us are receiving more than a few glares, and I know it's thanks to our calm exteriors. To be fair I guess it could ~~totally~~ be taken as snotty—and okay, maybe Travis is—but I'm not. I just think it's stupid to care so much about theatre and yet get psyched out by auditioning when it's going to be something you'll theoretically do for the rest of your life.

"Group Three, girls."

"That's me. See you guys." I get to my feet, relieved despite my auditioning mantra that soon this part will be over. It would be better, obviously, if Mira weren't in Group Three as well.

We go in one-by-one first. I'm the fourth one in our group of ten, and I belt through my chosen sixteen bars of "Now You Know" with as much ease as I can manage. Mr. Deans smiles encouragingly at me, even though the other teachers (who I don't know) are basically expressionless. The whole thing takes less than three minutes, and then I'm back in the hall waiting for the rest of the group to finish so we can have the chorus and dance auditions all at once.

"Just so you know." Mira walks over to me so directly I feel like I'll get pushed into the wall. There'll be a Devan-shaped outline between photographs from last year's productions (*Spring Awakening* and *Urinetown*). "Seniors almost always get the leads in the shows here. I don't know how it was before you moved."

School shows are one area I know tons about. "It's always like that."

"I just don't want you to get your hopes up," she says. "People transfer here from little schools where they're the most special, and it's not like that here."

"I didn't say that it was," I reply. "Or that I was."

She rolls her eyes. "The way you look when you sing . . . you think you're great."

I flex my hands because I don't want to ball up my fists and let her know how fast she can make me mad. And I don't have the words I want, the right way to tell her that singing is the only thing I never have to worry about. Singing is the most natural part of me, like how my heart beats and my lungs breathe air. So of course I don't have to worry about doing it. But if I say any of that to Mira, she'll laugh in my face.

Luckily people join our little circle, and Mira has no choice but to stop being publicly rude to me. And I'm not, like, BFFs with any of these girls—or with anyone here, except maybe Travis ~~and Sai~~—but it hits me that no one but Mira's a jerk. Really, no one but Mira even looks at me weirdly. People are nice here, and considering the whole thing with my mother and her ruined life, it's a good realization.

Even if it's also a pretty weird one.

After our dance audition (very basic considering New City's standards, but *Merrily* isn't exactly a dancey show) I head outside. My mother's text this morning made me feel a little better, but it's still a relief that it's Brad's Jetta waiting for me.

"Thanks for picking me up," I say.

He turns down the music from blaring to normal. "Absolutely no problem. It was a good excuse to leave work early, as it were. How was your audition?"

"Pretty good, I think. How was work?"

"Not bad. No fights with anyone so perhaps a banner day," he says.

I can't imagine Brad fighting with anyone, and I tell him so.

"You know what it's like," he says. "Sometimes you must absolutely say everything that you're feeling about something, whether you should or not."

"Um, no. I've seriously never felt like that."

He chuckles. "You and Reece have quite a great deal in common."

I seriously doubt that, but I stay silent.

"I hope you don't mind, but I must run to the grocery store," he says. "You don't need to rush home for anything, do you?"

"Totally not. I don't mind at all." I glance over at him. "Um, this might be a weird question. Just—do you think it's weird that, like, before, we moved a lot, and I hardly ever had friends, and here people are nice to me like that's normal?"

"Isn't this school much more suited to you?" he asks. "With all of the singing and dancing in the halls and such?"

I laugh, even though his actual point is fair. "It's just so different here from how it's been everywhere else. That's all."

"I can certainly understand it," he says. "I went through it a bit when I moved here for university, and suddenly spent all my time with others who were interested in everything I was. Quite a shock."

"Totally," I say. "Was it weird being in another country, too?"

"Somewhat, of course. I suppose that much was easier to adjust to, though."

"Do you go back a lot?"

"Not too often," he says. "It's a long trip, and I'm honestly not all that close to my family. Los Angeles feels far more like home to me. Especially now that I've"—he clears his throat and makes some froggy gulpy noises—"met Reece."

I wonder if anyone will ever feel that way about me.

He turns the car into the grocery store's parking lot. "Speaking of Reece . . ."

I try to act all natural like my insides aren't twisted up like a giant pretzel.

"She quite often speaks before she thinks."

I wonder how she said it to him. *I screwed up* or *I accidentally told her the truth.* "But she means what she says," I say.

"Well," he says, turning off the car. "It isn't that simple. Rarely with anybody. Never with Reece."

I shrug as I follow him inside. "Probably easier for you."

"Well, yes," he says. "But only by comparison."

I trail behind him into the produce section, where he begins squeezing a bunch of avocados with an insanely serious expression on his face. "Do you want help?"

"Absolutely. I need them for this weekend, so you don't want one that's soft like this." He hands me a mushy-feeling avocado. Gross. "Or one that's too hard. Right in between."

I get to work hunting for something just right, feeling a lot like Goldilocks. "How did you learn all of this? Like how to feel avocados and cook amazing dinners and stuff?"

"I've honestly no idea; I just began picking it up somehow," he says. "Also I look up a great number of things on the Internet."

I grin because it feels good to share that nerdy quality with someone else, especially someone else in my mother's life.

After the avocados, I help with tomatoes as well as a bunch of fruit so we can have a fruit salad tonight with dinner. Brad explains his selection process for each, so at least I feel like I'm contributing and not just standing there.

"Perhaps you're like your mother, and believe ordering delivery constitutes making a meal, but if you're interested in learning, I'd be happy to teach you whatever you'd like," he says as we emerge from the produce section.

"No, I'd love that."

He folds the shopping list in half and carefully tears down the crease. "Would you like to take the last two aisles? We can make better time."

I agree to that and dash off with a basket to get through my part of the list. Brad is bizarrely organized, to the point that the list is in order of how I walk down the aisles, so I don't have any trouble locating anything. It's weirdly satisfying when I find Brad still finishing up his part of the list. Suddenly I think about telling him about my notebook, about the list I work on constantly (though obviously not the subject or contents), about how between that and music and Google I feel kind of connected with him. But it seems weird to say aloud. Today especially.

"Nicely done." He takes the basket from me as he steers the cart into the checkout lane. I want to ask him how someone so freaking nice could end up with someone like

Reece Malcolm, but I rearrange the question so many different ways that by the time I get into his car, it comes out as something else entirely.

"Were you mad when you found out I had to move in?" I ask him. His eyes fly off the rearview mirror and to me so quickly, I'm afraid he'll back into something.

"Devan, certainly not. I don't know why you'd ask such a thing."

"Not *mad*, I guess. Just—"

"Well, it was . . . it was quite a surprise."

I chew on a hangnail on my thumb. "Because you didn't even know I existed?"

"Devan, there's a great deal I'd be happy to discuss with you, but I'm not certain this, specifically, is something we *should* be discussing."

"I can't just *talk* to her," I say.

"I realize she's . . ." He laughs softly, turning out of the parking lot and onto the street. By now I've chomped my thumb into a bloody mess. "She can be difficult. But she's also astonishingly reasonable."

I don't mean to, but I let out a noise like *unghhhh*, which makes Brad laugh. Luckily. It feels rude enough insulting my own mother, but insulting someone's girlfriend is somehow worse.

When we get to the house, my mother breezes in to help with the grocery bags like it's any other day. I don't know what I expected; I guess to her the text counted as an apology. And maybe technically it did. I want more from her, though, and not just in that vague way I always want more. If she didn't mean it, couldn't she at least tell me so? And if she did, isn't there a way to still make me feel better? I didn't exactly ask to be born. Who would ever ask for that?

She shoves something in my back pocket while I'm stowing Diet Coke in the refrigerator. I wait until I can slip into the next room before extracting the mystery item, which turns out to be a bracelet that matches my favorite necklace (white Bakelite from a vintage shop in St. Louis). I slide it onto my wrist right away even though I wonder what it means. I have a bracelet so I can't hate how Reece Malcolm feels about me? It makes me think of my full closet and my shiny MacBook and the phone in my pocket. Are they supposed to wipe out everything else? Because they're nice but they aren't what I actually want from her at all, if I had to pick. Can't she just love me and want me here? Or, you know, try?

Still, I walk back into the kitchen with the bracelet heavy on my wrist. "Thanks."

"You're welcome," she says, instead of any of the million things I'd like her to say. Instead of any of the million things maybe she *should* say. "Kate dragged me out shopping and I spotted it while she tried on about five thousand items. You two are way too much alike."

"I'm not that bad," I say, even though I am, and even though I'm not sure I'm on board with this casual conversation. I guess it's better than the alternative.

"Devan, are you helping me tonight?" Brad asks, arranging pots on the stove.

"Totally."

"I'm teaching Devan how to cook," he says to my mother.

"Let's hope that's wise," she says. "I'm not entirely sure anyone related to me should attempt anything in the kitchen besides eating."

Then Brad blushes, and they laugh really loudly, and I try really really really hard not to think about what else has been done in the kitchen. Their lives must have been a lot different before I moved in.

It's weird, though, how a bad morning can turn into a nice night. I learn how to mince garlic and how to cook chicken breasts in olive oil so that they're done inside but not all dried out either. Eating food you made yourself (or at least partly yourself) feels rewarding, like I really earned this meal.

It'd be nice to stretch out that feeling to the rest of my life.

Chapter Ten

Things I know about Reece Malcolm:

24.

Travis is waiting at my locker after the last class on Friday. He grabs me by the shoulders and gives me a semi-scary, intense look. "I have to prepare you for something, and I want to make sure you're *actually* prepared. Are you prepared? Actually?"

Is that even possible? "I guess so."

He spins me around, where, off in the distance, Sai is standing near Nicole, like he often is, but they are definitely holding hands, like he hasn't done, at least where I could see him, before. It isn't unexpected or shocking or wrong in any way, but I'm still fairly convinced my heart drops to a new, lower, sadder location.

I just shrug, though. Travis doesn't need to know about my heart's southern migration. "Figures."

"It's so boring and expected," he says. "Are you okay?"

"Of course! You're so weird."

"Duh." He waves and takes off down the hallway.

My phone rings as I'm going through my locker to make sure I have everything I need for the weekend (and concentrating on not looking crushed). I don't recognize the number, but considering I hardly have anyone's, I still take every call that comes in.

"Hey, sweetie, it's Kate. What are you up to? Big Friday night plans?"

"Totally not." Tomorrow I'm going out for karaoke with everyone—even if maybe I shouldn't give Mira more chances to be mean to me—and on Sunday Travis invited me to go shopping at Fashion Square for new jeans. It's weird to have this crowded of a weekend, but I'm trying to dwell on the positive and not the weird.

"Oh, good, because I know this is such short notice, but let's go get dinner and chat. I want to hear about everything, and I know there's only so much we can talk about in Reece's presence." She laughs, and I can't help joining in. "So tonight? I've already run it past Reece, and I can pick you up."

"Um, sure. What time?"

"Our reservations are for eight, so seven-thirty-ish? See you then, Devan."

After double-checking I have everything in my bag, I slam my locker door and head out to the parking lot. My mother's car is right up front, and I get into it like everything with us is fine. I guess everything *is* fine, or as fine as it's going to be.

At home I start to email Justine about auditions and karaoke and the updated list of songs from Nation and my upcoming dinner with Kate Logan, but I feel weird that it's been so long and I do have this phone and all, so I close my door and call.

"Hello?"

"HiJustineit'sme," I say, because I didn't expect that hearing her voice would bring a billion things crashing around in my head and heart. Home and Dad and my old room and how far away everything is now. "Sorry, it's me."

"Oh my God," she says. "Finally."

"Sorry, I've been—it's busy—I . . . " There actually isn't a very good reason for why I haven't called her, so I don't know why I'm trying. I guess because actually saying that would make me sound like an awful friend.

"What's it like there?" she asks. "Do you live near the beach?"

"No, the beach is like an hour away. I haven't been there yet."

"Have you seen anyone famous?"

"Um, yeah, my mother's friends with Kate Logan—"

"Oh my God!" Justine's voice shoots up practically a whole octave when she's excited about something, and I can picture her face reacting to this Kate Logan news. "Is she amazing? Kate Logan, I mean?"

"Kind of, yeah. She's taking me out to dinner tonight, actually."

"Your life is amazing," she says. "Oh, so auditions for

the fall show are next week. It's *Guys and Dolls*, but I think I have a good chance at playing Sarah."

"You do, totally," I say. "Ours were yesterday. I think they went okay."

"Of course they did," she says. "When have you not gotten a role?"

It's true, but why does she have to say it like it's my fatal flaw?

"I have to tell you everything that's up with Noah," she says, and launches into a whole speech about how he's been texting back really fast, not like before, and it clearly means something. Hopefully I'm not awful for not hanging on her every word. Sai's often taking up space in my brain, but I manage to keep him there.

Maybe that isn't fair. Maybe if I actually ever kissed someone, it would be different.

I hope it wouldn't be, though.

After Justine's monologue on The Tenor is over, we both sound happy to end the call. It's weird how only a year ago I couldn't have imagined cutting a conversation short with Justine unless someone needed the phone.

I'm ready to leave when Kate arrives, but only because I'd been changing clothes for an hour, trying different combinations. I settled on an apple-green skirt with a black sleeveless shirt under a yellow cardigan (totally sounds like it shouldn't go, but it's so wrong it's right) and black flats. It's good I put this much care into it, because like always, Kate looks perfect, tonight in a simple dress printed with bright flowers and tall strappy sandals that are classy not trashy.

"You look adorable," she tells me in a way that isn't

condescending at all, as we walk outside to her Prius. "Though it's still surprising—shocking, even!—that Reece's daughter would manage to wear anything other than jeans and a T-shirt."

"So she's always been like that?"

"Since I've known her, yeah." She giggles a little. "Reece is Reece." She pauses from buckling her seat belt and makes very direct eye contact. "How are you doing? You've had so much to adjust to."

I shrug. "I'm fine."

"You," she says, tapping my shoulder, "do not have to be nice when it's just us. Reece has been one of my very best friends for years, so I'm more than familiar with what a pain in the ass she can be."

"Did she say something to you?"

"I figured out that much on my own," she says, which makes me laugh. "And no. Was there something to say?"

It's probably dumb to hold back, considering how much I still have left to find out about Reece Malcolm and how willing Kate seems to be. "Can I ask a question?"

"Always! I insist."

"Did you, um, know about me? Before I moved here?"

"Well, yeah. One of my best, best friends, remember?" She gives me a huge smile like that's so obvious. "I know, Reece keeps it all here"—she holds her hand to her heart—"but it breaks through sometimes. I treat her like . . ." Kate's brow furrows. "A wild squirrel. Yes! If you sat on your lawn every day, a squirrel would eventually trust you enough to eat out of your hand. But you have to be *so still* and patient."

"Aren't *all* squirrels wild?" I ask.

"Don't ruin my metaphor, Devan."

"Reece Malcolm's a wild squirrel." I say it like a question.

Kate snorts. "Most definitely."

"I ruined her life," I say, which makes Kate's expression fall immediately. "Trust me. I did."

"Trust *me*, sweetie," she says. "You didn't."

I think about quoting my mother, but proving Kate wrong isn't worth reliving those words. They run through my head enough as it is.

"So how was your audition?" she asks, and I'm grateful for the change in topic.

"Okay, I think. We find out about callbacks on Monday."

"I was thinking that you have so much competition coming up, between school and then college and then, well, life! So maybe I could work with you, help you improve, etcetera. What do you think?"

"Do you seriously want to do that?" I ask, instead of *oh my God, that's the best thing I've ever been offered. Ever ever ever.*

"I seriously do," she says. "And, sweetie, sometimes you'll only get one chance at something. Stop questioning what comes your way and just grab hold. Don't be . . . "

"A wild squirrel?"

"That," Kate says, "should be your new mantra."

❁ ❁ ❁

My mother leans into my room the next evening. "Your friends are here. Red-haired girl and boy with eyeliner. Guyliner? Is that what people call it?"

"I guess some people do."

"There goes my last attempt at sounding cool." She laughs and heads out of my room. I wait a moment before running downstairs, where Lissa and Elijah are waiting, both admiring the painting over the fireplace. It's weird to see them standing here, like worlds are colliding or something, but I'm also glad. Travis's friendship is practically too good to be true, and who knows what's up with Sai, and of course Mira's my enemy or whatever, but Elijah and Lissa are chill and easy to be around.

"Hey," Lissa says.

"Hey, Devan," Elijah says. "We just heard from Kennedy that Lawrence can't make it."

I just got a text with the same info. And am trying not to be ~~devastated~~ disappointed by it. Probably it's best my first karaoke attempt isn't in front of Sai anyway. Now I'll be way less worried about looking like an idiot.

Little Osaka is not what I expected. It just looks like L.A.—shops and strip plazas and chain restaurants—and nothing exotic or international in comparison, considering all around town it's normal to see signs in other alphabets and languages.

Travis and Mira are waiting for us in front of one of the strip plazas, and I follow them into a dark lobby filled with video games (which Elijah investigates immediately) and wait for Travis to get us a room. It turns out to be a little cramped, covered with mirrors, and filled with enough chairs and a couch so we can fit if we squeeze. Squeezing is scary with Mira around, but she's laughing with Lissa about something on her phone and it's like I'm not even there. And when Mira's involved, I love my invisibility status.

Travis has his *signature song*'s code memorized, so he punches it in immediately. This means we're serenaded with that old George Michael song "I Want Your Sex" while we flip through the karaoke catalogs.

"Who do you think Kennedy's singing to?" Elijah asks. "I'm putting my money on me; I'm looking good tonight."

We all laugh at that, which makes Travis glare at us—though not enough to interrupt his routine, of course. I locate a code for one of the million songs I wouldn't mind singing, and I think about punching it in, but then hold back to let everyone else go first. Except then I think of what Kate said, and I just lean forward and type it in. And no one looks at me funny at all.

Right, and then I sing ("Total Eclipse of the Heart," which is a very cheesy and ridiculous song, but it gives me a chance to belt it to death). And even though almost everyone (Elijah excepted) has heard me sing in choir, this is obviously something different, because they do stuff like stare at me with their mouths open and cheer for notes I hit and stop paging through the catalogs so I have their full attention.

"Holy crap, Devvie," Travis says when I've finished. No one has lined up a next song yet, so the room is suddenly very very very quiet.

"That was incredible," Elijah says. "Why didn't you say you could sing like that?"

"I, um." I squeeze back into my spot on the couch and pick up a book to see what I want to sing next. "Thanks."

"I can't believe you're from *Missouri*," Travis says.

"Right, because Los Angeles is definitely the center of true talent." Mira rolls her eyes. But she looks over at me and nods. "You should let loose like that in choir sometime. Deans won't know what hit him."

"Thanks," I murmur.

"Does anyone else think Deans is hot?" Travis asks.

"Oh, *no*, not this again." Mira punches in a code and jumps up. "I'll save you all from listening to that."

Everyone is actually better out of class, where we can be ourselves and sing what we like. Even Elijah, who isn't in any choir classes, has this husky kind of rock voice, and if I hadn't already asked my mother if I could go to his show, it'd be first on my priority list.

After singing for nearly four hours—the last of which we devoted entirely to show tunes (even Elijah)—we cross the street to a little restaurant where plates of sushi circle the room on a conveyor belt. It's a relief I've already been out for sushi with my mother and Brad so I don't feel like an idiot. And it's fun racing each other to grab the plates as they go past us, and even without my new mantra I would happily accept that these people ~~minus~~ including maybe Mira are now my friends.

After we assemble a towering stack of empty plates, we walk outside to the two cars. I kind of want to ride back with Travis, since I figure Elijah and Lissa should be alone at the end of the night, and I guess Mira thinks the same thing.

"Travis, you can take her, right?" she asks, gesturing to me.

"Of course. I always have room in my car for Devvie."

"It's probably easier for me to," Elijah says. "But thanks. See you guys Monday."

I'm so surprised they didn't pawn me off that I just kind of wave to Mira and Travis as they get into Travis's car and sit down in the backseat. Lissa turns on Elijah's stereo, cranks it way up so that everything in the car vibrates with the bass and drums. Of course I'm a huge musical theatre nerd whose iPod will verify my taste in music doesn't often deviate, but actually I like the beat and the singer's wail, and the way the sound literally shakes through me.

I definitely expect—even with not getting pawned off—to be taken home first. Seriously, won't they want to make out or whatever once they're rid of me? But Elijah pulls up to a house I assume is Lissa's, since it isn't mine. She must have assumed what I did, because she gives him sort of a look before calling good night and hopping out.

"You staying in the back?" Elijah turns around and grins at me. "I feel like a chauffeur."

I laugh as I get out and then back in to the front seat. "It's only like five minutes to my house."

"Not the point." He drives to the end of the street, pulls up to a stop sign, and looks over at me. "I wasn't kidding earlier. Your voice is the best thing I've heard in forever."

"Thanks," I say. "Seriously. That's like the nicest compliment."

He sets his hand on my knee, which sends little shock waves through me. What exactly is *this*?

"I, um," is all I get out before he leans in and kisses me. A lot flies through me, right up front that isn't Elijah basically with Lissa and what he's doing is wrong wrong wrong. But also that I'm *finally getting kissed*. And, oh my God, kissing feels really good, because Elijah's lips are soft with peppermint lip balm (I saw him use it earlier) and he's gentle. I know we shouldn't be sharing this kiss but my brain kind of shuts off thanks to the soft gentle peppermint action.

"I, um," is what I say again after he leans away, glancing kind of shyly at me like he's awaiting my reaction. "What about Lissa?"

"What *about* Lissa?" He shrugs. "We made out once. Okay, tw—four times. Or something. I like her a lot but she makes it hard, makes excuses not to hang out with me or—I don't know. Liss is a great girl. But it just keeps not happening."

"Does she know you feel that way?" I turn around because we're still at the same stop sign, and won't someone pull up behind us and start honking soon?

"Trust me," he says. "She does."

And that is how I end up kissing Elijah for *four whole minutes* until a car does eventually pull up and honk. I mean, I didn't sit there watching the clock the whole time. I just happened to notice while we were talking, and then again when Elijah squeals the car through the intersection. I'm out of breath from the kissing, and feeling tingly all over. *Actually* tingly.

"I knew that was going to happen," I say, and Elijah laughs and reaches over for my hand. "The car honking, I mean!" Oh my God, this is so weird. Right? This is very strange. "My house is actually—"

He laughs again and parks the car on this random street, totally not mine at all. "You need to get home?"

Oh.

So then we're back to kissing, a few nice and gentle like before, but soon it's rougher, somehow, even though his lips are still soft. I've always worried being queen of inexperience meant I wouldn't have any idea what to do, but kissing is easy, and even though I'm a box of nerves, I don't do anything weird or jumpy when Elijah's tongue slides into my mouth. I'm not dumb; I know we've probably taken closed-mouth kissing to its limit tonight.

"Dammit," Elijah says, and I realize it's because his phone is ringing, and not a reaction to kissing me. "Sorry, it's my mom. Hang on." He clicks his phone and holds it to his ear. "Hey, sorry, am I late? I've still gotta take Devan home. Yeah, as soon as I can."

I run my fingers over my lips, wondering if this makes me different than I was just a half hour ago. Honestly, I worried I wasn't ever going to get kissed, unless it was onstage. "Are you in trouble?"

"Nah, I just told her it'd be an early night and I guess it's later than she expected." He shrugs, starting up the car and taking off down the street. "She worries. My brother's kind of wild, and she thinks I'm gonna get into trouble like him."

"At least you know she cares?"

"Yeah, trust me, that's not something I ever worry about."

I have a lot of questions for him as he drives to my house, like if he thinks Lissa will kill us, and does this mean anything other than it's pretty nice kissing each other, and if we're supposed to be quiet about it or not. I keep them all in, though.

"Talk to you soon," he says, touching my knee.

"Definitely."

He kisses me again before we officially say good night, and I get out of the car and walk up to the house feeling a little floaty, and still tingly. Except then all I can think about is Sai. Stupid freaking *Sai*, who basically has a girlfriend now, who is not interested in me at all—despite the crazy things my mother says—and who was definitively not the boy kissing me mere moments ago. What is *wrong* with me?

It doesn't help that my mother sees me when I walk in and asks, all excitedly, "Whoa, who did *you* make out with tonight?"

Since I'm new to kissing, I didn't think about the fact that my lip gloss would migrate around my face.

"Don't look so horrified." She jumps up from her chair. "Brad's still out with his friends; it's just us. You should feel absolutely free to share details about sucking face"—yes, she actually says *sucking face*—"with Sai. I have to live vicariously through someone, after all."

"I didn't make out with Sai," I say in kind of a crazy voice.

"Oh." She grins at me. If she were a cartoon character, a light bulb would go off over her head. "The boy who picked you up tonight."

I give up, because she's clearly relentless. Also if she's bad at tons of things I need her to be good at, I should probably take what I can get. "Yeah."

"Everything all right?" she asks, finally getting the picture that maybe I'm not as thrilled as she is about this development. Also, no one's mom should ever be this happy her kid made out. What is *that* about?

"I don't know." I flop down on the couch and kick off my flats. "I know it's dumb to like Sai, but I do, so maybe I shouldn't have kissed someone else. Also there's someone who totally likes Elijah, who I'm sort of friends with, so that feels wrong. But also he's really nice."

"And really cute," my mother points out, sitting down across from me. "Are you making too big a deal about this?"

I hold back from laughing and saying that I make too big a deal out of everything. Because she has a point. "It's just— This is so dumb."

"Say it." She grabs a bag of cookies from the coffee table and holds it out to me. "Macadamia nuts will help, right?"

A few bites of a cookie prove her right. "I've never kissed anyone before, except, like, in plays. So . . . is it stupid that I didn't expect it to happen? Or, like, especially with someone who's just like a guy I know?"

"It's definitely not stupid. But don't stress. You'll kiss many more people in your life, and some of them will mean a lot, and some won't. And it's all good either way."

I think about that and then about the hypothetical boys still to be kissed. But mostly I think about how it's a relief to spend a few moments more worried about anything other than my mother for once.

Chapter Eleven

Things I know about Reece Malcolm:

24. *She is a wild squirrel.*
25. *Her boy advice isn't so bad.*

Even though I am wearing new and kind of expensive jeans picked out for me by the very choosy Travis, I am ~~terrified~~ a little nervous walking into school on Monday morning.

And not because the callbacks list will be up.

Elijah is waiting at my locker. He's just leaning there, all casual. "Hey."

"Oh, um, hi. Good morning." *Good morning?* Why am I so weird?

"I was going to text you yesterday," he says, "but I didn't have your number."

"Oh," I say. "Okay. Do you want it?"

He laughs, and his laugh is somehow really hot. I didn't know guys could have hot laughs. "Yeah, I want it."

I give him my number, and he texts me right away so I have his. Is this just how it happens? You get randomly kissed, and then you find yourself wanting to be around that person? For some reason I expected way more complications than that.

(I mean, besides that there's Lissa. And that there's Sai. Not that Sai counts. Lissa is something real to Elijah, obviously, whereas Sai might as well be someone whose poster I tore out of a magazine.)

"Are you doing anything after school?" he asks.

"Well, um, maybe," I say, because that much is true. If I get a callback, Kate said I could come over and work with her. But if I don't—which, okay, I don't think is very likely but *is* possible, especially since I'm so new to New City—I'm completely free and could totally use that free time for kissing Elijah more.

Wait, I should find out if I have a callback.

"Sorry, I—" I try to gesture in a way that will explain everything but I probably look crazy as I dash off from my locker and toward the Music Hall. There's a swarm of people in there, and I have no idea how I'll make my way to the sacred piece of paper and still get to Women's Choir on time. Also, oh my God, I was so rude to Elijah, and do boys stop being interested in you if you're weird *and* rude in the span of, like, two minutes?

I text him while trying to squeeze my way to the sheet. *Sorry, I forgot callbacks were up. I didn't mean to be rude.* My phone beeps almost right away: *no prob. good luck!*

Mira appears out of nowhere and tugs me by the arm down the hallway toward Women's Choir. "I'll save you the trip."

"I'm not on it?"

"Devan, shut up," she says. "Your whole shtick is getting annoying. Can you drop it?"

"I, um, I don't have a shtick."

"Right. The Little Miss Timid thing is just you."

All I can think to say is that I'm working on not being a wild squirrel, but that isn't going to help my cause.

"Of *course* you're on the callback sheet," she says. "You didn't actually doubt that, did you?"

I shrug. "It's my first audition here. I didn't know."

"Trust me, you're the only one feeling any surprise over it." She glances around us, and pulls me all the way into the choir room. "Just so you're aware? Everyone knows what happened Saturday night. Liss and I do, at least."

Crap crap crap.

"It's fine," she says, like suddenly Mira's in charge of banishing my worries. "Lissa's freaked, but it's fine."

"I don't think you get to say it's fine." I didn't mean to say something so honest and borderline bitchy to her, but once it's out I feel brave. Accidentally brave, at least.

"Okay, I don't get to say it's fine." Mira sighs. "And Liss doesn't get to say it's not fine, either. She's rejected Elijah enough times by now to lose whatever claim she has over him."

I don't know why suddenly Mira's so nice, but I'm not

going to question it. I take my seat before Lissa walks in and keep my eyes to the front of the room, which hopefully makes me seem innocent and not like a boyfriend-stealer. I'm not a boyfriend-stealer, right?

I get the weird sensation someone's looking at me, so I glance at Mira (who isn't) and then to Lissa. She's watching me, but she doesn't give me a dirty look or anything. We just kind of hold each other's gazes for a second. Then Mr. Deans is there and we're on our feet for warm-ups, and I tell myself to dwell on the callback and the potential for kissing later. And maybe everyone will be okay with things.

Travis is somehow already outside the Women's Choir room when class lets out. He grabs my hand and yanks me down the hallway. I feel like I'm getting pulled around a lot today.

"So?" he greets me.

"So what?" I ask, as if I'm any good at playing it cool.

"Oh my God, Devvie, so something *significant* happened on Saturday night and you didn't tell me *any* of it on Sunday when we spent *our whole day* together?"

"I—"

"Why didn't you say anything? Elijah's so hot in that whole rock and roll way. I didn't even know you *liked* him, and—"

"Stop talking so loudly," I say, and not just because we're walking by Sai and Nicole. His arm is wrapped tight around her shoulders, but he still looks over to smile and wave at us. How can I hate him for being with her when he's so nice? (Also when I'm maybe with someone, too? But that's just a technicality. Wait, a technicality? Do I think of Elijah as a technicality? The situation, yeah, but not Elijah at all.)

"Who told you?" I ask.

"It doesn't matter," he says. It does, but I don't point that out. "How did this happen? You have to tell me everything."

I shrug. "I don't know. He's . . . he's nice. It just did. And I know I suck because of Lissa and everything—"

"You *do not*," he says. "Lissa and Eli are like this big complicated mess, but one thing they're not is a couple. He's fully available. So is he, like, the best kisser in the world? Musicians are *so hot*."

"You're so nosy." Though maybe he isn't nosy, and I'm just too closed-off or something. I really don't know how to share a little when I can never share everything. "Can we not talk about this at school?"

"Ooh, choice details for later? Okay."

I roll my eyes but find myself kind of leaning in and giving Travis a hug. "Thanks for not hating me."

"You're too adorable to hate. See you in Nation."

By lunchtime, even though honestly no one's being weird to me, I feel weird walking outside like things are normal. Things are the *opposite* of normal, and my brain can't even handle the entirety of the situation. Like that maybe I, no matter what people are saying, am a bad person to Lissa. And maybe I'm not a good friend to Justine, considering how easy it is for me to ignore her now. And maybe I'm not even a good friend to Travis, because he clearly wants me to pony up every detail about whatever is going on, and all

I want to do is hold them closely against my chest with my arms wrapped tight.

So I sit with my usual sandwich at an inside table and text Kate to see if it's still okay to come over later. My phone buzzes in my hand, but it's not Kate responding at lightning speed; it's Elijah.

where r u?

I respond, and before long he's inside sharing my table and stealing part of my sandwich. (It's okay because he shares his Cheetos with me.) It's sweet of him to be in here, but also maybe it draws more attention to us. (Still, it's not like I tell him to leave or anything.) I wonder if this makes me the kind of girl who picks a boy over her friends. Except I didn't, really—the boy picked me.

Since Kate eventually texts back that of course we're still on for tonight, I let Elijah know I can't hang out. He offers to drive me home, and I take him up on it. My mother will know something's up if we're really late, but he still parks at the other end of my street and turns off the car.

I unfasten my seat belt, which suddenly feels like this big bold move, and lean in toward him. This means I'm technically the one who's kissing him, which I like. (Also it's not like Elijah isn't returning the kiss immediately.) He pulls me as close as possible—which isn't very close thanks to his car's design—but it still feels romantic. I'm not sure what to do with my hands, so I put them on his shoulders. We're kissing softly at first, and it's slow and warm, and then before I know it the kisses are blending together. Elijah leans away a little and I'm afraid he's going to say he should take me home—even though he should—but it's to kiss my earlobe and then my neck, which makes me shiver. I thought when people said things like that they were exaggerating, but I literally do shiver.

"Are you sure you have to go home?" he asks in his low husky voice. It's just how he talks but I still like it, like it's just for me.

I want to lie but I don't. "Yeah, I'm sorry, just, callbacks tomorrow, and my mother's friend is going to work with me, and—"

"I know," he says. "Callbacks are a big deal."

I shift around so I'm sitting properly in the seat again, and buckle my seat belt even though we're all but at my house already. "Thanks for understanding."

"It's no problem," he says as he pulls the car down the street and into the driveway. "See you tomorrow."

"See you." I wave and walk inside, where my mother is—as usual—typing on her laptop. "Hi."

She looks up at me. "Hi yourself."

"Um, I think I mentioned something about this the other day, but in case you forgot, Kate said I could come over tonight and work on some vocal stuff. She's going to pick me up and everything. Is it still, like, okay?"

"Like, completely."

Whenever she mocks something I say, it's done so lightly I can't bring myself to get offended anymore. Also I've realized maybe it's just her, having witnessed her repeating back to Brad his Britishisms, as if there isn't a whole country where people talk like him. He always bursts into laughter, though, mocking right back because while her impression is good, her fake accent is like something out of a bad high school play.

Kate picks me up about an hour later. It would have been enough time to finish my homework if I'd done that instead of spending my time picking out a perfectly casual singing outfit (I switch out my jeans for yoga pants and my flats for my gray and blue sneakers) and looking at pictures of Elijah ~~and Sai~~ on Facebook.

"Hi, sweetie," Kate greets me as I get into her car. "So I hear there's a boy." Her eyebrows rise conspiratorially, and then: "Already!" like the entire word is the exclamation point.

"It's not a big deal," I say, not sure if that's a lie or not.

"I hear he wears *guyliner.*"

I don't know how to tell Kate Logan not to call it that so I just kind of shrug.

At her house in her piano room, I sing through "Like It Was," wishing I could have used it for my initial audition instead of "Now You Know," which is bigger and faster and showier. I'm not sure how I can blow anyone's mind with this one.

"So here's the thing, sweetie," Kate says when I've completed the song to her very barebones accompaniment. "You, of all people, should stop worrying so much about hitting the right notes. Of course you're going to! Try to feel the song more."

Normally it's like I can't *stop* feeling things to my very core. Real life things, at least. It's hard to wrap my brain around needing the opposite for music.

"I feel like you've got the sadness down," she says. "But

there's more in there, you see that when you think about it, right? Anger? And also a sense of humor about it?"

I nod as my brain catches up with that.

"Also, you don't need to"—she flings her hands into the air—"attack each note with such *gusto*! This phrase here . . ."

I lean over her shoulder to follow along in the sheet music.

"What if you let that be a quiet moment? Trust me, I used to be scared of those, too, and I probably would have forsaken them even more if I'd had your pipes."

"Yours are—"

"Oh, please! You have such the gift. But we won't forget that if sometimes you dial it back a notch."

I'm not sure about that, but I try again, keeping all of what she said in mind. Afterward we both laugh because it's seriously so so so terrible. I've never sung so badly in my life—and in front of *Kate Logan*. You'd never think I could just laugh, but I guess Kate is right about a lot. I know I have something, and one bad rendition isn't going to disprove anything.

"You are thinking way too hard," she says. "Just absorb it all, and let it go."

I raise an eyebrow at that.

"My God, you look exactly like your mom when you do that. Come on, let's walk around the house, get your mind off of this for a minute."

I follow her out of the room and down the hallway. By the time we're back in the piano room, I don't feel any more ready to tackle the song again, but I don't really have a choice. This time, though, I start actually understanding what Kate means. This time I do feel it all.

"That was amazing," she tells me. "Okay, let's do it again."

"But—" I feel weird that it's supposedly amazing but I have to sing it another time.

"If this is how good you are after a few tries, imagine how you'll be when it's effortless," she says. "Just because you're brilliant doesn't mean you can't be better."

This might be kind of dumb, but it's a revelation to hear. Obviously practice isn't just for people who aren't that great, but I generally sail through songs so easily on my first attempt. *Of course* there are levels of greatness, of nailing it. For caring so much, maybe I've been kind of complacent.

So I go through "Like It Was" at least five more times with Kate, and then "Now You Know," even though I don't need it for tomorrow. My head feels hollowed out, between the complacency revelation and working my voice harder than ever before. But who knew utterly drained and lightheaded could feel so good?

Kate drives me back home, where Brad is putting dinner on the table and my mother has her MacBook on top of her empty dinner plate.

"You're just in time," Brad says to me, which is a nice way to be greeted. My mother doesn't look up but she does wave. "I'm relieved someone will talk to me during dinner."

"I'm almost finished with this scene," my mother says. "Thanks for cooking. And putting up with me."

Brad laughs. "Devan, how was school?"

I think about telling them I got a callback, but I don't know if it sounds like a very big deal to a TV writer and a Pulitzer Prize winner. So I just say it was fine, which I guess it was. My mother eventually does close her computer and let Brad serve her spinach quiche and salad, and Brad tells us a story about getting really great sandwiches for lunch but makes it sound way more exciting than sandwiches should be. They let me do the dishes—completely on my own—after we eat, which feels like a big step in helping them out, and then I head up to my room to do my homework.

When I check my phone there's a missed text from Elijah. *u have time to talk?* I don't, but it's enough that he wants to. (I have another text, too, from Justine, about The Tenor, but it doesn't feel like a response is required.) I text back an apology to Elijah, and he gets it, because he's nice, and so I concentrate on my English lit.

My phone rings a couple minutes later, and I wonder if Elijah didn't actually get it, but it's not him. It's Sai.

I answer right away.

"Hey!" he says. "You aren't nervous about tomorrow, right? You're gonna nail callbacks. You're the best singer in Nation."

We've never talked on the phone before, but I love how you'd never know that from how normal Sai makes it. I'm sure he's never been awkward one day in his life.

"Thanks," I say. "And, no, I'm not really nervous. Are you?"

"Probably more than you. Not used to being in the chorus; afraid that's what I'll get stuck with. But it's all good. Character-building? That's what people say?"

"Yeah, sure," I say.

"Heard something about you and Cross," he says.

Who would have told him? Travis? (Probably.) I wish Sai didn't know. Is that bad? "Oh, um. Yeah."

"Yeah? Didn't know you were—"

"It just kind of happened," I say, which is—well, as my mother would say—a-*ma*-zing. When Justine arrived home from choir camp and told me about the first night she made out with The Tenor, that's how she put it. And I listened faux-enthusiastically when all I could think was, *How does anything like that* just happen*?*

"Yeah, I know how that goes," Sai says.

Of course he does.

"I know it's kind of weird," I say so he knows that I don't think it isn't. "Especially because of Lissa or whatever. Maybe I shouldn't have—"

"Him and Lissa aren't official or anything, far as I know. I don't think you did anything wrong. Not sure you could do anything wrong if you tried, Dev."

It's one of the nicest things anyone has ever said to me. And Sai isn't just *anyone*. I never felt the way I feel about Sai with anyone else. I know it's bad, but to be fair I never felt the way I do about Elijah with anyone else, either. Sai might be gorgeous and confident and talented and a not-so-secret nerd, but I know I could never just lean in and kiss Sai. Elijah has a lot going for him, too.

Still, it's amazing Sai thinks such kind things about me.

"Man," Sai says. "Bad night."

"Are you . . ."

"Am I what?" he asks after I fade out. Somehow Sai can smile with his voice.

"Are you okay?"

"My dad just, ya know . . ." Now it's Sai who fades out. "Spent a lot of tonight yelling at me. It sucks because you'd think the one tradeoff for it happening all the time is I'd get used to it."

I shrug, even though that's stupid over the phone. "I got used to it. From my stepmom, I mean. But, like, only that I expected it. It's not like it ever felt any better."

I say it before I think about it too much. My old life isn't something I want people at New City to know about, because its disappearance is pretty much required for me to seem normal. But sometimes it's like Sai isn't part of my New City world at all. My brain stores him somewhere else, somewhere I can't even pinpoint.

"That sucks," he says. "Dunno. Still think maybe you got to a better place with it than me."

"Maybe so," I said.

"I only have two more years," he said. "Less than. Gotta get through school, and I'll be okay. But it—" His voice breaks only a little but I feel it like I'm being choked. "It gets worse. He hates me a lot more than he used to. And don't try to be nice and say crap like I'm wrong, he doesn't hate me, I'm his son so he doesn't hate me. Trust me. He does."

"I wasn't going to. I was going to say I was sorry."

He's silent for a while. It's a good thing that thanks to my mother I've grown comfortable with silence, so that I don't blurt out anything annoying like *are you there? can you hear me?* "Thanks, Dev."

Out of nowhere, I think about nights like this a billion years ago, or really just a few months back. I wish I had a grimy old key to a music room to offer out to Sai right now. Those nights I slipped off with Justine saved something in me. It seems silly that Sai could need that kind of salvation, but I still wish I had it to give to him.

It's weird how at this moment, it's not Justine but the key that I miss—well, what the key brought me, because technically the key is strung on a ribbon and tucked into my jewelry box. Back when the key was the only escape we had—me from Dad and Tracie, her from an empty house because while her parents were great, they weren't always around a lot—I figured I'd never feel so connected to anyone as I did to her. And now all of it is gone: the key, the connection, and me.

Chapter Twelve

Things I know about Reece Malcolm:

26. *She knows she's someone who has to be put up with.*
27. *She trusts me enough to help her out (a little).*

My previous schools didn't usually do callbacks. Even if there were a lot of people who wanted to be in the musical, I think teachers usually found it easy to choose who was good enough to be cast. (Sometimes I was pretty sure they picked the show based around who they wanted to cast.) But at New City we're being whittled down, and even though maybe it's silly, it makes me feel closer to someday doing this for real.

Everyone in every choir seems distracted, but Mr. Deans doesn't call us out on it, just makes us sing pieces five and six times instead of two and three, and I know he must understand. At lunch (inside again) I don't bother to eat and instead stare at my sheet music. It's not that I'm nervous, but I have to know I did everything I could to be ready.

"Hey." Elijah sits down next to me with a soda and a sandwich. "You need to be alone to get into the callback zone?"

"I don't have a callback zone," I say. "And hi."

He kisses me, very softly, totally okay on school grounds. I still hope no one sees us. "I expected some kind of haze. Glazed eyes, foaming at the mouth, the whole thing."

"You are weird," I say. "I'm actually totally calm about auditions."

"I'll believe that when I see it."

"Shut up." I grin and look back to my music. I think about last night, and my mother's computer-covered plate while Brad and I started dinner. I guess we'd both postpone food for art. (Also lots of food—especially anything with dairy—can make your throat mucusy. Gross but true.) "Sorry I couldn't talk last night. I had sort of a voice lesson in the afternoon, so I still had all my homework left."

Also obviously I talked to Sai for like an hour but that has nothing to do with anything. Right?

"It's cool," he says. "Maybe you can hang out tonight, though?"

"I can ask my mother, sure." I do want to be alone with him again, where we won't have to worry about anyone seeing us kiss, where I can let myself be someone who kisses a boy she doesn't really know but—maybe breaking laws of logic—likes a lot anyway.

After school we crowd into the Music Hall, but it's a much smaller group than last week. Even though the list was publicly hung in the hallway yesterday morning, there's still a lot of scoping out the competition. My whole lunch table—minus Elijah, of course—has made it this far. It makes me feel kind of special until I remember whatever's going on with Elijah means they're not really my lunch table anymore.

"Whoa," Travis says, as the door opens and Elijah slips in. "Devvie, did your boyfriend get a callback?"

"He's not my boyfriend," I say really quickly, hoping that Lissa and Mira, who are sitting on the opposite side of the room, didn't hear that. Well, or Sai. Except of course Sai heard. He's sitting right next to me.

"Hey." Elijah walks over. "I had to see it for myself, you actually calm."

"She's an old pro," Sai says, resting his hand on the back of my chair. *Old?*

"Yeah, I know," Elijah says.

"You're not in the choir room with her every day," Sai says.

"I still *know her*," Elijah says, in the sexy way he says things sometimes. I really hope Sai doesn't think Elijah means *know* know.

"What are you doing after this?" Elijah asks.

"Ooh, coffee, maybe," Travis says. "We could all compare notes on—"

"I was," Elijah says, "talking to Devan."

I do my best to subtly glance over at Lissa and Mira. Their eyes are not so subtly trained on us. "Um. My mom's picking me up. When I'm finished. But, um, later, maybe? After dinner?"

"Yeah, just call me."

I nod, feeling my face flood with heat as he retreats from the room.

"Devvie." Travis shakes his head. "You have no game."

"What's she need *game* for?" Sai asks. "That guy's got it bad."

"Text him and tell him you'll definitely hang out later," Travis says. "And then just let your mom know."

"She doesn't have to," Sai says. "Not if she doesn't want to."

"Lissa Anderson, Jasmine Murray, Devan Malcolm."

"That's me. See you guys." I get to my feet, way way way grateful for the interruption. It would be better, obviously, if Lissa wasn't being called at the same time.

They call Jasmine into the choir room first, *of course*, so I'm left alone in the quiet hallway with Lissa.

"Hey," she says.

"Um, hi."

She nods, tucking her hair behind her ears. "I can't believe how E and Sai were acting in there." She nods toward the waiting room of sorts. "Peeing all over you."

"What?"

Lissa looks back to me, a smile slowly sliding across her face. "Marking their territory. That's what I meant."

"Oh!"

"It's Mira's joke; I just lifted it." She shrugs a little. "So you're not hanging out with E after this?"

I shake my head.

"Wanna go to Starbucks?" She leans in a little closer, drops her voice down to a whisper. "Promise I won't invite Mira along, okay?"

I don't think I can refuse her after spending so much time kissing her okay-not-technically-boyfriend-but-still.

Jasmine walks out into the hallway and points to me. "They want you next."

"Good luck," Lissa tells me, which is nicer than I feel like I deserve.

I walk into the room, and it's the same teachers as last time. Hardly any time passes before the accompanist begins, and I try to forget about how much hinges on this song. I even try to forget all the amazing advice Kate gave me, because I don't want it to clog my brain. I just sing.

Afterward I wait in the hallway for Lissa, and she walks out with her mouth in a straight line. I've seriously never seen Lissa look anything but happy.

"Are you okay?" I ask, even though maybe I shouldn't acknowledge anything.

"I hit a couple bad notes," she says. "A *couple*."

"A couple isn't bad," I say.

"Enough people will try out without missing any," she says. "It's okay, though; I don't think I'm the lead type. I'm not even sure I want to be in a musical, but I felt like I should at least try."

I text my mother that I have a ride home, and then walk outside with Lissa to her car. We're quiet and I still have no idea what to expect.

"I'm sorry," I say, because I am. Regardless of anything. "If I shouldn't have—"

"Listen, to be honest I'm not a huge fan of E going out with you, but . . . " Lissa shrugs. "Obviously we had our chance together, and it kind of fizzled. And I knew he still liked me and I like him—as a person, you know. But I didn't want to go out with him. So who am I to say what he can't do now?"

I sort out the information, piles in my brain.

"And, Devan, you are lucky, because I was the first girl he kissed, and he was *awful*. You have me to thank for any fun you've had as far as that's concerned."

I laugh, against my better judgment. "Thank you?"

"Oh, you are welcome." She turns her car into the parking lot behind Starbucks and slides right into one of the first spots. "You could have talked to me, you know. It's so weird you were acting so scared of everyone."

I know I shouldn't say it's because a lot of the time I basically *am* scared of everyone. Time to work on my wild squirrel mantra more.

We walk into Starbucks and get into line to order. I check my phone to see if my mother has responded, and she has. *Of course it's fine. Be home for dinner if you can because Brad's making burgers on the grill and they will amaze you. xo*

"Do you think burgers could amaze anyone?" I ask without thinking about it. Then I feel really dorky. "Sorry I asked that; my mother just sent me a weird text."

Lissa looks over my shoulder and laughs. For a moment it's like I'm two thousand miles away with Justine. It's surprisingly nice. "How *will* burgers amaze you? Do they do magic?"

"Brad *is* a really good cook," I say. "My mother's boyfriend."

"You're lucky. My parents are both terrible cooks."

She steps up to order, but I kind of push in so that I can pay for her drink, too. I feel like I should do *something* for sort-of-not-really stealing her sort-of-not-really-boyfriend.

"I felt so weird when it happened," I say once we have our drinks and we sit down at the only open table. "Like he was kissing me and I kept thinking about you and how I was a terrible person."

"Well, definitely don't think about *me* when you're kissing E," she says. "God, don't stress. Seriously."

Then she laughs kind of hysterically. "I guess it's pointless telling you not to do that."

"Ugh, kind of," I say.

"Yeah, E and I had . . . something. We didn't *not* have something. But if you like him . . . "

"You're being too nice about this," I say, as if I'm an authority. Maybe people act like this all the time, who knows. "I just feel—"

"How you feel *kind of* doesn't matter," she says. "Not to sound like a bitch, but, you know? If you're worried about me, and I say it's okay . . ."

I'm not sure I could be this reasonable, considering I have way less claim to Sai than Lissa does to Elijah—well, no claim at all, let's be honest—and I still hate Nicole for being his girlfriend. "You have a point, yeah."

"You and Mira are kind of the same," she says.

"What?"

"Ha, sorry," she says, which I guess means I look as alarmed as I feel. "It's just that she freaks out over everything, too. You admit it, which is a big difference. Mira's a lot crazier than she used to be."

"I hate that she hates me." It's way more honest than I intended, but there it sits, right in the air, between us.

"She hates *everyone*," Lissa says. "Even me, and we've been friends since kindergarten."

"I guess to be fair she was kind of nice yesterday," I say. "Nice for Mira at least."

"See? Don't take it personally."

I'm not sure I can manage, but I know it's good advice.

We finish our Frappuccinos and then walk back outside to Lissa's car. I feel about twenty times better than I did this morning, with the callback behind me and Lissa clearly not mad.

"Do you still want to go together to E's show on Friday?" Lissa asks as she pulls up to my house.

"Um." I do want to, but I don't know if I *should* want to. Is it weird? Is it weirder not to? But here's the thing: I want to be Lissa's friend. And if I'm going to follow Kate's mantra, I have to reach out. Right? "If that's okay with you."

Lissa shrugs like it's a no-brainer. "Definitely. And you have to tell me tomorrow if the burgers are literally magical."

"Maybe they'll all get letters from Hogwarts."

We laugh, and I wave and get out of the car. My mother is working in the living room, but Brad is in the kitchen and recruits me to help. He teaches me how to make burgers, which is pretty easy even though touching raw meat is ~~completely~~ a little gross. It feels like a dumb thing to get hung up on when someone so nice is being so patient with me. And then it makes me think about how Brad will be a really good dad someday, if he wants to be, though I guess that would be if he and my mother break up. I can't exactly imagine Reece Malcolm and kids would mix; I barely count, really.

After dinner (the hamburgers don't perform magic or anything but it is incredible how amazing they taste), my mother says it's fine if I want to hang out with Elijah, so I text him. I know I should probably spend a little more time on my homework or reviewing my callback in my head, but I don't end up thinking about it nearly as much as I normally would. You think you know how you'll react to anything, and then a boy shows up and kisses you, and some of that just vanishes. I wonder what else of me is waiting for life to erase it.

Elijah shows up a little while later and is polite to my mother and Brad, and I feel special that it's for my benefit. Maybe it's silly that I can still hardly believe a boy likes me—because to be honest lots of people end up being liked, and I can accept I'm not less special than *all* of them—but maybe it's okay it feels rare and amazing.

Outside, in his car, we kiss once, twice, lose-track-of times. Until my brain kicks in full-strength and I remember a question I should have already asked.

"Um, hey." I pull away from him. Just a little. Our cheeks are still kind of grazing. "How did Lissa and Mira find out?"

"Liss is my best friend." He backs out of the driveway and pulls onto the street. "Of course I'll tell her. As for Mira, Liss must have told her. You mind that I said something to Liss?"

"No," I say. "I guess you could have told me you told her, though. I could have been prepared on Monday at school."

"Don't worry so much." He reaches over and touches my hair before taking my hand. "You're one of those people who's gonna have a heart attack at twenty."

"Shut up." I shiver as he traces a couple of his fingertips over my palm. "If that's true, you'll feel bad when it happens."

Elijah laughs. "True that. So you want to come over? I was thinking maybe since you're so into music you could hear my band's demo. Lame?"

"Totally not lame. I want to hear it. Can you play for me, too?"

"I mean, I *can*," he says. "But bear in mind I play bass, so it's just gonna be like *dum dum dum dum dum dum dummmm* over and over."

"You totally *have to* then."

"Then you have to act like it's actually cool."

Elijah's mom is out, so at his house we head up to his room, since that's where the bass as well as the demo CD are. And I feel myself getting nervous, because I'm in a boy's bedroom where there is an actual *bed* and once you kiss someone, isn't it assumed more will happen?

"Okay, you have to keep up your end of the deal." He slides his black bass's strap over his shoulder before plugging it into his amp. "I expect total groupie behavior."

I pretend to rock out, head-banging to his playing, which, okay, is pretty lame without the other instruments. But he's *good*, and now I get why he likes us theatre geeks, because at least we have passion for music in common.

"Okay, this'll be better." He puts the bass back on its stand and hits a few buttons on his computer. Music blares out of the speakers—punk, which I expected, but at least it isn't just loud and fast, but melodic and fairly polished, too.

"You guys are really good," I say.

"Thanks," he says, pulling me out of the desk chair I was sitting in. Safer than the bed, right? "You should sing with us sometime."

"Right, my voice is *so suited* to it."

"Seriously," he says. "You should stretch yourself, put yourself out there. Bet you're capable of stuff you never even imagined."

I kiss him for saying that, which leads to more kissing, and standing-up kissing eventually leads to sitting-down kissing, which—even though it's on the bed—feels fine. Well, you know. More than fine.

"How was your callback?" he asks when there's a lull in kissing. "Do you find out soon?"

"Pretty good. And, yeah, tomorrow morning." My stomach flips a little thinking about that cast list hanging in the hall, how right now Mr. Deans or whoever must have already printed it, how if my name's not on it I don't know how I'll get through the next few months at New City. "Do you guys have auditions and stuff in the music department?"

"At the end of the year before so we know what classes we'll be in," he says. "Some people try out to be in the orchestra for the musical but they don't always do shows that need a bass. This one doesn't. Last year I got to play for *Spring Awakening*, so that was cool."

"I'm so glad I don't go to a normal school anymore," I say, which makes Elijah laugh. "I'm being serious!"

"I know. It's cute." He takes my hand and spins my bracelet around on my wrist. "So you're glad you moved and everything? Don't miss St. Louis?"

It's like one moment my brain is full of things like kissing and cute boys and how it feels to exist in a world where everyone I know seems to care about the same things in life, and then the next it grinds to a stop.

"Yeah." I'm not even sure it's a real answer, and I know it's nothing like how I actually feel about my situation. Not how guilty I feel for ruining my mother's life twice—once by being born and once by moving here—or how I never felt so alone as when I lived just with Tracie for those three months before her lawyer figured out where I was supposed to go. And maybe I shouldn't love being here, because of the guilt thing, but I kind of do.

And I'm not going to tell Elijah any of that.

"I should probably go home," I say. "I still have a lot of homework."

"Same, unfortunately," he says, and we walk downstairs and out to his car. Of course we kiss for a while before the car's actually pulling up to my house, and I'm glad. All the heaviness in my brain hides away again.

"See you at school tomorrow," he says. "Good luck, but you won't need it."

"Thank you." I kiss him once more—not just for saying that, but it's part of it for sure—and head inside. Brad's alone in the living room with his laptop.

"Hello, Devan," he says. "Reece is in her office, as we don't always work well in the same room. How was your evening?"

I'm pretty sure there's no part of hanging out with your sort-of boyfriend you should have to report to your mother's boyfriend, so I just shrug. "Fine."

"I was talked into making dessert after you left, so if you're interested . . . "

"Totally," I say, following him into the kitchen. It literally seems like he's still opening the refrigerator when my mother appears in the doorway.

"Hey, kid," she greets me. "Good night?"

"Sure," I say.

"I believe you have superpowers when it comes to the sounds of pie being served," Brad says, which makes her laugh.

"Hell *yeah* I do. Don't you remember? That's almost exactly the first thing you ever said to me."

Brad laughs as he makes sure I get the first slice of chocolate pie. It's impressive, given how closely my mother seems to be all-but-circling it. "I nearly forgot that."

My mother glances at me. "We were at a catered party, and I'm pretty great at intercepting caterwaiters before their trays are empty."

"I regretted saying that quite a lot," Brad says. "I was only trying to find an excuse to talk to you, and it seemed to be bordering on an insult."

"Eh, I didn't take it as one," she says. "Also your accent helps."

I laugh because it's so true. Also right here in the kitchen, over chocolate pie, I can feel how much they love each other, and it's kind of funny how I feel better off for it. What if Dad died a year earlier and there was no Brad in the house when I moved in, and therefore no pie and no excuse to stand in the kitchen at night? Not that I wanted Dad to die *at all*, obviously. My brain feels like it could cloud with darkness again, and so I try to overcome that with pie and replaying moments with Elijah. I wonder if my mother feels comfortable telling Brad the dark, horrible things about her. There must be dark, horrible things somewhere in Reece Malcolm, right? And does Brad feel okay telling her all his hopes and dreams and whatever else?

I can't imagine ever feeling that way about someone else. I hope that doesn't mean I'm a completely screwed-up person.

"You look serious," my mother says, and I realize she's talking to me.

"Sorry."

She laughs. "There's no apology required for that. Everything all right?"

"Totally. I should just do my homework and sleep."

"In that order." She grins at me. "Good night, kid."

"Good night, Devan," Brad says.

"'Night." I wave and walk upstairs, where I focus on homework only, definitely not picturing the cast list sheet or Elijah ~~or Sai~~ or every single thing and person I'm scared of.

Chapter Thirteen

Things I know about Reece Malcolm:

28. *She has a superpower when it comes to pie.*

The next morning I run straight to the Music Hall. I mean, callbacks were one thing. A cast list is another entirely.

I don't even worry about being polite as I navigate my way through the mob crowding around it, though I do notice people are kind of stepping away to let me through. I don't spend time debating if it's a good sign or not, just look at the cast list, run my finger down until I find my name, and even though I'm only the third person listed—*ohmy godi'monlythethirdpersonlisted*—still run my finger over to confirm I've gotten the role I wanted.

And there it is in black and white: *Mary Flynn: Devan Malcolm.*

Considering how tight the crowd is getting, I excuse myself, running into Sai as I attempt to cross the hallway to Women's Choir. Like, literally. My face smacks into his chest.

Oh my God. It's really firm.

"Man, watch out." Sai laughs and grabs my shoulders to keep me from bouncing off of him and into someone else. I notice there's a huge splotch of my lip gloss on his T-shirt where I face-planted into him. "Congrats, by the way. You're gonna be awesome."

"Thanks." I grin at him. "Oh my God, I didn't even look at anyone else. You got something, though, right?"

"I got something," he tells me. "See you in Nation."

"See you," I say, waving before—"Sai!"

He's already too far down the hallway, past the gathering crowd, to hear my warnings that my MAC Dazzleglass (in the embarrassingly named shade of Love Alert) is currently giving the illusion that some girl (who is definitively not the girlfriend he's about to have class with) had her mouth on him this morning. For a split second I cross my fingers for some Love Alert–motivated suspicion and jealousy. Wait, no, I don't. That would make me a terrible person.

"Devan!" Lissa runs up behind me as I walk into Women's Choir. "Congratulations. Are you completely psyched?"

"Totally," I say, which makes her laugh.

"Sometime I want to see you go really crazy. You just got a huge role."

"This *is* me really crazy."

We laugh even though obviously it's kind of true.

"How were the burgers of magic?" she asks.

"Oh my God, pretty amazing. No actual magic but close."

Mira walks into the room and makes a beeline for us. "Liss, I'm sorry."

"It's fine," Lissa says, and I realize her name must have not been on the list. I was so used to checking only for me—or me and Justine—but now there are other people I should have looked for, too.

"They're stupid to leave you out," Mira tells her, before glancing at me. "I can't believe the lead female role calls for someone who can be sarcastic and bitter, and yet of course it's the year you show up and basically already land the part your first day."

"I, um, I didn't mean to."

"Devan." She knocks her shoulder into mine. "Don't be stupid, of course you did. Your act has to stop."

Last time she accused me of having an act, she was wrong, but right now I feel pretty stupid. Of *course* I did. This is the most important thing in my life. I mean, after everything with my mother. Or is it the other way around?

"Seriously, congratulations, even if we all saw it coming. You really deserve it."

"Thank you," I say, thrown by this gush of niceness from her. Who is this new and nicer Mira? "What about you? I'm sorry, I totally forgot to look."

"K.T.," she says. "The journalist. It's a good featured role considering I've never even been in the chorus before."

"Definitely," I say. "Congratulations. You get to be in, like, one of the best scenes."

"I know." Mira grins so fully it's almost like she's a different person. "Thanks."

Mr. Deans tries to lead us through a warm-up and then "Down to the River to Pray," which is the latest song he's added to our repertoire, but the mood's super distracted, from girls who didn't get roles and girls who did. He excuses the crappy performance on it being one of our newer songs and leads us through a Haydn piece, which is silly because if we can't manage English today, Latin is not going to happen.

"Why doesn't everyone use this period to study?" he says after the second sloppy rendition. "Devan, can I see you up here?"

I used to love getting called up individually by choir teachers. Not to sound ~~completely snotty~~ ~~egotistical~~ full of myself, but it would inevitably be about something good. Until the day it was about the worst thing ever.

But I walk up to Mr. Deans as normally as I can and hope I don't blurt out something stupid. "Um, hi. Is everything okay?"

Mr. Deans laughs. "I love how quickly I'm learning how high-strung you are. Everything's fine. I wanted to tell you how excited I am to have you as Mary. When you sang 'Now You Know' your first day, I hoped you'd have a great audition for the others, because I was already sold."

"Thank you so much," I say. "I'm really excited. It's, like, one of my very favorite shows."

He smiles and nods. "I had a feeling."

I talk to him a few more minutes about *Merrily* before returning to my desk. Of course no one is studying, and Mira and Lissa gesture for me to take the empty seat near them.

"Are you okay?" Lissa asks.

"Yeah, you look more freaked out than usual," Mira said.

I'm not about to tell them that the last time I got called up in choir it was because my dad was dead. So I shrug and try to play it off as one of my weird things I guess everyone is used to by now. And it actually feels okay getting teased, and not just because it's better than talking about Dad. It's like—in spite of everything—life is becoming good and normal. And I've been waiting a long time for that.

❋ ❋ ❋

Today Elijah says we should eat outside, and considering how Lissa seems fine with everything and Mira's being less randomly mean, I know he's right. So after getting through the sandwich line, I follow him outside, hoping it's not super weird that we're walking together. We're not doing anything like holding hands or even standing closer than usual, but I do feel everyone's eyes on us as we approach the table.

It's the weirdest thing that for so long I would have killed for a group of friends, and now that I—sort of?—have them, I find myself longing at least a little for the days when I didn't have to worry about what anyone else thought. Having a boy around who wants to kiss me would be way better if everyone else wasn't thinking about it, too.

He leans in a little like that will make our conversation private at a table full of people who're following us like a hot celebrity couple. "What are you doing after school?"

"I have Nation," I say. "Sorry."

Travis sits down on my other side, and I grin at him. We didn't get a chance to talk in Nation because I guess after losing control of Women's Choir, Mr. Deans ran a tight ship.

"Congratulations," I say.

"For what?" He rolls his eyes. "I can't believe what a small role I got."

"Some people didn't get roles at all," I say as lightly as I can. At least Travis has a featured chorus role. But also of course I know if I'd ended up with a featured chorus role I'd be completely ~~devastated~~ depressed right now.

"You don't get it," he says, which I guess is fair, but still. I'd try to understand. "And I should have known you wouldn't."

I open my mouth to respond, but I don't know what to say, and he moves back to his original spot anyway. Almost immediately, someone else sits down next to me.

And that someone is Sai.

"I meant to talk to you in Nation, but, man, Deans was going crazy," he says. "I was thinking for our Acting project, we could do a scene together."

Elijah glances at Sai and then at me. But we're not doing anything wrong.

"Sure," I say. Sai's the only other junior in the class anyway, and even if I didn't want to spend time with him—not, like, romantic time, I just like hanging out with him—it would make sense for us to pair up. Still, I glance at Elijah to make sure he doesn't look suspicious. Then I realize I haven't known Elijah long or well enough to know what suspicious looks like on him. I guess he seems neutral enough.

Elijah and I kind of take off on our own to head to class as lunch is ending. To everyone else's credit, despite that there seems to be *a lot* of watching us going on, no one follows us or anything. And I remind myself I *like* being around Elijah. I have to stop overthinking things.

"So tonight you have Nation—tomorrow?"

I shake my head. "It's the first night of rehearsals."

"Friday's my show," he says. "You think we can manage to hang out before then?"

"I, um, I don't know," I say. "But I'm definitely coming to your show. Just so you know, between the musical and Nation, I'll be busy basically all the time."

"I know," he says with a shrug. "I just like hanging out with you."

"Why?" I ask, totally accidentally. Luckily he laughs, and leans in and kisses me. It's funny how an action like that goes: I'm calmed by how nice he is, how already this feels familiar, how my heart also races in this really clichéd way. (I guess clichés come from somewhere.) All from his lips against mine for just a moment.

My mother picks me up from Nation rehearsal after school, but drops me off at home alone so she can run errands. I'm actually glad to have the house to myself. I don't want to slack on my homework again (like last night), plus I'm not used to having so little time on my own here. Being alone has advantages, like belting songs at the top of your lungs without disturbing anyone or embarrassing yourself.

Also, of course, trying to figure out Reece Malcolm. Sometimes—obviously—it's easier without her around.

I slip into her office. My mother's recent email is really no help. The discussion with Brad regarding a television in the living room is still, somehow, going on, but my name hasn't come up again. (Also there's nothing preceding Brad's comment about apologizing regarding me, so that must have come from a real life talk, not an email. I'm not sure if that's a relief or not.)

There are emails with Kate about getting lunch, and emails with Vaughn about business stuff (royalty checks and her latest advance), and plenty of other random emails to and from Brad about the house and dinners and plans and some subjects I'm blocking from my brain until science invents a bleach or other very selective memory deleter.

The thing is, though, as far as emails go, I really don't exist.

Is that a good thing or a bad thing?

I feel like I've done everything I can in the office, so I brainstorm for a bit before heading upstairs to my mother and Brad's room. There I learn that they both keep the closet and shelves meticulously organized, that T-shirts—most bearing names of bands I've never heard of—take up about 80 percent of Brad's closet space, and that despite her being prone to fashion ignorance, my mother owns several pairs of amazing shoes, mixed in with the Converse of varying colors.

I sit down on the bed to examine all the framed photos

on my mother's nightstand. There are none of Brad and, of course, none of me. One is of my mother and a woman who looks enough like her—and me, I guess—and is old enough that I figure she's her mother. (She looks normal, not overly Botoxed like I guess I imagined.) Why haven't I met her yet? There are also a few pictures of my mother with Kate, and with Vaughn, and one of Kate and Vaughn getting married. (Kate's dress is to die for, of course.) The only unidentifiable photo is a black and white picture of an old-fashioned couple on their wedding day; I figure maybe they're my mother's grandparents. It's weird to have so much history that doesn't feel like mine at all.

It's annoying I was brave enough to search through the room and still end up empty-handed. But also deep down I know I shouldn't be surprised. It's not like if anyone searched my room really hard they'd figure everything out about me. I mean, I lived with Dad and Tracie my whole life and it usually felt like I would never understand them. Why did I think I'd have better luck with Reece Malcolm?

I look around to make sure nothing's out of place before heading back to my room. And maybe it's dumb, but I open my desk drawer and take out some of my favorite theatre programs so I can tack them up on my walls here, just like they'd been back in my Missouri room. There's a lot I'm afraid to tell people, but I don't want to be a mystery in my own room.

❊ ❊ ❊

We have our first rehearsal the next day after school, though it mainly just involves passing out scripts and rehearsal schedules and introducing ourselves like we don't all have Nation or Honors Choir or Acting together anyway. Mr. Deans has either totally forgotten what high school is like or is a sadist, because he basically seats us from biggest to smallest part, which leaves Travis glaring over at me, as well as Sai, who is playing Charley. I tell myself it's way safer with him in that role and a senior I hardly know, Aaron Finley, as the other lead, because I really don't want to act unrequitedly in love with Sai with a whole audience present. Even in character.

Mira, unlike Travis, looks thrilled—the new Mira is still in control, I guess—to be there, wedged in between the chorus and the bigger roles. I tell myself if I were in their shoes I'd be more like her than Travis, but who knows? I've always gotten pretty big roles in school productions. Chorus—even featured chorus—would depress me, too.

That night my mother and I have a very quiet dinner out at the very loud Mexican place on Ventura. Afterward we walk down the sidewalk in the cool evening air, and when I do a double-take over a pair of red shoes in the window of a shoe store, she makes me go inside and try them on.

"I have enough shoes," I say, even though I don't believe that's actually possible.

"Who cares?" she says. "Let me do something nice once in a while, all right?"

"You do nice things all the time," I say, even though that's different than actually *being* nice. I don't know if I think Reece Malcolm is nice.

"Too kind." She flops into the chair next to me. "How is everything?"

"Everything's okay." I slide out of the new shoes and back into my old ones. "You really don't have to get these."

"Eh." She gathers them up and carries them to the register. I wait by the door, and thank her only a thousand times as we keep walking. Then I summon the courage to bring up something that's been nagging me a little since last night when I saw those pictures in her bedroom. Okay, a lot of things nag at me but this one feels safe-ish to ask about.

"Why haven't I met anyone in your family?" My heart starts pounding before it's even past my lips, so it's more than a minor miracle I get it out.

"If we're technical," she says, "I only have one person in my family: my mother. And she's in New York, which isn't exactly conducive for you two meeting. Trust me, she's tried. My mother's just . . . exhausting. I wanted you to be settled in a while longer first. And if we're not being technical, I'd say you've already met my family: Brad. Kate and Vaughn. Chosen family counts for more in my book."

Something about that phrase cuts through me roughly. She didn't choose me at all, and deep down I know I count for less. Hearing it sucks, though.

"How are things with the boy?" she asks.

"Fine, I guess," I say. "But he wants to hang out more than I can, since I have so many rehearsals after school . . ."

"Yeah, I swear, half a relationship is time management," she says, then sighs. "Not actually. I know."

"Are you okay?" I ask, because there's something about the way she exhaled that seemed like she's really rattled.

"Brad wanted me to go out with him tonight," she says. "Some concert I don't care about, that he does, and maybe if I cared enough about him, I'd go."

"Is that what he said?" I ask. "I mean—sorry. It isn't any of my business."

"I'm the one who brought it up," she says. "And, no. He didn't. But I worry he thinks it. I worry I— *Shit.* It's just . . . the possibility exists this is all I am, this is all I have to give." She gestures at me. "I'm no fucking better here, am I? As if shoes will fix everything."

"Shoes are pretty important to me, though," I say, because right now staying silent seems rude, and I don't like seeing her this way at all. Also that she realizes something is here to fix lights a tiny flame of hope deep down in me. I glance at the bracelet on my right wrist, feeling better that it's her trying her best, not buying me off.

"There is that." She links her arm through mine, leans in a little. Her hair brushes my cheek. "I'm sorry I'm such a screw-up. Hopefully it isn't genetic and you'll be fine."

"You're totally not a screw-up," I say. "You're like a rich and famous writer with a house and a boyfriend and friends you think are family."

"You," she says, "are far too kind. My money is mostly thanks to my trust fund, and I'm sure I'll ruin things with Brad eventually."

"Still," I say.

"I'm going to warn you," she says. "Because something tells me I should. But I'm planning on hugging you. Don't freak."

The warning is a good thing, because I might have had

a heart attack. She wraps her arms around me, tight, and kisses my cheek.

"Thanks, kid," she says.

"I didn't do anything."

"Being as kind as you are is something," she says. "I don't take such things for granted. All right, let's get ice cream and head home. I have work to do, and I'm assuming you probably have homework as well."

It's the first night I bring my backpack downstairs and do my work sitting across the room from my mother as she writes. But tonight it feels right, and I hope tomorrow it will, too.

Chapter Fourteen

Things I know about Reece Malcolm:

29. *Shockingly, she owns some amazing shoes.*
30. *She cares more than I figured. Even about me?*

"So I was wondering," I say, walking up to Lissa on Friday morning. I'm a little nervous even though haven't I learned by now she's not someone to fear? "What are you wearing tonight? What should I wear?"

Lissa laughs. "Really? The fashionista is asking my humble opinion?"

"I am not a fashionista," I say. "It's L.A.! Lots of people look nice."

"Mmm hmmm." She points at my shirt (blue and sleeveless, layered over a white tank top for some contrast), then my skirt (kind of poufy and knee length, printed with flowers that look kind of retro), then my shoes (I took a chance with my silvery flats, which don't entirely match anything I'm wearing but my necklace—I think they work anyway). "It's a compliment, you know. I know a lot of people wear nice stuff, but you put everything together in a very . . . *you* way."

"No, I . . ." I shrug. "Thank you. Still, I don't think I can go to Elijah's band's show dressed like this. Right?"

"Not everyone there will be straight out of Hot Topic or whatever you're thinking," she says. "And I think E likes you because you're so . . ." She gestures to me. "You. But I can come over and help you pick out something that's less—"

"Me?"

"No, fashionista, you can still be yourself. Just less flowery."

I didn't intend on inviting her over, but firstly, it would be rude to say she can't, and secondly, I really do need help getting ready. And thirdly—if I admit there's a thirdly—Lissa is someone I hope I can actually become friends with, especially now that Travis seems to hate everyone who has a bigger role than him in *Merrily* and because even though Mira's being pretty nice, I don't totally trust her. I'm just a little worried if Lissa spends more time in my mother's house there's something that gives away what a freak I am.

If there is, though, Lissa doesn't act like it when she shows up a bit before we have to leave for the show, and she doesn't seem to realize that my room still looks like a sort-of-lived-in display room with hardly anything personal up on my walls except for a few theatre programs. Yeah, Sai was in here, too, and that didn't stress me out—well, not for that reason—but I don't feel like boys notice that stuff as much, and, anyway, he's new to L.A., too. He would shrug off anything strange as having to do with that.

Lissa flips through my closet. "You have a lot of really nice stuff."

"My mother got me a bunch of new things when I moved," I say. "Since I didn't have a lot of notice I was coming or anything."

"Really?" she asks, and I feel the weirdness of my statement hanging in the air around us. Crap. "What happened?"

"Nothing, just." I sit down on my bed, dragging one of my toes across the rug, staring at the line it makes. "My dad died."

"Devan, oh my God." She spins around to face me. "I'm really sorry, I—"

"It's not a big deal," I say, because I don't want to bring down the night's mood.

She turns back to my closet and takes out a pair of dark jeans and this stupid shirt from Pizzazz, my old show choir, that I somehow packed and brought here. "Wear this."

"Really? Isn't it lame? I only wore it to sleep in or for rehearsals."

"It's so lame it's kind of amazing. Trust me."

Considering Lissa always looks cool, today in a shirt that says The Damned (she had it on inside-out at school) and faded jeans (I realize her and Brad have basically the same uniform, albeit different tastes in music), I do trust her. So I slip into the bathroom and change from fashionista mode to something that my reflection in the mirror promises won't look too out of place. I step into my silver flats and put on my white bracelet and necklace, so I also still feel like myself.

"Where are you guys going?" my mother asks as we walk downstairs a few minutes later. She's curled up in her usual chair in the living room with her laptop propped on her knees.

"Um, Elijah's concert?" I say, worrying she's about to change her mind. "You said I could go, remember?"

"Yeah, of course you can go, I just forgot when it was," she says, a note of exasperation in her voice. "Do you need money?"

"No, I'm fine, thanks. See you later."

She waves, but her attention is already back on her computer, so I lead Lissa outside. I wonder if it's obvious how weird my whole situation is. Suddenly I don't want to be here, not with Lissa, not on my way to a place where I know I won't fit in, not in this stupid stupid stupid Pizzazz shirt.

"Maybe I should—"

"Maybe you should what?" Lissa sticks her tongue out at me and shoves me into the passenger seat. "Come on. If we hurry, we can eat before they go on."

I buckle myself in and lean my head against the window. It's so easy to want to be the girl who isn't scared by everything, but at the moment it feels impossible to actually be her.

"Are you still worried about that shirt?" She backs out of the driveway and throws a glance at me. I can't tell if she's making fun of me or not.

"No, just." I spin my bracelet around on my wrist. "Sorry. It's probably annoying I get nervous about everything."

"A little! Mostly I don't get it. When you sing you're this force of nature, all fearless and bad-ass. Then you switch off, and it's weird. It's like you really are in a musical, where you can only express yourself through song or whatever."

I laugh because it's a way better metaphor to get labeled with than, you know, a wild squirrel. "I never really thought about it like that."

"If I could be like that all the time, I definitely would." She shrugs. "I'm no force of nature, though. Maybe a chance of rain."

"In L.A. a chance of rain seems pretty good," I say.

She laughs and cranks up her stereo, shouting something over The Clash. (I'm savvy mostly when it comes to show tunes, but I'm not a complete lost cause, either.)

"What?"

"I said, I'm glad you came."

I wish I could bottle how I feel right now, the music at a deafening level, the twists and turns and hills of Laurel Canyon flying past us, the possibility I could be like them, too, part of nature. Could feeling fearless not turn off when I wasn't singing? I like it as a goal.

Lissa finds street parking not too far from Molly Malone's, where Killington Hill is playing, and walks right up to the burly-looking bouncer outside like he isn't large, scary, and glaring at everyone in the vicinity.

"Hey, Red," he greets Lissa with a sudden smile. "Where's your guy?"

"He's playing tonight," she says, more enthusiastic than

I've ever heard her before. "He's not my guy, though." It's said like an afterthought, and I wonder if she would have added it at all if I wasn't there.

"Go on in," he tells her, and Lissa grabs my hand and yanks me through the door. I don't know what I expected, but it's just like a bar with a stage in back. And I don't look out of place; there are plenty of girls in jeans and vintage-esque T-shirts.

"I don't think we have time for food, but I'll get us beers." Lissa riffles through her bag and takes out what is a very good but fake ID. "Though you don't seem like a beer person."

"I'll have a beer," I say, because it seems like the right thing to be drinking here, and I know it's totally Afterschool Special of me to hope Lissa thinks I'm cool and therefore will drink a beer to try to prove that, but, okay, I do. Beer turns out to be pretty gross, but I sip mine anyway because I'm thirsty and also because of that whole cool thing.

"I love *right now.*" Lissa nearly has to shout into my ear thanks to the noise from the crowds of people. "Five minutes before a show."

"Yes!" I can't believe we're speaking the same language. "The air is, like, electric."

"Exactly," she says and clinks her bottle against mine.

"Devan?"

The first and only time I've had alcohol, I run into my mother's freaking boyfriend?

Brad makes his way to us through clusters of people surrounding the bar.

"I, uh—"

He laughs and shakes his head. "Devan, I was sixteen once. Well, as it were, I was sixteen and far too socially lacking to be out doing anything illicit but—relax."

"What are you doing here?"

He laughs again. "Having a drink with friends, seeing a few bands. You? The same?"

"E's band is the first one up," Lissa tells Brad like he's a friend of ours. "It's so amazing for him."

"Who is E?" he asks. "Oh, is this the guylinered one Reece spoke of?"

Lissa cracks up. "I'm *so* calling him that from now on. The guylinered one! Oh, hey, I'm Lissa."

"Brad Harper." He shakes her hand. "Well, enjoy. I'll see you later, Devan."

I wave and hand my beer off to Lissa. "I can't drink this with him watching."

"Who *is* that?" she asks. "He's cute, and the accent—"

"He's my mother's boyfriend," I say before she can continue and scar my psyche. "So please stop."

"Got it," she says. "Oh, they're out on stage. Come on, let's get closer."

We squeeze in, slipping through gaps in the crowd, until we more than halve our distance to the stage. Elijah is completely absorbed in connecting cables and tuning his bass, but right before the drummer counts off, he throws a look to the crowd and grins at Lissa and me. My body fills with warmth that this boy who is so passionate and talented has a smile like that for me, has kissed me more times in the past week than I can count, can even remember I exist in the rush of lights and noise and music.

Lissa and I jump up and down for the entire set, screaming more enthusiastically at the end of their songs than anyone else. Not that the crowd isn't responsive or anything. People are paying attention, nodding along with the beat, directing all their attention at Killington Hill. Pride swirls around in me, for Elijah and also for myself. It isn't just that he's my sort-of boyfriend, it's that I can be in this crowd, Lissa at my side, finally part of something that isn't show choir or the school musical.

When their set is over, Lissa gets us another beer each (I can't even see Brad at this point, and I guess I'm getting used to the taste), and we watch as the guys hurriedly pack their equipment before Elijah bounds off of the stage and makes a beeline for us.

"Hey!" Lissa holds out her arms, which I guess he doesn't notice, because the first person he hugs is me.

"I'm so glad you came," he says, and kisses me. He tastes like the stage: lights and sweat and adrenaline. "What'd you think?"

"You guys were amazing," I say honestly. "I'm so—"

"Where'd Liss go?" he asks, pulling away from me. We spot her making her way to the door, and then Elijah takes off without another look to me. I decide to wait before going after them: give it a couple minutes, then finish my beer, then weave my way through the crowd and walk into the crisp night air.

They're sitting close together on the curb, Elijah's arm wrapped around Lissa, her head on his shoulder. My stomach does a few backward flip flops, and I think about turning around and going inside, but they notice I'm there.

"Hey," they say at exactly the same time.

I notice that Lissa's eyes are red and wet, which is sort of hard to entirely accept. Lissa is way too tough to cry in public like someone like me would do.

"Hi," I say.

Lissa whispers something into Elijah's ear, and he nods.

"I'm gonna talk to Liss for a minute." He gets up and pulls Lissa to her feet. "Wait here for me, okay?"

I nod, and then watch as they head down the sidewalk and around the corner. My stomach is still flopping, so I wrap my arms tightly around myself as if that will help.

After a few minutes, I sit down and get out my phone to check that I don't have any missed calls or texts. After what the clock on my phone verifies is ten more minutes, there's still no sign of Elijah or Lissa. I wonder how long I'm supposed to sit alone on the sidewalk before going inside or looking for them.

"Devan?" Brad walks outside with a couple guys who I guess are around his age and who immediately take out cigarettes and lighters like their lives depend on it. "Is everything all right?"

I shrug and try to look very casual about sitting out here alone.

"I'll be just a minute," Brad tells his friends, before sitting down next to me on the sidewalk. "Where are your friends?"

I shrug again. "Around the corner. They needed to talk."

"Ah." He surveys me, probably catching onto the signs I've been here for a bit: my phone out, my notebook in my lap. Just habit—I have nothing to add to my Reece Malcolm List. "Why don't I wait with you?"

"No, I'm totally fine, and your friends—"

"Trust me, any excuse not to stand over there with smokers is a very good one. So your guylinered one is very talented," he says. "I always wanted to be in a band, especially when I was younger."

"Why weren't you?" I ask, eager to move the subject away from Elijah. "I mean, you're obviously totally obsessed with music."

"Sadly, it takes more than that. I've accepted I've no musical ability at all." His phone beeps, and he takes it out of his back pocket. After reading the message, he chuckles softly and taps out a response. "It's Reece, letting me know she can't make it tonight, as if that's any sort of news."

"Does she, like, hate music?" I ask.

"Definitely not," he says. "But she's, at times, a bit antisocial, and getting her out with people other than Kate and Vaughn is tough. Some of my friends are convinced she's imaginary, considering they've never met her since we've been together."

"Does it bother you?"

"A bit, I suppose. I certainly don't mind that we aren't one of those couples that does everything with each other." He laughs as he puts away his phone. "I don't love garnering a reputation as someone with a fictional girlfriend, though."

"Hey, Harper," one of Brad's friends calls. "We're heading back in."

"You should go," I say.

"I think I'll wait a bit," Brad calls back. At the guys' semi-disturbed glances between Brad and me, he adds, "This is Reece's daughter, Devan."

They both shake my hand and end up sitting down with us, which is fine because they're friendly and funny and clearly the kind of guys who would think it was gross for Brad to be talking to a teenager who wasn't his girlfriend's daughter. But it doesn't leave the back of my mind that now I've been out here for maybe a solid half hour with no sign at all of Elijah or Lissa.

Finally, when Brad's friends are ready to head back inside to see the next band, Brad gives me a little glance. "Shall we just head back to the house? See if we can at least drag Reece out for a late dinner?"

I nod, getting to my feet. "I mean, if it's okay. If you want to go back inside—"

"Of course it's okay." He says good-bye to his friends while I text Elijah and Lissa to let them know I have a way home, and we take off. We're still sitting at the very first stoplight we hit when my phone beeps with a text. *sorry lost track of time . . . call u l8r? –E*

I'm not sure how I want to respond, so I don't. In my head I type out lots of responses, though. *You should be sorry. Lissa's not the only one who has feelings, you know. How could you just LEAVE ME THERE? Please stop saying 'l8r'! Aren't I worth typing the whole word?*

At the house, my mother is already in pajamas and curled up with her laptop, so Brad and I make a salad and grilled sandwiches instead of suggesting going out. (I normally geek out only where musicals and clothes are concerned, but the panini maker is pretty great.) After we eat, my phone rings. I start to hit *ignore* but I've probably done enough ignoring tonight already. I take the call.

"Hey," Elijah says. "I'm sorry about earlier. Liss just . . ."

I give him a lot of time to finish his thought, but he doesn't.

"Liss felt really bad, too, especially since she was your ride. You got home okay?"

"Yeah," I say. "Thanks for making sure. Like, two hours later."

"Devan, I'm . . ." He sighs really loudly.

"You're what?" I ask after another endless pause. Is it so bad to need just a little *sorry*?

"Never mind. Are you busy tomorrow? Do you want to hang out?"

I'm not sure I do, but I agree, and he promises to pick me up at noon. Neither of us sounds very thrilled, but I try not to take that to heart as I lie down in bed.

Chapter Fifteen

Things I know about Reece Malcolm:

31. *She's probably an annoying girlfriend.*

Elijah picks me up on Saturday like we didn't have the most awkward evening less than twenty-four hours ago. Brad asks him a few questions about his band, and he answers them politely and enthusiastically but without the geeky ramble of Sai's responses. I can't figure out which I prefer.

"I was gonna check out some amps," he says as we get into his car. Then kisses me. Then nods at his bass in its case in the backseat. "You cool with that?"

"Sure," I say, even though the first time we hung out we listened to his demo, and last night I went to his show.

I can't imagine Lissa would mind doing tons of band stuff with him.

Not that I'm competing with Lissa.

Should I bring up Lissa?

Should I bring up the show?

"Then we can do whatever you want." He slides his arm around my shoulders. "Unless you're dead from boredom. Then it's straight to the funeral home for you."

Okay, I can't actually be annoyed now. Right? Also I don't end up just standing by in the music store. Elijah plugs his bass into amp after amp, making sure I hear each one, and gets my opinion (not that I'm some amp expert, but it's funny how understanding music means you understand a lot more than your little corner of it) before finally deciding on a vintage model we both agree is best at thundering through you.

I watch as he counts off bills from a huge wad of cash in his pocket, and he shoots me a little grin. "I worked all summer, and my mom still gives me an allowance, but it's taken a while."

Thanks to my clothing habit, I've never been great at saving my babysitting money in any impressive amounts. "Where did you work this summer?"

"Interned at Liss's mom's office, filing and stuff, but it paid okay and I didn't have to wear a uniform or wait tables, so it wasn't bad." He thanks the cashier and hoists up the amp from the floor. I hold the door for him and grab his keys so I can open the trunk for him as well. Lissa has a billion things in common with him and got him the job that got him the amp, but I can at least be helpful with doors and keys.

"Hey," he says to me.

"What?" I'm eager for an apology or an explanation, but instead he says "Hey" again, this time with a grin, and loops his fingers through one of my belt loops to pull me close to him. And there is no way to say that making out in the parking lot behind a music store isn't completely tacky, so I won't try.

Probably I should bring up last night at some point, but my anger has faded. If it were really a big deal he wouldn't have texted and called later, right? And we wouldn't be here now. (Well, not *here*, specifically, but out with each other.) I'm more than willing to let it go for today. Maybe for forever.

Elijah has plans to hang out with the rest of Killington Hill that night, and the house is empty when he drops me off. There's a note on the counter from Brad, who has handwriting so perfect it looks like a font, saying there are leftovers in the refrigerator for me, and an addendum to the note from my mother in her crazy scrawl, letting me know they'll be out late and to text if I need anything.

I let myself into my mother's office, but there's nothing of note. My goal of figuring her out is still important, but I'm realizing how it isn't like you can totally judge a person by her stuff, even her email. Unfortunately email is really all I have to go on.

After I microwave leftovers (grilled chicken and asparagus over quinoa), instead of worrying about my mother, I go up to my room and open my computer to worry about other people instead. Thanks to Facebook, I figure out that Travis is with a bunch of other people from Nation and

Honors Choir who are in the *Merrily* chorus, which *sucks*. I guess part of me did worry our immediate friendship was too good to be true. Maybe I was right.

And even though I don't like explaining my feelings to people, if Travis wasn't being this way, maybe I'd have someone to talk to about this whole Elijah/Lissa situation. I pick up my phone and start to text, delete, start to text again, delete *again*, and then finally just click on her name. Probably she won't have time on a Saturday night anyway.

"Devan?"

"Oh, um, hi. Yeah. Are you busy?"

"Not at all, Noah and I were going to go out, but he's sick with food poisoning or something like that," Justine says. "Hopefully he's not lying."

I don't feel, like, great about things with Elijah right now, but at least I'm confident that if he told me he had food poisoning, I'd believe him.

"I got a role in the fall musical," I say.

"I figured," she says. "I saw people congratulating you on Facebook."

"Sorry I didn't tell you sooner," I say. "It's been, like, a really weird week."

"Bad weird?"

"No. Yes? I don't know. Things are—"

"Hang on, someone's calling."

Justine pauses, and it's like I can feel exactly what's about to happen.

"Hey, it's Noah. Can I call you later?"

"Sure." I wonder if there's one right thing to say when

you feel your friendship isn't what it's supposed to be anymore. "'Bye."

Justine doesn't call back, but I distract myself by watching approximately two billion clips of different productions of *Merrily* online. Also Elijah starts texting me about the weird things his bandmates are up to (*parker just got his foot stuck in a cheez-it box*) and it feels way less like I'm alone as I guess I am. Also less like he's going to end things so he can be with Lissa.

My phone beeps again, but this time it's not Elijah. It's my mother. *Just checking that you're behaving. xo*

I grin and text back. *Of course. Tell Brad thanks for dinner.*

Did you have fun with the boy? xo

I feel like my answer is way more complicated than *yes* or *no*. But also, I guess I did. And even though there are kind of a lot of crappy things going on—like how everything is clearly not the way it used to be with Justine, and how maybe Travis and I won't be friends anymore, and how ~~probably~~ ~~maybe~~ ~~I don't know~~ possibly Lissa wants Elijah back—I'm kind of okay for the moment.

✽ ✽ ✽

Sai walks up to me Monday morning while I'm still at my locker. He looks really good in a just-rolled-out-of-bed way, but I try not to notice that.

"Hey," he greets me with a grin. "Good weekend?"

I shrug. "It was okay. How was yours?"

"Not bad. So I was wondering, you busy after Nation rehearsal tonight? We could get started on our scene."

"No," I say. "I mean, no, I'm not busy. I can check with my mother and find out. Probably it'll be okay, though."

"Awesome," he says. "Let me know later."

Travis walks by as Sai walks away, and I try to make eye contact. Travis very obviously looks away and keeps walking. I slam my locker shut and head over to the Music Hall where *of course* the first person I see is Mira. Apparently today is just going to keep getting more annoying.

"Hey, are you okay?" she asks me. "You look extra dour."

"Don't," I say.

"I'm not doing anything," she says. "Seriously, what's up?"

Fine. I will continue treating Mira like she no longer hates me, even if nothing actually happened for her to change her opinion. "It's just Travis."

"Ugh, I know. He's been completely snotty to me, too. Don't take it personally."

"Did this happen with the spring show?" I ask.

"I signed up as the accompanist last spring," she says. "I realized recently I'd rather be in the show. So Travis was the only one of us to actually be in *Spring Awakening*, so even though it was only the chorus, it was different. Sophomores don't really ever get roles."

"Back at any of my old schools, Travis probably could have gotten the lead as a freshman," I say.

"Yeah, New City's great, but then I think about how if I went somewhere else I might actually end up with more opportunities." She shrugs, shoving her hands into the pockets of her jeans. "But I guess I'd rather deal with real competition now than think all of this is easy until I go to college."

"Right? Me, too, totally."

Lissa rounds the corner, and her expression goes blank when she sees the two of us standing there.

"Hey," Mira says. "Why is everyone acting weird today?"

You can tell she expects us to laugh, but *obviously* we do not.

"Can we talk?" Lissa asks, and it's obvious Mira thinks this is directed at her. But I nod and take a few steps farther away from the Women's Choir room. Mira gives us a look I can't interpret at all before heading into the classroom.

"Hi," Lissa says. "So I'm really sorry about Friday night."

It flies out of her in a big jumble, just like words betray me sometimes, and even after everything, I feel this weird kinship with Lissa, who days before I would have dismissed as way too cool for me. "It's okay."

"It's not," she says with a groan. "What's *wrong* with me? I was completely over whatever we had, but the second he's with you I turn into some girl on a reality show. And—because crying at freaking Molly Malone's isn't bad enough—I had to tell him."

"What did he say?" I ask, even though it isn't technically any of my business. I can't believe how open Lissa is, how she could just say all of this to me.

"Not much." She shrugs. "I think he was too surprised to know what to say."

"Right," I say.

"Also, he *likes* you, Devan. I'm old news."

I laugh at that, even if I don't know how much of it I can believe.

"I'm really sorry we ditched you," she says. "I'm such a bitch."

"You're not."

"*I am.* I ditched you and tried to hook up with your boyfriend."

Boyfriend. Wow, I'm not prepared for that word.

"Anyway, we should get to class," she says. "I'm glad you got home okay."

We walk silently into the choir room. I feel how it's different between us now than it was on Friday night before everything unfolded. It's not like I actually think Lissa is a bitch—just that she can be so honest with me right away feels foreign from how Justine had never freaking come out and said that she needed to, I don't know, prioritize The Tenor now. When her best friend's life had totally fallen apart.

Ugh, I don't want to spend today thinking about Justine or her tenor or Friday night. Time to take out my sheet music and let that clear my head.

By lunchtime things are officially weird. Travis is being quiet—well, quiet for Travis, which means speaking only to Lissa and Elijah. Lissa is avoiding eye contact and conversation with Elijah, and that means Mira is soaking up all her extra attention. Also Mira is clearly happy to pretend Travis isn't snubbing her, and clearly unaware that something totally awkward went down on Friday night.

I seriously want to hide. But instead I am next to Elijah, wondering if he's technically my boyfriend now, and if Lissa will keep telling him she wants him back, and if things here can ever just be *normal.* I don't need everything to be perfect, but sitting here it's hard to ignore how freaking weird everything has gotten.

"What are you doing after school?" Elijah asks me. "No, wait. Monday is Nation. Can I pick you up after so we can hang out?"

"I, um, might have to work on this acting thing."

I'm not doing anything wrong by working on a class project with Sai, but I still feel the need to hide information. Is that bad?

"Something for Acting One?" Travis asks like I'm a little kid. Now I wish he'd go back to fully ignoring me. "You're lucky you have a good voice. They don't like casting people in leading roles who aren't at least in Acting Two."

"Well, she has a kickass voice," Elijah says. "And she already got the part. So your point's pretty moot."

Everyone ends up laughing at Elijah because *moot* seems like such an odd thing to say, but I squeeze his hand under the table and smile at him. Because he's great. Because no matter what happened on Friday, and even though I hope I get better at defending myself, someone here who is new to me cares enough to say something.

And thinks I'm kickass.

"I wanted to tell you something," Elijah says as we're walking to class from lunch. "I know I keep asking to hang out and you keep having Nation and your show—"

"I'm sorry, it's just that—"

"No, listen, I want to make sure you know that I get it. Trust me, wish I could get my band together for more practices."

"Why are you so great?" I ask, and he actually *blushes*. Oh my God, it's so cute I can hardly handle it. I kiss him there, right in the middle of the hallway, without checking that Sai or Lissa or anyone else is around. I don't care. I'm full of feelings I never expected to have for a boy I didn't even know last month.

And I could lie, but I won't. After Nation, when Sai and I let ourselves into the spare rehearsal studio (we're allowed to sign up for it, so it doesn't exactly replicate letting myself into the choir room with Justine), I'm suddenly full of feelings again. With Elijah I feel safe and special, which is seriously more than I thought I could feel for a boy. With Sai I don't even know how to name what I feel, but my head buzzes with it. It feels like a betrayal of Elijah but I'm not sure if it actually is. I would kill to suddenly have boy experience to draw from.

"Your phone's beeping." Sai sits down on the floor with the script for *Proof*. I wonder if he picked a scene for us already, and I wonder if it's the one where Hal is kind of drunk and kisses Catherine. Is it possible to want and not want that, badly, all at the same time? "Probably Cross, needs help at the makeup counter."

"Why would he need help?" I ask. "Elijah knows what he's doing."

"He's gonna branch out," Sai says. "Needs more glitter, probably."

"Shut up," I say, getting my phone out of my purse. The text is indeed from Elijah, so I act like I'm on my own working on my acting project before I go home for homework and dinner. All of it's true, just leaving out the one tiny detail sitting next to me. I hope that doesn't mean I'm becoming a good liar or anything.

"Kennedy still acting weird to you?" Sai asks, and I shrug.

"Yeah, unfortunately. You, too?"

"Me, too. Honestly, bet the guy's just confused because he thought his audition went so well."

It's nice Sai wants to believe something good about Travis.

"Yeah," I say, "I heard it was *an epic triumph*."

Sai cracks up. I love making ~~him~~ people laugh. "Man, he must have said that ten times after."

"I wish I was more like that," I find myself admitting. "That part, I mean, not the jerk part later."

"The mildly delusional part?"

"No, just . . . " I consider my words carefully, but for some reason it feels safe to say it. "Less scared, I guess. I knew I did well with mine, but I'd never go around calling it *an epic triumph*."

"Yeah, well, you're also not an asshole, Dev," he says. "Not that Kennedy is."

"Not about *that*, at least."

He grins at me. "It's a fine line. I'm glad you're on this side of it."

"Me, too." I page through my script. "Should we get to work?"

"Sure," he says. "You doing okay with everything?"

"What's everything?" I ask. "School and the show?"

"Yeah, I don't know. Being in L.A. working out for you?"

"Sure," I say quickly. "What about you?"

Hopefully since he asked me it's fine to ask him.

"School's good," he says. "Excited about the show. My dad's still . . . "

"I'm sorry," I say.

He reaches out and tucks this stray lock of hair behind my ear. His fingertips trace little lines on my cheek. It's weird—there is no denying that. I think about what it would be like to pounce on him and let go of everything I'm holding inside in this moment—there is no denying that, either.

"Your hair was in your face," he says like all friends take care of that duty for each other. "Okay, I had one idea for the scene, but I'm open if you do, too."

I've kind of lost the ability to speak but I do manage to nod. And I do manage not to pounce. If I were to pounce on anyone it should be Elijah, but I can't imagine that at all, and it's easier if I keep myself too busy the rest of the night to dwell on that any longer.

Chapter Sixteen

Things I know about Reece Malcolm:

> 32. *She'd probably handle boy stuff better than me. (She has Brad, after all.)*

There's no rehearsal on Friday night, which leaves me completely free to hang out with Elijah. I guess it's kind of an official date. Considering how there are a billion things that are great about Elijah, and only one I don't love—how who knows if he'd like me at all if Lissa would have figured out she still liked him a couple weeks sooner—I know I should be tingly-heart-pounding-thrilled in anticipation. But I'm pretty much like I always am, just with less lip gloss because I expect there will be some serious kissing.

Elijah's mom is, again, out, so we go to his house. We have this list of plans as he's driving us there from my house:

order something for dinner, watch this weird horror movie he claims is more unintentionally funny than scary, listen to the cast recordings of *Hedwig and the Angry Inch* and *Bloody Bloody Andrew Jackson* because I'm determined to make him like at least one musical, if not two. But as soon as we get inside I stumble over something and fall into Elijah, and it's like the excuse we need.

We kiss for a long time standing there, barely inside the front door. We're both wearing jackets and, between the heat of the room and *the heat of the room*, I'm way too warm. Still, I'm worried if I take mine off it'll look like I'm starting to remove clothing. I like Elijah lots but I am not ready to remove clothing around him. (I mean, more clothing than a jacket.) Kissing is great—more than great, bordering on amazing—but I know I'm not ready for anything more than kissing right now. Despite how at this very moment I can't imagine not being wrapped up in Elijah's arms.

And that means I'm ~~almost~~ ~~completely~~ not thinking about Sai at all.

❀ ❀ ❀

I sleep in a little late the next day, though the aroma of Pancake Saturday wakes me up eventually. My mother's downstairs with Brad when I walk into the kitchen, though of course I'm already dressed and she's in her pajamas.

"Hey," she says. "Good night?"

"Sure," I say. It's not that I was out that late with Elijah, it's that they were out later than me. For some reason it made me super relieved to realize when I let myself in last night because hopefully that meant my mother was being less anti-social and there wouldn't be any drama between her and Brad. Maybe it's weird that I'm totally invested in them being happy together, but I am.

It had been one of my first chances in a long time—thanks to rehearsals and the fact that Reece Malcolm doesn't leave the house that often—to check her email or look in her room, but after an evening of making out with Elijah I hadn't exactly been thinking about investigating.

Honestly, it had been kind of nice to forget about it for at least a while.

"Do you have plans today?" my mother asks. "Brad and I were going to see a movie, maybe. If you go you can be our tiebreaker."

"I don't have to." I take a plate of pancakes from Brad and sit down. "If I'll be, like, a third wheel."

"You absolutely won't be," Brad says.

"Unless you're busy, I demand you go with us," my mother says.

"We'll go to the ArcLight," Brad says. "You'll love it. They have reserved seating, and it's much nicer than your average movie theater. And there's an excellent music store next door, though I know people your age don't really buy CDs anymore."

"I still totally do. I love having a little book of lyrics and photos," I say. "Probably normal people who don't only listen to musicals don't, though."

"I think we'd be pretty disappointed if you were normal," my mother says.

I know she's joking, but it's weirdly nice to hear anyway.

They force me to choose between two movies—without telling me which sides they're on—and I pick the documentary over the indie comedy, which turns out to be what my mother wanted. After she gets ready, Brad drives us over the hill into Hollywood, and when we walk inside Amoeba Records I have this rush of whatever religious people probably feel when they step into church.

"Oh. My. God." I stare at the expanse of CD bins, at the stairs ascending into the second level. "This is . . ."

"I know!" Brad scurries ahead of me. "I know that musicals and such are in the back, if that's what you're interested in."

My mother glances between us. "I have no idea who'll be less annoying to hang out with. Devan, maybe?"

"You're very funny," Brad says, and then continues scurrying. My mother and I walk to the back, where together we manage to find the musicals section (it's always a great sign when it's separate from the movie soundtracks section, and it is here).

"Everything good?" she asks me.

"Why? Do I seem like it's not?"

"No, paranoid one, I just like to check in with you."

I study a recording of *Follies* I don't own. "Things are fine. School has stupid drama, but I guess that's normal."

"Unfortunately. Anything you want to talk about?"

"Totally not." I flip through the C's. "Is it ever just easy to like someone?"

Ugh, why do I ask such weird questions without thinking?

"Yes," my mother says. "Believe it or not. Sometimes people make it pretty easy."

❀ ❀ ❀

By next week we're in the midst of rehearsals already. Normally it takes longer to feel like you're really *doing* something because it requires so much time for everyone to learn their songs and their lines and, sometimes, what show they're even performing. Here it is some kind of well-oiled machine. Seriously, Week Two and we're running lines like *actors*. I guess we *are* actors.

I did hope Travis would end up with the other lead role, and not just because I wouldn't have to deal with his dirty looks and silence. Luckily the senior playing Frank, Aaron Finley—who I never really talked to before *Merrily*, even though we're in Nation and Honors together—is a nice guy. Unlike some people I've heard whispering, he doesn't seem to care that the other two leads are only juniors, and brand new to New City at that.

That's especially good today because the three of us are working on "Old Friends," and Mr. Deans keeps telling us we'd better seem comfortable, like we've known one another half our lives. I'm glad I'm pretty good at acting because I'm not sure I've seemed comfortable, ever.

"What are you doing after this?" Sai asks me, poking a finger in my side while we're sitting onstage after our scene, waiting for notes. Boys should learn not to do that. I'm pretty much okay with how much I weigh and all, but they still shouldn't treat you like the Pillsbury Doughboy. Luckily I don't let out a weird giggle to further solidify that imagery. "Wanna hang out?"

Well, *yes*, I do. Even if him asking is weird. (I mean,

the asking is weird, right?) We've done stuff with a group and we've worked on school projects, but we haven't just *hung out.* Even though I have free time, maybe I should call Elijah. Or maybe I should see if Travis is free, so he'll hopefully get over being mad at me.

But all of that stuff is just my brain giving me better options. I don't take any of them. I totally go over to Sai's house.

"Just warning you." He unlocks the door from the garage to the house. "It's not awesome like yours. It's not even *nice*."

It actually *is* nice, sort of, because the house itself is big, bigger than my mother's. It's just empty. The living room holds only a TV and a recliner, and the kitchen has all the major appliances, but not even a table or chairs.

"See?" Sai gestures around. "How much does this suck?"

"Once you get more stuff, it'll be fine."

"Yeah," he says. "Maybe. Come on, my room sucks the least."

Maybe it's weird that he's asking me up to his room, but he's been in mine. It isn't a big deal.

"See? Sucks less." He opens his door and makes a dorky grand gesture. Sometimes I wonder if Sai is actually some huge geek who made a deal with the devil: his soul in exchange for the hair, the abs, the shoulders, the curve of his biceps—

"What are you staring at?" he asks me.

Ohhh my God, Devan. Get a grip.

"Nothing, sorry," I say. "Your posters."

"Oh, man, I know, it's lame." He laughs and runs his

hand through his hair, pluming it up a little more than usual. "Nic gives me crap about 'em, too."

I actually am only looking for any excuse that doesn't involve a detailed list of his best attributes. But even though I'm not Nicole's greatest fan (nor do I love thinking about the time she's spent in this room), I can't argue that a bunch of literary posters like you'd see in English class or at Barnes and Noble aren't lame. "It's great you're so into books, though."

"I'm rebuilding my collection." He points to a bookshelf in the corner. "My sister convinced my mom to start sending my books out to me."

I wonder what became of all my stuff once I was gone. I can't imagine Tracie doing much besides tossing it or ignoring it forever.

"Why is your sister still there?" I ask. "Since you had to move here?"

"Man, it's a long story." He sits down on his bed, and since it's the only furniture besides the shelf and a nightstand, I, after hovering for a few moments, join him. Unlike mine—which I make every morning—it's a mess with sheets and pillows tossed every which way. My bed only looks like that after not sleeping much at all.

"Everything okay?" I ask, because I hate seeing this bed, hate how much Sai hates this house, hate that his own mom would need to be convinced to send him the things he cares about most.

"Same as always," he says with a shrug. "Glad we're doing the show. Once Kennedy gets over his epic dickishness, it'll be a good time."

"Totally. I never feel so much like myself as when I'm—"

"Playing someone else?" he asks with a grin.

"Well, yeah." I smile back at him. "You know what I mean, though. Right?"

"Right." He leans forward and wraps his arms around me. I don't know what is happening or what I should be doing, so it's probably the worst hug ever. Him embracing, me like stone. My heart beats like I'm having some kind of medical episode. Offstage I've only stood so close to one other boy before, and that's only been when we're kissing. "Glad you came over, Dev. It's been shitty lately."

"Not the same as always?"

"Guess I don't even know anymore." We stay like that for a long time. I turn from stone, though, slipping my arms around him, hugging tightly, too. It's funny, really, how normally I think of Sai as the hottest guy ever, but right now he's just my friend who needs me. It breaks my heart, actually, how much he needs me.

We don't really talk any more. Eventually Sai extricates himself from the hug, curls up next to me, shoves a pillow under his head. I can't explain it, but I know he'll sleep better if I'm here, so I lie down as well (not too closely). We both doze off, which—when I wake up a bit later—I realize is kind of crazy considering I've never slept next to another person before. Sai's still asleep, and I wonder what proper etiquette is for hanging around after your friend who's a boy but most definitely not your boyfriend but in a completely different way than your gay friend who is a boy but not your boyfriend sleeps.

I glance at the clock on his nightstand and decide since

I'm in no rush I can hang around at least a half hour. That's a normal amount of time for a nap, right? Then I notice the other stuff on his nightstand: a book by Hemingway I've never read, the newer *Merrily* cast recording, a box of condoms.

I guess in a way I thought Sai and Nicole might be having sex. That's what people who go out do, at least eventually, right? Not that I necessarily think Elijah and I will, even eventually. Obviously I've thought about it, and not just when we're in the midst of making out. Our making out is pretty tame, after all, and I guess that's why sex doesn't seem inevitable. I know, obviously, that I'm sixteen and a half, and lots of people who are sixteen and a half have already done it, but right now it just doesn't seem like something I should even be considering. Everyone's got their own speed, and mine is currently set to Doesn't Totally Feel Comfortable Even Taking Off Her Jacket In Front Of Her Sort Of Boyfriend. You've definitely got to get past that one before you can think about having sex.

My stomach and head are spinning a bit out of control, doing their best not to imagine Sai and Nicole, trying not to hate the thought, knowing I shouldn't hate it like I do. If I call it what it actually is, anyway, it isn't hate. It's jealousy. And anyone who has a boyfriend shouldn't be filled with this much jealousy regarding another boy's sex life.

I lie there, stiff like a mannequin, until Sai is eventually awake again. He reaches over and rests his hand on my waist. It's warm from sleep, and I feel my gaze snap to it almost magnetically.

"Thanks for being here," he says. "Weird maybe, but sometimes I sleep better if someone else is here."

"It's not that weird." I slide my hand over his. He squeezes me a little and pulls me closer. Kiiiiind of full-body contact. Something about the moment feels dangerously out of control. But also I want to lock out the rest of the world and even time from passing to stay right here in whatever this is.

Sai's phone buzzes in his pocket. We're close enough that I actually feel it against my hip. He digs it out and holds it to his ear in what seems like record time. "Hey, Nic. No, I'm just hanging out after. Going over some stuff. Yeah, later? Awesome."

He clicks off his phone while I try not to overthink the fact that he totally just lied to his girlfriend.

"I, um—maybe I should go," I say. Not because lying next to Sai in bed isn't nice, but maybe because it's too nice. Too something, for sure. "Do you mind?"

"No, let's go." He gets to his feet, stretches his arms into the air so that the hem of his T-shirt rides up a little and I can see a stretch of his stomach. I tell myself it's okay to look, okay to think about how it would feel, because I have something terrible to do as soon as I get home.

The weird thing is that after Sai drops me off at my house, as I'm gathering up the strength, Elijah calls me. I almost ignore it so I can be completely ready, but when am I really going to be? "Hi."

"Hey." He takes one of his now-usual pauses. "I heard you went to Sai's."

I'm still getting used to people realizing I exist, much less *talking about me*. "Um—from who?"

"Does it matter?" he asks.

Well, kind of.

"Are you guys—"

"Are we what?" I ask, instead of just letting him finish. Oh my God, am I turning into Reece Malcolm?

"It just seems like . . ." Insert Elijah pause. "You know what it seems like."

"Maybeweshouldn'tgooutanymore," I say all at once.

"I *knew* it," Elijah says, all triumphantly. The boy I kissed is not a boy I would have thought would be so gleeful at *catching me* or whatever.

"We aren't anything," I say. "I wouldn't do that while you and I are . . . I just— Probably it's not fair to feel anything for him if I'm—"

"What's that supposed to mean?" he asks.

"It's not *supposed* to mean anything!" It dawns on me what he thinks. "Do you still feel things for Lissa?"

Pause pause pause.

"It doesn't feel very fair for you to yell at me about Sai, then," I say.

"I'm not yelling."

That much is true.

"I think you're right, though," he says. "Maybe we shouldn't go out."

"Fine," I say.

"Fine."

It seems like we're going to hang up on each other, but neither of us does.

"I *was* over her," Elijah says. "Then that whole thing happened . . . after my show."

"I know what thing you're talking about." Like I've forgotten getting abandoned already. I'm pretty sure getting abandoned is one of the only constants in my life.

"You're great," he says.

"I know," I say, because I'm still kind of mad at him. But also because it hits me maybe that's not untrue.

Elijah laughs his hot laugh. I am totally not immune to it, even now. "At least you have a chance," he says. "Liss and her issues . . ."

"Oh, right, I really have a chance. Are you forgetting Nicole?"

"I'm not," he says. "I think *he* does sometimes."

"Probably we're both guided by stupid emotions," I say, which makes him laugh even harder.

"Probably so. How was your rehearsal? You knock a few people out with your voice yet? I mean literally, too, one second they're on their feet and the next on their asses."

I giggle at the image. "I wish. It's good to have a goal, though."

"My mom's yelling," he says. "Garbage has to go out. But we're cool? No drama?"

"No drama," I say. Honestly, too.

Chapter Seventeen

Things I know about Reece Malcolm:

33. *She actually seems to like that I'm kind of a geek about things (like cast recordings).*

I really don't feel like walking into school like things are okay the next morning. Obviously ending whatever Elijah and I had was the right thing to do—and I know that—but as awkward as everything and everyone already is, this can't make things any better. It's not something I can exactly talk about with Sai—obviously—and Travis is still on Project Ignore Devan. Justine's never felt so much a part of my past and not my now. And Mira's at my locker, and that can't be a good sign.

"How are you?" she asks.

"I'm fine," I say.

"They just have this thing they can't get over," Mira says. "It's not about you."

"Okay." I'm not sure what else there is to say, especially to freaking *Mira*.

"It was a good sign that Elijah was going out with you. I thought they were finally over each other. But sometimes it's hard to give up on someone you've felt that way about for forever." Mira sighs and starts off down the hallway. "See you in class."

I seriously have no idea why this is the topic that seems to have made Mira stop hating me, but mysterious as it is, I'll take it. Plus it makes it way less scary at lunch to sit down at our table, even though today Lissa's in the spot next to Elijah. After all, I wish Sai was in the spot next to me. But even after what happened—well, almost happened—last night, Sai is sitting next to Nicole, and his arm is around her shoulder. I haven't admitted to myself until seeing them that I hoped he made the same call I did last night.

But I guess I'm not really that surprised he didn't.

❊ ❊ ❊

Rehearsal is short tonight because it's Parents' Night, the Nation is performing, and everyone in Nation is in *Merrily.* So we change out of our rehearsal clothes (well, the girls do; the boys always rehearse in whatever they're already wearing, except for Travis) and into our performance clothes for the first time. Up until now, all the show choirs I've been in required guys to be in tuxes, girls in embarrassingly sequined dresses. Luckily New City continues its reign as better than my previous schools, because the guys are in black pants with black shirts, and we're in swingy black dresses. I'm not saying I'd wear the dress for any reason other than the Nation, but it's still a lesser fashion offense in the scheme of show choir couture.

"Your mom here?" Sai asks me as we're waiting backstage in the auditorium for our cue. We haven't talked much today so it's a relief this immediately feels just like normal. Just like pre-lying-in-bed-next-to-each-other, at least.

"No," I say with authority, even though it's not like we ever discussed it. I just figure Reece Malcolm has way more important things to do. "I'm assuming your dad's not?"

"Nope. My dad doesn't even know I'm in Nation. He's a cliché of a person."

"Oh, are you supposed to be on the basketball team or something?"

"Something, yeah."

Mr. Deans's voice goes out over the PA system, so we get into our actual line (I'm side-by-side with Travis, which neither of us is thrilled about) and walk out. We open with an old Cure song Mr. Deans is obsessed with, "Friday I'm in Love," which gets way more than the requisite parents-are-proud applause. I think that gears everyone up enough to do even better with "New Music" and then another old song, "Where Is My Mind," by another old band, the Pixies.

I know how it sounds when parents are humoring us, and this is definitely not that. Actually entertaining people is ultimately what it's all about, right?

"I'm gonna take off," Sai says afterward, as we're walking out of the auditorium and back to the hallway. "You need a ride?"

"I feel so annoying being the only one without a car," I say instead of *yes*.

"I don't mind."

We take off down the hallway together, as parents pour out of the auditorium. I got over it a long time ago that my relatives hardly ever came to see me perform, but I can tell from the look on Sai's face it's something he's still getting used to. I wish I knew what to say, but there's nothing comforting about the fact that eventually you do accept that your family won't be there.

"You were really good tonight," I finally say. "I wish I'd been paired up with you instead of Travis."

"You only think that 'cause he entered his ass phase," Sai says, and then we both laugh over the fact that *ass phase* sounds a lot like *ass face*. "And Deans is really hung up on the complementary heights thing, which I don't even get."

"Me neither, but maybe if I were better at math?"

"Devan!"

The voice is immediately recognizable, but since it seems impossible, I ignore it. It's more likely I've started hearing voices than that she's actually *here*.

"Hey." My mother catches up with us, clearly out of breath from dashing down the hallway. "Didn't you hear me?"

"What are you doing here?" I ask.

"It's Parents' Night," she says, her face falling just a bit. "I'm sorry, maybe I should have asked when I got the email newsletter from your school—"

"No, I mean, it's fine—it's great," I say, as Brad catches up with her. I notice neither of them is in their uniforms; Brad is in brown pants with a green sweater, and my mother is actually in a dress, and miraculously it's blue and fitted and makes her look amazing. Oh my God, are they trying to look like grownups for my sake? "I just didn't know you were coming. I'mreallygladyoudid."

"I figured it went without saying." She tugs at one of her sleeves. "And I'm assuming because you don't look horrified that Kate didn't lie and this looks all right?"

"It looks great," I say. "You should totally dress up more often."

"I wouldn't hold my breath. Listen, we have to, you know, meet your teachers and everything, but we'll bring food home and talk more then, yeah?"

"Sure." I'm suddenly aware of the nametags they're wearing, suddenly very aware that Sai is staring at the neatly-written-by-Brad REECE on my mother's.

"Are you Reece Malcolm?" he asks her, his eyes wide like a little kid in line to meet Santa at the mall.

"The one and only," she says, total monotone, before laughing. "Yeah."

"Oh, man, that's awesome. *Destruction* is like my third-favorite book of all time."

That only makes her laugh harder. "That's a flattering ranking."

"Why didn't you tell me your mom's Reece Malcolm?" Sai nudges me. "Didn't you notice I had all of her books in my room?"

"No," I lie, as my mother mouths *in his room?* just at me but not exactly subtly.

"Are you writing a book now?" Sai asks.

"I don't talk about what I write while I'm writing it," she says. "I am, though."

"She always is," Brad says. "Her work ethic is impressive."

This sounds dumb, but sometimes I forget there are probably lots of things about my mother Brad likes besides that she's pretty, and famous in a strictly literary sense.

"We should get to class," my mother says with a smirk.

"Will you sign my books if I bring them over?" Sai asks.

"I'll sign anything you bring me," she says. It kind of throws me, because I've never been able to use that tone when talking to a boy, not even Elijah, who I felt comfortable enough, you know, making out with. Reece Malcolm can just toss it out at a very cute boy (who, okay, is half her age, so maybe not as intimidating) in front of her boyfriend like she does it all the time. Maybe she does. "Devan, we'll see you later. Sai, I'll have a Sharpie ready."

Brad waves at both of us before dashing off behind my mother. Normally I'd be immediately figuring out how weird my relationship with my mother seemed to anyone who saw us at the same time, but I feel that fading a little, and not only because maybe Sai's situation is as off as mine in its own way.

"Man," Sai says. "I seriously can't believe you didn't say anything."

I shrug. Even if Reece Malcolm weren't my long-lost mother, even if I had a completely normal childhood and felt close to her, would I bring it up? *Oh, by the way, my mother's someone super important*?

"Yeah, guess it's not like you ever say much." His tone is casual but nothing means nothing. Right?

I hold open the door to the parking lot. "It's not a big deal."

"It *is* a big deal," he says. "You're lucky to have a mom like that."

Am I?

At the house I finish my homework and sing through one of my solos before walking into my mother and Brad's room to rummage around a bit, though I find nothing of note. Maybe it's time to cool it with this whole investigation. Reece Malcolm was there tonight, had slapped on a nametag that proclaimed to people she was my mother, made appointments with my teachers like what they say about me matters (hopefully they'll have good things to say). This house doesn't feel so loaded with dangerous traps anymore—and neither does Reece Malcolm.

So I head to my room and go back to singing until I hear the garage door open. Always a good warning to end the belting out of show tunes.

"Devan!" my mother calls. "We have Thai and word from New City that you're an overachiever!"

I walk down the stairs into the living room. "I am definitely not an overachiever."

"You have quite high marks so far in all of your classes." Brad sets out the takeout containers on the coffee table. I notice he and my mother have switched nametags. They're such dorks. "Considering how much time your choirs and your musical take up, I'd say that's fairly overachieving."

"Oh, God, speaking of choir!" My mother grabs my arm. "I had no fucking idea. You are incredible."

"It's show choir," I say. "All of us. You wouldn't even know if I—"

"Devan, while I don't possess your level of show choir insight, I'm not an idiot." She takes off up the stairs. "I have to change out of this thing before I can eat."

Brad and I get plates and silverware from the kitchen, and the three of us sit around the living room coffee table divvying up all of the appetizers and entrees. I keep trying to think of a way to thank them for going tonight, but finally it hits me I'm probably making it way more complicated than it has to be.

"So, um," I say, "thanks for going tonight."

"I think it was required," my mother says, or at least I think that's what she says, because she's in the midst of shoving a spring roll into her mouth.

"Still." I look down at my plate, hoping they'll attribute my red face to the panang curry. "Dad didn't always come to see me perform. So . . . it was nice you did."

"Someone thought Brad was a student." My mother laughs. "I told him not to shave today; it always makes him look twelve."

"Oh, I'd say at least fifteen," he says, laughing too. "How many twelve-year-olds do you know who have to shave?"

"To be honest, I don't know *any* twelve-year-olds. It's possible." She throws a packet of chili sauce in my direction. "Seriously? You don't need to thank us. We're doing what we're supposed to. And getting to see you perform more than made up for basically being back in high school all night."

"Perhaps I'm wrong," Brad says, "but isn't Show Choir generally a bit more . . ."

"Lame? Embarrassing? Totally cheesy? Yes," I say. "This one's really good."

"Quite." He nods. "That Pixies song was excellent."

"Brad, can you get me a soda?" my mother asks. "Devan, do you need anything?"

I don't, and Brad goes into the kitchen. Right away, my mother leans in my direction.

"You were in the boy's room?"

"Platonically," I say, even though I'm only mostly sure that's true.

"Is that even possible with him?"

I laugh instead of answering, as Brad walks back in with a soda for my mother and a beer for himself.

"So I heard through Kate that you actually have one of the leads in the school musical," my mother says.

"Oh, yeah, it's . . ." I was going to say it isn't a big deal, but it *is*. Not sharing is pretty much my default setting, though. When I first started making it into show choir and getting roles in shows, I saved up the news, waiting for the perfect moment to tell Dad and maybe melt through some of the silence that was settling in around us more and more. And it wasn't that Dad didn't care—I really was sure of that—but he just didn't get why it was so important. Dad was a practical person; he couldn't understand me giving so much time to music. And occasionally Tracie would flat-out call it a waste of time, which I worried was what Dad was already thinking. So I stopped talking about it.

"I didn't think you cared much about musicals or whatever," I say to my mother. It's weird, but a hurt look flickers over her face. I'm pretty bad at backpedaling but it never stops me from trying. "I mean, I know people think they're cheesy and stupid."

"I wouldn't say I care about musicals in general," she says. "But I do care, specifically, about any you're doing."

"Didn't someone want to make a musical out of one of your books?" Brad asks, while I feel a warm flush fan out over my face.

People care about me.

"Oh, God, *yes*." My mother cracks up. "*Destruction: The Musical*."

"It's not the worst idea ever," I say, kind of surprised at myself for taking an unpopular point of view. "Some really good musicals have, like, really serious source material."

"Hmmm," is all she says. And then laughs again. "I'm dubious but it's not as if *Destruction: The Musical* is ever going to happen anyway. Brad, could you go get me another Diet Coke?"

"You've only taken three sips from that one," he says.

"First of all, why are you counting my sips? Second, take a hint."

Brad picks up his plate and gets back up. "I'll be in the kitchen, love, until I hear otherwise from you."

My mother stares at me for a few moments once Brad is out of the room. "So you've read my books?"

"Yeah."

"You've read *Destruction*?" she asks. And I know that actually means, *You've read the dedication?* "When?"

"Last year," I say. "For school."

She furrows her brow at that. "High schools teach *Destruction*?"

"No, it was like an extra-credit thing. We got to pick whatever book from this shelf of modern classics my teacher had." I leave out what had happened at home, when Tracie saw me reading it. I leave out never having the nerve to ask Dad about it or about her.

"And you randomly picked *Destruction*."

"I liked the cover."

She laughs. "Fair enough. So what happened with Guyliner?"

Everything in me feels lighter with the subject changed. "I guess we kind of broke up," I say, even if that doesn't sound entirely right. It's not like we were ever officially together; he was my Almost Boyfriend, not my Actual Boyfriend. And it's weird how I'm okay with that now.

"I'll kick his ass if you need me to."

I laugh, trying to imagine that amazing scenario. "I was the one who broke up with him. I just . . . I guess it's stupid when Sai has a girlfriend and all, but it didn't feel fair for me to go out with Elijah if most of what I thought about . . ."

"Good for you," she says. "That was the right thing to do."

"He's interested in someone else anyway," I say. "So we're both okay with it."

"That's a relief. There's nothing worse than breaking up with someone who's still hung up on you," she says. "Not that I'm any sort of relationship expert. I've had approximately two and a half of those."

I almost ask how it's possible to have half of one, but then again I would totally count myself as having half a relationship myself. It's so weird when stuff that people with actual life experience say makes sense to me.

"I really like your books," I tell her, even though we're probably both grateful to be on the safer topic of boys. "You're an amazing writer."

"Thank you," she says.

We smile at each other, and I swear something solidifies then. Like maybe we'll never be great, but we're okay, and that's a lot. I wasn't sure I'd ever get to feel that, but now I do.

Chapter Eighteen

Things I know about Reece Malcolm:

34. She's worn a dress at least once.
35. She cares about what I'm doing.

"Okay, so." Travis flops down next to me in the auditorium while we're watching Sai sing "Franklin Shepard, Inc." for maybe the ten-thousandth time in the weeks since rehearsals started. It's a crazy song, with a billion lyrics, and super emotional because it's when Charley explodes thanks to Frank's soul-selling ways. "I've forgiven you."

"*You've* forgiven *me*?"

"Oh, fine," he says. "You know what I mean."

I go back to watching Sai, because I'm not sure I should forgive Travis just because he's willing to talk to me again.

I want to though, of course. It's funny how much I miss someone I haven't even known for that long.

"I'm in the *chorus*," he whines. "And I'm a *junior*."

"But that's not my fault," I say. "Or anyone else's."

"I would nail that line," he says, as Sai jumbles the lyric about the gross percent and the billing clause. I sing it in my room all the time and can verify it's a tricky verse to get through, which I tell Travis.

"Well, of course *you'd* defend him," he says. "Big shock."

I really hope he means because we're friends, not because my ~~obsession~~ crush is that apparent.

"It's going to look awful on my college applications," he says.

"It's a smaller part but at a really good school," I say. "Also, seriously, if you wanted to complain about it, I would have been here for you. I'm your *friend*. And you acted like I was invisible, which is one of the meanest ways to treat someone."

I can't believe how easily it rolls out of me. I'm so used to composing text messages and wannabe-snarky replies in my head. It turns out saying the truth out loud feels kind of great.

"Okay, Devvie, point taken." He slides his arm around my shoulder. "I'm sorry, okay? Is that what you want?"

Obviously it is, but after weeks of him all but ignoring me it's not like everything's just automatically fine. But I guess maybe it'll get there.

I pull away from him—which is really all for show—and get out of my seat. "Apologize to Sai and Mira later."

"Fine, fine. Where are you going?"

"He'll probably get through this better if we aren't sitting here staring at him."

"You're way too nice," Travis says, though he does follow me to the back of the auditorium and around the corner. "Ohhh my God! Are you being way too nice because something happened?"

"Nothing has happened," I say. "Nothing's going to happen."

He sticks out his lower lip like a little kid put into time-out. "That's so boring. You have to make something happen. Especially since you and Elijah came to a tragic end."

"We didn't come to a tragic end," I say. "And Sai has a girlfriend. And even if he didn't . . . he's him, you know? And I'm just me."

"What are you talking about? You're talented and always have the best clothes and you're cute and you have really good boobs."

I cross my arms in front of my chest without even really meaning to. Still. I don't want Travis looking at them. "Thank you. But lots of people here are talented."

"Not like you," he says. "I hate you for how you sing. And you know what I'm saying! Sorry if you don't want to believe it, and I know he's all godlike and one of the Popular Ones but, no, you guys are clearly right for each other."

It's kind of weird because the other day in the hallway I caught sight of this familiar-looking girl with great hair and an amazing dress, and then I realized that she was my reflection. Inside I'm pretty close to the same me, but on the surface I'm just not her anymore. It's weird trying to see yourself the way other people do—and I'm totally not saying I'm in Sai's league exactly, if there's such a thing as leagues anyway—but maybe Travis is only a little crazy, not completely.

"Devan! We need you!"

I run to the stage, apologizing to Mr. Deans as I make my way up.

"Man," Sai says. "Can't believe how much I screwed that up."

"It's a hard song," I say.

"I'm glad it's yours and not mine," Aaron says.

Sai rakes his hands through his hair, which makes him look like a really hot mad scientist. "I'm never gonna have it right by opening night."

"Opening night's in four weeks," Aaron says. "Not tomorrow. Chillax."

Sai and I exchange a look at that, because who says *chillax*? Then I think about Travis and what he said and how Sai and I always seem in sync about everything. There's seriously no one who I've felt this way for before, most especially not someone I also wanted to make out with.

It's weird and possibly stupid, but for a split second I wonder if I'm falling in love with him. But he's ~~probably definitely~~ not interested in me at all. And even if he was, he has a girlfriend. Also, I'm sixteen, and I'm pretty sure when you're sixteen you aren't supposed to do things like *fall in love* anyway.

Still. Maybe I feel *something*. Something bigger than just make-outability.

"Old Friends" is a much easier song, which means I can

focus on getting the (totally simple) choreography down completely. I also keep reminding myself of everything Kate told me, and I try to look for more in the lyrics so I can use more emotion. It's there, too: anger, annoyance, eagerness, love. I love that I can find it when I just think to look.

Sai and I are free to go after we run through the short scene after the song a few times, since Mr. Deans will be working more with Aaron for his solo that comes next. I check my phone to discover a text from my mother (*Going out with Brad tonight, can you get a ride home? xo*) and text back a fast response without checking (*Yes of course!*).

"Um," I say, because it's weird asking favors from Sai, "is there any way you can take me home?"

"Yeah, of course, Dev," he says. "Was gonna stop and get food, that okay?"

I like *Dev* a lot better than *man.* "Totally, if I'm not intruding on your plans."

"Nah, think my book'll take it okay I'm spending my time with you and not it," he says, gesturing to the paperback in his back pocket. "Come on."

We stop for pizza, the only thing we can agree on, because apparently Sai doesn't like Mexican, Chinese, Thai, Japanese, or Indian. I want to ask him if that was weird growing up, with a mom who's Chinese and Indian, but I don't know if that's an okay thing to ask.

"What do you think of Nic?" Sai asks as we sit down with our giant slices (me: one, him: three).

"What do you mean? I barely know her."

"Really? You guys have some classes together."

I'm still not sure what it means that Sai seems to see no

differentiation between the group I'm in and the one he mainly hangs out with. "Yeah, but . . . we're not friends."

He nods and plows through more of his first slice.

"Why?" I ask.

"Doesn't matter," he says. "Just—not to complain or anything . . . Nic's a great girl. I think she just wishes I wasn't depressed all the time. Not like I don't."

"Right." A tiny thrill dances on my fingertips and down my spine. Now I have a legitimate reason to dislike her. "I wish . . . Back in St. Louis, my best friend had this key to our choir room; she got a copy so we could practice our solos. Anyway, whenever we were having crappy nights, we'd sneak in to use the piano and sing and . . . " Out of my mouth it doesn't sound like salvation, though, it sounds incredibly geeky.

Sai slowly grins at me. "Wouldn't have pegged you for a breaking and entering girl, Dev."

"It was just entering! We had a key!"

His eyes are all crinkly and distracting. Just like he can smile with his voice, Sai can smile with his eyes, too. "A *stolen* key. So do you miss St. Louis?"

"Not really. Sometimes I forget to even think about it." It feels physically buried in my chest somewhere, like I only feel it when I move certain ways. Justine and Dad and Tracie, pushed as far underneath as I can keep them.

Sai looks at me, jutting his chin up into the air a little.

"You don't believe me?"

"Neither of us has been here that long—it's interesting you don't think past the last few months."

Really, Sai? What about you, guy with a girlfriend,

seeking solace in someone else, if we're talking about being *interesting*?

Wait, am I mad at Sai?

"It's complicated," is what I finally say.

"Yeah?"

"My dad died," I say. "Which you know already, sorry. Just . . . before I moved, I never knew my mother. I don't know why, but I didn't. She didn't have anything to do with me, and if my dad hadn't died . . . "

This thing that's almost everything about me that I don't want anyone to know didn't just slip out. I said it because no matter how weird things can get between us, I trust Sai. And I can't say that about anyone else in my life, at all. Travis could turn on me again with no warning, Mira makes no sense to me, Justine only knew my superficial dreams—and not even those anymore—and Lissa and Elijah are both a little awkward to talk to now about anything, much less the most personal stuff. But Sai has this honesty practically pulsing in him. It's like even if he wanted to he'd never be able to keep his true feelings under wraps.

"Whoa," Sai says, which is a fair—and honest—reaction.

"Yeah."

"You want to talk about it?"

I laugh while trying not to cry. "I thought I *did* just talk about it."

Sai reaches forward and touches my face for, like, the briefest of moments. "Fair enough."

Only one other boy has touched my face like that, and it was Elijah while we were kissing. If it were someone else or if I were someone else maybe it would mean something—something beyond that Sai knows this is a tough topic for me.

"How bad do you think I did today?" he asks.

It's nice of him to ask—it's like he knows exactly how much I need the subject changed. "It's a hard song, but you have time. Just recite the lyrics to me. That's the hardest part, right? Like, that there're so many of them? The melody's pretty straightforward. I mean, for Sondheim."

"I guess," he says. "Yeah, I'll do it."

So he does, and I make him start over when he messes up, and it only takes him a few times through to get each line right. We're finished eating by then, and we walk out to his car where I make him sing it through right there and then, *a capella*. He still flubs a couple lines, but it's not like before.

"You're good at this," he says. He's leaned in close to me, and I can almost pretend we're cozy in his car for a reason other than this song. "Thanks, Dev."

"Maybe Aaron's right," I say. "Maybe you just need to chillax."

❁ ❁ ❁

It's still early enough in our rehearsal process that we have nights off, so on Friday I agree to hang out with Travis. Even if maybe I'm still mad at him. The alternative—hanging out at home alone—sounds worse.

Also right now the only person I seem to be totally capable of talking to is Sai. And despite that Sai is great, I don't want the only person I hang out with to be the boy I'm ~~obsessed with in love with~~ crushing on.

"So what do you think about Aaron Finley?" Travis asks me over pasta (mine) and ahi tuna (his) at Firefly, which he likes because of this one room that looks like a library but is actually the bar, and he feels like he's getting away with something to be out at a place with a bar (which we're not even sitting in). Considering by now I've been places like Molly Malone's, which actually *is* a bar, it seems like lame reasoning. Still, it's comforting knowing I'm not the only one who makes decisions for lame reasons sometimes, and it's nice imagining sitting in the fake library with Sai the Book Nerd, holding hands or even making out in the dim light.

Yeah, something is clearly wrong with me to devote so much brain space to him. I am well aware.

"Aaron's a really strong singer," I say. "And actor. When he was rehearsing that fight with Sai the other day, I seriously almost cried."

"*Un*important," Travis says. "What I'm saying is, what team do you think he's on? His sexuality confounds me!"

I laugh. "Hmmm. Confounding to me, too. He is cute, though."

"Oh, really, so you notice other guys? Guys who aren't—"

"Shut up," I say with a lilt in my voice, hoping it'll sound adorable and not bitchy.

"Do we have a plan yet?"

"A plan to unconfound Aaron Finley's sexuality?"

"Like I need a plan. I'll just wait till the cast party and make my move."

Maybe this sounds crazy? But sometimes I wish I were more like Travis. "What if he's straight?"

"If he's straight he won't even figure it out, and I'll be spared humiliation as well as further pining. But, no, we need a plan for you and S—"

"Don't say his name."

"—for you and Troy Bolton," he says. "Fine."

"Oh my God," I say. "Don't even."

"You can do what I'm gonna do," Travis says. "But somehow I don't see you jumping him unless I physically throw you at him."

"Can we stop talking about this?" I pull on my cardigan, even though the outdoor heaters are on in the dining area that looks indoors but actually opens up to the trees and sky. It's weird how chilly L.A. fall nights are. "It's totally depressing to act like it's a possibility when it really isn't. I'd rather unravel the mystery of Aaron Finley. Or, better, not talk about boys at all."

"Tell me. Boys are so stressful." Travis perks up in his chair. "Oh my God, Mira's here! With her *parents*. Tragic."

"Hanging out with your parents is not tragic." I follow his line of sight to Mira, sitting with a couple definitely at least ten years older than my mother.

"Your mom's cool," Travis says. "Not everyone's is. Case closed. Let's go embarrass her. Mira!"

He's out of his seat before I can do anything, so I follow him over.

"Oh, hey." Mira ducks down a little in her chair. Her fauxhawk is dehawked, just lying there like boring hair, and she's wearing a pale blue sweater over her T-shirt and jeans. "What are you guys doing?"

"Eating, obviously," Travis says. "Hi, Mira's parents."

They say hello to him and introduce themselves to me. Mira's dad is wearing the kind of casual-but-clearly-high-end-label clothes I've noticed Brad's Hollywood friends wear. I guess that's pretty normal for L.A. in general, though, not just Hollywood types. Her mom is very mom-like, the kind of woman I pictured back in the pre-*Destruction* days. Light brown hair, sweater set, nice-but-not-too-trendy jeans. Hopefully it isn't bad that occasionally I still wish I went home to someone like her.

"You should come with us," Travis says, because for someone who gets good grades and so is theoretically smart, he never figured out that Mira and I sometimes hate each other, and at best have a wary, awkward acquaintanceship. Boys can be dense about that stuff, even if they know who you're secretly in love with. "Is it okay, Mira's parents?"

"Maybe you should ask if I even *want* to come with you," she says.

"Mira, that's no way to talk to your friends," her mother says. "But if you want to go out with them, it should be fine, as long as you're home by curfew."

"Are you sure?" Mira asks, starting to stand up.

"Go with your friends," her dad says. "We'll see you at eleven."

"Eleven thirty, Dad," she says. "You promised."

"You're right, I did. Have fun."

Mira carries her plate (the same pasta I ordered) over to our table and rolls her eyes at me.

"What?" I snap.

"Don't make fun of my sweater," she says. "Or my stupid hair. My mom has a heart attack whenever I look too—too casual. Just don't."

"I wasn't going to," I say, though I do feel sad about her pathetic outfit.

"Is it because you're Asian?" Travis asks. "Like Asian parents are extra strict or something?"

"Travis, you don't get to ask me that," she says. "And, *no*. It's not."

"Do you want to switch sweaters with me?" I ask her.

"What? Why?"

"Because that'll still look okay with what I'm wearing, but this'll look way better with your T-shirt and jeans."

She eyes me for a minute before pulling off her sweater and handing it over. "Try not to stretch out the chest too much."

"I'm not that big!" I say while Travis guffaws.

"I guess this is better." She slides into my cardigan. "I trust your judgment, all hail to the fashionista, etcetera."

"Too bad your hair's still all limp," Travis says, to which we both respond, "Shut up," at the same time. Uh oh. Being in sync with Mira seems like a very bad thing. "So we've been talking about Aaron Finley."

"'We'?" Mira asks. "So that translates to *you* talking about Aaron Finley while poor Devan is forced to listen."

I try not to giggle but not really that hard. Mira joins in.

"So what are you guys doing after this?" she asks.

"Sorry about my curfew. My mom watches way too much daytime TV. She's so convinced I'm going to these sex and drug parties that I don't even think exist."

"Yeah, seriously, *if only*," Travis says. "And like you'd get invited!"

Mira laughs and shakes her head. "I know, right?"

"Um, maybe this is dumb," I say, surprised at my own bravery. "But maybe we could just go to your house? Then we don't have to worry about your curfew."

"Perfect," Travis says. "Ooh, we can use your piano."

"You guys actually want to do something that lame with your curfew-less Friday?" Mira asks.

"We're eating here so Travis can pretend he's out at a real bar," I say. "How is going to your house any lamer?"

"Devvie, I'm gonna kill you," he says, as Mira holds up her hand.

"What?" I ask her.

"I'm high-fiving you, stupid."

I slap my palm against hers. When I see this side of Mira, I actually want to be her friend.

When we get to her house, we go to her room first so we can digest a bit before singing. Travis lies down on the bed immediately, but I glance around the room, wishing my own had as much character as her framed photos and posters, and the bookshelf with everything arranged by color.

"How do you find anything?" I ask, hoping she won't revert back to Other Mira and bite my head off.

"That's what my dad says. But sometimes that's the fun of it; I come across stuff I wouldn't otherwise." She lifts her shoulders in a shrug. "Also I love how it looks."

"No, me, too, I should have said that first." I notice the red, white, and black spine of *Destruction*, neatly nestled in the maroons. "Your room's really nice."

"It's just a room, no big deal. Lissa said yours is amazing, some great view of the hills, huge closet, your own bathroom."

I shrug. "It's pretty nice, yeah. I just haven't . . ." *Shut up, Devan.* Why am I tempting fate and nature? Mira is not to know anything about me that isn't surface.

"You haven't what?"

"Found a way to make it my own," I say, even while telling myself not to. "It's still, like, a room my mother set up for me."

"Maybe you can ask for your birthday," she says. "That's what I did. It was still all pink and frilly until last year, when they let me repaint it and get new shelves and the bed. God, is Travis asleep?"

I laugh when I see that he actually is. "So I hope he apologized to you."

"He did but he didn't even have to. I understand what it's like not getting what you want the most. Sometimes it turns you into someone else."

Mira's so hard for me to figure out that I can't even imagine what, or who, it is that she wants the most. Since she seemed so angry when Sai and I first showed up, was it something to do with Travis? Did she have one of those embarrassing and pointless crushes on a gay boy? (It happens.) I hope for her sake it's something else.

Travis is awake before long, so Mira's parents let us take over the living room. We sing what feels like every last piece of sheet music Mira owns before Mira's dad walks back in to (nicely) suggest Travis and I go home. The car seems quiet after the nonstop singathon, and I notice that Travis is grinning at me.

"What?" I ask, preparing for a perverted comment about Sai or Aaron Finley.

"I'm really glad I forgave you, Devvie. You're one of the best people to hang out with."

I pretend to look exhausted. (Okay, to be fair, it's almost one in the morning, so I *am* exhausted.) "Don't even think about starting that again."

He grins at me even more as he pulls into my driveway. "It's so easy to make you crazy. You know I missed you. See you Monday."

Chapter Nineteen

Things I know about Reece Malcolm:

36. My friends think she's cool.

Rehearsals are consuming more and more of my life, which is exactly what's supposed to happen. There's comfort in getting up early and staying late and devoting most of your waking life to this living, breathing *thing*. When you share that with others it makes sense that it's bigger than yourself, but if I was asked I couldn't even put into words how much bigger it actually is, like sizing up the universe.

We've stopped rehearsing the show as separate scenes, and now work on the acts themselves, when we aren't polishing a particular song over and over again. The pieces are finally adding up, though. And while I definitely live for performing, I try not to hurry past these parts, either.

I'm actually telling Travis this while he whines about being ready to open, even though *oh my God I'm so ready to open*. We've already run through all of Act One after school, and are now watching Sai, Aaron, and Mira rehearse "Franklin Shepard, Inc." (It's Sai's song, really, but they have to sit onstage with him and react.)

"I thought you were pessimistic," Travis says with a pout.

"I'm just saying! We rehearse for *two months* and then we have ten performances, total. If we make it all about those ten shows—"

"But it *is* all about those ten shows," he says. "That's how it works, Devvie."

We wince as Sai lands on a really wrong note.

"I just don't want life to be like that," I say. "Living two months for ten shows in two weeks." Up until now I pretty much have been living like that. Each day something to get through to hopefully bring me closer to the one where I met my mother. And now I'm here, but it's not like all of life immediately fell into place like I was so sure it would.

"Sai, come on," Mr. Deans calls out. "I know you know these lyrics by now. You should, at least."

"Mr. Deans should kick him out," Travis says. "Replace him with someone who can hit notes and memorize lines."

"Like you?" I shake my head while feeling super embarrassed for Sai. "It's about more than hitting notes and memorizing lines, you know. Sai's such a good actor."

"Are you saying I'm not?"

"No, just . . . " Sai is still singing (it's a long song) and giving it a lot, but it's so obvious—at least to me—he's trying to fight off melting down. I think about Sai's dad, and Sai's sad empty house, and I wish I could carve out something safe and easy for him right here. Not flubbed lyrics and bad notes. "Stop enjoying him not being perfect so much."

"You're useless," Travis says. "You're *way* too *in love* to think clearly."

"You're in love?" Brian Fredricsson—who plays Joe, the Broadway producer who gives Frank and Charley their big break . . . and whose wife eventually leaves him for Frank—sits down between us, even though we're already pretty close. "With Aaron Finley?"

"I'm not in love," I say. "With Aaron Finley or anyone else."

Travis shoves his hair back from his face. "I think I could be in love with Aaron Finley."

"You barely even know him," I said. "That isn't love."

"You sound like my mom."

I glare in his direction, which is tough to do because of Brian sitting so close and all. From the way Brian looks downward with an expression like he's eaten something that went bad, I guess he hoped Travis didn't have eyes (or anything else) for Aaron.

Grownups don't seem like this. They're just *with* each other. When does that set in? Sitting around obsessing over people who aren't available to you is pathetic. And still. Here we all are.

✽ ✽ ✽

I go straight home that night (thanks to a ride from Travis) instead of getting food out with some or most of the cast, like I've been doing more and more lately. It isn't a matter of avoiding the house or anything; it's just how life gets during a show. Especially this show. But today I got a text from my mother during school: *Never see you these days. Dinner, just us? xo*

Like I could turn that down, life-consuming show or not.

"Hey," my mother greets me when I walk in. She's curled up on the sofa, *sans* laptop for once. "Dinner ideas?"

"Um, whatever's fine with me." I regret saying it immediately. Reece Malcolm does not like *whatever* answers. "Sushi?"

"Not sushi," she says. "Mexican?"

"Sure," I say. "Are you okay?"

"Just tired. And ready for dinner." She sits up and slips her feet into her Converse. "How was rehearsal?"

"It was pretty good," I say as we walk to her car. "I feel like we're almost there, which is good because tech week starts next week, and we open the week after that. And mostly it's only this one song that's still an actual problem, everything else just isn't perfect yet. But I think it will be."

"So is New City crazy?" she asks, once we're heading down Ventura. "Your rehearsal schedule's fairly unbelievable to me."

"No, I've had longer hours before," I say. "Though we'll be rehearsing this weekend and next, too, just so you know, now that opening's so soon. We need a lot of time to get everything perfect."

"I suppose it's how you prepare for your goals in life, but

I can't imagine I would have given up this much of my time when I was your age."

"You didn't write all the time?" I ask, even though we're still not totally on comfortable terms about her books or anything. I can't imagine either one of us ever bringing up the dedication.

"Well, yeah," she says. "But I was home at my desk."

"But, like, if it's the thing that matters most to you, it doesn't feel like a sacrifice."

"So how's everything?" my mother asks once we're seated on the patio at Mexicali (it's always way too loud inside to talk), munching on chips and salsa. (Theirs isn't too spicy for me.)

"Everything?"

"You know." She gives me a look like I'm pretty stupid. "School, the show, the boys, whatever else."

To be fair, I guess that was obvious and I *am* being pretty stupid. "Boys are nonexistent, really. School's fine, I'm keeping up with my grades and everything."

"Of course you are," she says. "Brad and I were saying we sort of feel the need to mock you for it—"

"Good grades?"

"Your overachieving nature." She shrugs. "But we were the same way."

"Probably especially Brad," I say. "He's so OCD about doing everything perfect. I mean, in a good way, but still."

"Trust me, you don't have to convince me of that." She unzips her purse and takes something out of it. "Anyway. I wanted to do something for you, since you've impressed me pretty tremendously with managing everything lately."

"It's really nothing," I say, though I do hold out my hand.

She places a key ring in my open palm. It's the nicest one I've ever seen—who knew key chains could be fancy?—a square of luxe red leather, kind of like my favorite flats. "I thought about putting a copy of my key on it for you, but I was afraid you'd think I was giving you a BMW—I'm not. But I am teaching you to drive as soon as the show's through, and you will get your own car as soon as you're ready."

"Oh my God." I stare at the empty ring, until she hands me a copy of her key, and then I get out my old key chain to move my house key over, too. "You don't have to get me a car, though."

"Honestly, don't think it's an entirely altruistic move. Brad won't have to drive you in the mornings, and I won't feel guilty when I can't pick you up after school. It works out for all of us."

"A cheap car," I say, even though I'm not sure there's any such thing. "Okay? Nothing really nice or anything."

She laughs. "Nothing nice, sure."

"Thank you," I say. "Really."

"So I wanted to—" she starts as a waiter arrives with our sodas and to take our food order. We get our usuals, enchiladas for her and the chile relleno for me, both orders to be split in half and shared. I still can't predict what she'll say or do, but it's nice we've gotten into this routine with food. Maybe it's silly that it makes me feel more connected with her, but in this tiny way it does.

After the waiter leaves, and I'm about to ask my mother to continue saying whatever she was about to say, which I figure can't be too terrible considering that it followed up the key chain-giving, Lissa walks by down the sidewalk. And despite the weirdness post-me-and-Elijah, I call out her name and Lissa turns around, and we end up talking until the food shows up.

And so it isn't until I'm at the house later, sliding my old choir room key onto the key chain, that I remember my mother wanted to talk to me about something. I'm tired enough to tell myself it isn't a big deal, and that sleep is way more important. So I tuck the key chain into my purse, get into bed, and let it go.

❃ ❃ ❃

Tech Week is suddenly just *there*, which is how it always goes. It's hard to remember a time before rehearsals are your whole life, but at the same time it goes so fast. Now there are costumes and props and lighting cues. Boxes of programs are stacked in the lobby (though of course it's bad luck to look at them before we open).

Sai can finally get through "Franklin Shepard, Inc." with no huge flubs. There are still usually a couple of minor ones, and I worry about opening night. Okay, this isn't Broadway, but it's New City, and the standards are high. Aaron heard from Liz Geier (who plays Frank's first wife, Beth) that she heard from Mr. Deans that there are actual talent scouts from UCLA's and USC's drama departments attending, though that seems unlikely to me. This is musical theatre, not football or anything colleges take seriously.

I know Sai is worried. Okay, to be fair, he calls me almost

every night, and he says it a lot. *Man, Dev, I'm worried. I'm the only one who's still screwing up.* But I'd know anyway from the look on his face whenever it happens, from the way he paces when he isn't onstage, from the sheet music he's rarely seen without. I think it's better to mess up a little and still be one of, if not the most talented person in the show, who just happened to get the trickiest song.

But I never say that on the phone, and I never say he'll be fine, either. I don't think it's fair to tell people anything like that. Maybe they *won't* be fine. Maybe flubbing one lyric is something they'll never get over, if it happens during an actual performance. Maybe rehearsals are bad enough. On the phone I just let him talk. I mean—about that. I talk, too; I don't just sit there and let him ramble (even though that probably would be acceptable, considering that Sai talks *a lot*). Just. On that subject, he can talk it out. I listen. It's our system.

Probably it means nothing that he calls me every night. I'm sure he'd call Nicole if she were in the show too and would know what he's talking about. That's something about theatre, how it's its own world. A couple months ago there were a few subjects I could talk about on a regular basis, but now it's pretty much The Show. What would it be like if Elijah was still sort-of-my-boyfriend? Talking nonstop about Tech Week and costume fittings and weird-but-not-entirely-bad choices by other actors (Brian's not-exactly-accurate New York accent comes to mind *a lot*) would probably be super annoying.

"Awesome costume," Sai says to me as we're waiting around backstage while they work out the kinks on some lighting thing. Unfortunately, my costume for the last song in the show, "Our Time," is this dopey pair of pajamas, while Aaron gets to look all hot-guy-in-an-Army-uniform and Sai looks all retro suave in jeans and a vintage Columbia University sweatshirt. Not fair, Mr. Deans.

"Shut up." I elbow him in a way I totally stole from my mother. Also an excuse to touch him, if just a little, and if *my freaking elbow* even counts. (I'll take what I can get.)

"It's not that bad," Aaron says. It probably sounds dumb, considering we're in the show, Nation, and Honors Choir together, and have a billion scenes together, but I still like that Aaron talks to me. I mean, he's a senior, and worthy of the Aaron Finley Sexuality Conundrum. I'm definitely not into him or anything, but I can still recognize he is a tall, hot, talented guy.

"Yeah, on the pajamas scale they're awesome," Sai says, messing with his hair even though I've overheard Mr. Deans *on multiple occasions* telling him that pompadours are not appropriate for Charley. Technically I don't think Sai's hair qualifies as a pompadour, but firstly it makes me laugh gleefully to remember (I have to bite my lip to keep from giggling inappropriately) and secondly, pompadour or not, Charley would definitely have normal hair that doesn't draw attention to himself.

"Hey, guys." Mr. Deans appears out of thin air like a magician or something. If magicians wear sweater vests and Adidas. "We're still having some tech issues; think I'm gonna call this an early night"—I don't mention that we only have one song and the curtain call left to rehearse anyway—"so you can change and take off."

"You guys want to do something?" Aaron asks.

"I should get home," Sai says. "Lot of homework to get caught up on. You want a ride, Dev? Or you want to go out with everyone else?"

"It's not everyone else, it's whoever I can round up," Aaron says. "But we'll find you a ride if you need, Devan."

I shrug, because I like rides home with Sai, but I like being included, too. "I guess I'll stay."

"See you tomorrow," Sai says, squeezing my hand before taking off. It's a friendly gesture, I'm sure. Right? Friends can touch hands.

I start to head to the girls' dressing room to change out of my costume.

"You guys are lucky you're both so good," Aaron says. "I figured it would suck doing a show where the other two leads are a couple."

"We're *not* a couple," I say, so quickly we're sort of talking at the same time. "Who told you that? It's totally not true."

"Whoa, Devan." He holds up his hands. "I just figured. Calm down."

"Good luck with that," Mira says, walking up to us. "Devan's never calm about anything. Anyway, I overheard you guys making plans. Lissa's at Dupar's with Elijah, and he has to take off but she was going to hang out for a while. Since I'm free and everything. If you guys want to come, and invite everyone . . . "

Aaron agrees, and even though Mira still makes me a little nervous—and I know I'll feel weird seeing Lissa and Elijah together out of school—I agree to go, too. So there

I am, as soon as I'm changed back into my normal clothes, squished into the backseat of Aaron's car with Mira and Brian (Travis claims the front seat). When we get to Dupar's, which is a diner I've actually been to with my mother more times than I can count, Elijah is still there with Lissa, but they're saving a giant booth for the few carloads of people from the show. Somehow I end up sitting next to Elijah, because by the time I realize it's happening, it would look rude to move, so I just sit down and glance at him. Hoping to convey I would sit somewhere else if I could.

"How's the show?" he asks, which is a fair question, because we try our best not to talk about it at lunch too often, since Lissa didn't get a role at all and Travis is still probably pissed about his chorus-ness.

"It's really good," I say. "We're close to being there, I think. You'd probably think it's totally nerdy, or I'd tell you to come see it—"

"Of course I'm coming to see it," he says. "You guys are all in it. Shows may not be my thing—I'm never going to be in Nation or sing in a musical—but it's not like I look down on them."

"How's Killington Hill?" I ask.

He makes a sound that's sort of like *guh*. "Don't ask. I think we're breaking up."

"Sorry. That sucks."

"I thought you had to leave," Mira says to Elijah from across the table. It's always nice when her attitude is focused somewhere else than on me.

"I was just going to," he says. "See you guys."

"Where's Pompadour?" Mira asks, which is I guess

what she's retired Aladdin for in reference to Sai. "Adding volumizer?"

Everyone laughs (including me), which makes me feel bad.

"He had homework," I say, to make up for it.

"If he doesn't figure out his part soon, I'm going to *freak*," Travis says. "It's so not fair he got that role. You know Deans must have *re*grets."

"It's not that bad," Mira says. Shockingly. "He's really good besides that."

"But that is like *the* main song for him," Travis says. Which I don't think is true. Sondheim doesn't write shows that center around big numbers or anything. They're way more complex than that. "He screws that up—"

"He won't," I find myself saying. "He's working really hard—he'll get it. And half the stuff he messes up, unless you're some geek who's got the whole thing committed to memory already—"

"Like all of us?" Mira asks, laughing.

"Well, yeah! But you wouldn't know otherwise. No one's parents are going to."

"Unless he makes the face," Travis says, and does an *amazing* impression of Sai's crestfallen expression. I won't lie—I laugh at its accuracy. "He needs to get a handle on it better."

That much is definitely true. And no one's laughing now.

Chapter Twenty

Things I know about Reece Malcolm:

37. *She's tremendously impressed by me.*

I've always wanted a ritual for opening nights, but considering I moved around so much and therefore rarely opened a show with the same group of people at the same place, it was hard nailing one down. Also I'm not very superstitious.

It's a good thing, too, because it—whatever that ritual might be—would be completely derailed on this opening night. I'm sitting outside of the boys' bathroom while, of all people, Travis throws up. (Obviously I bite back that he doesn't even have a big role.)

"I can get Mr. Deans," I call when it seems like there's a break in the puking. "Or maybe the school nurse is still here? Also maybe—"

"Devvie, I'm fine," he calls back, though there's definitely more puking following that assertion.

Sai walks past me and pats my shoulder. "I can take over vomit duty, Dev."

"You're sure?"

"Yeah, I'm ready to go." He glances back and watches me for a long moment. "You nervous at all?"

There are a lot of reasons to be nervous about opening night, like that my mother is in the audience (for the first time of anything I've ever performed, not counting three songs with the Nation); Kate freaking Logan is in the audience; and what if Liz isn't crazy and there *are* musical theatre talent scouts? If Sai messes up, Travis will never shut up about it, and also Sai could end up totally devastated.

"I'm fine," is what I say, though.

"You're interesting, Dev," he says. "I've seen a lot freak you out. But this? Nothing."

"I want to do this my whole life," I say. "I just can't let it."

"Makes sense," he says. "Sometimes you're bizarrely reasonable, you know."

"That's my goal." Wait, am I flirting? With a totally attached boy out of my league while my friend pukes a few feet away? "Devan Malcolm: alto, bizarrely reasonable."

"And seriously talented," he says with a smile, squeezing my shoulder. Shoulder-squeezing doesn't sound hot but his hand feels very right on me. "Don't forget that one."

And then he disappears into the bathroom while I have what feels like a heart attack but most likely is just a normal reaction to the nicest thing ever said to me.

(Or at least the nicest thing ever said to me by the hottest person to ever speak to me.)

Travis's throwing up has quelled by five minutes to curtain, and his complexion changes from ghostly pale to fairly normal as we gather around Mr. Deans. Mr. Deans has something to say to all of us, which is amazing with a cast of thirty people. Mine is to take my time, which reminds me of how Kate made sure I really feel each moment in songs, so it's good advice. He tells Sai to give himself a break, which is exactly what I would have said, too.

The orchestra blasts out the first notes of the overture, and I glance around the circle of us gathered here. I have a lot of favorite things about theatre, but this is definitely one of the best of them. The moments before the curtain rises are always electric, but standing backstage when it's *your show*, even more so. If I could capture what it feels like right now and keep it handy, life could never get too bad again.

Show mode kicks in, and all of a sudden I'm onstage with the entire cast, belting out the first number like my life depends on it. I guess in a way it does. Later on I'll be aware of everyone important in the audience, of how far we've come since our first rehearsal, of how much I'll miss this once it's over, but right now none of it matters. Maybe that's why someone like me connected so immediately to theatre. It's the only time in my whole life I can get completely caught up in a moment.

But maybe I'll get better at that.

The one time I come out of the moment is during "Franklin Shepard, Inc." I stand stage left with Jasmine

Murray, who plays Gussie, and hold my breath to see how Sai gets through. (Honestly I'll bet all of us are holding our breaths.) The bad news is that it's not perfect, but the good news is that it's close, and the kind of slips only we would notice. At least he holds back from making that horrified face.

Afterward we have a couple of seconds where we're waiting to enter the next scene, and I squeeze his hand without thinking about it. (Maybe the Live In the Moment thing is a little dangerous?) But he grins at me like we're on the same page.

"I didn't screw it up," he tells me once the curtain goes down after we close out the first act with "Now You Know" (totally my biggest moment in the show). "And that was *awesome*, Dev. Man, something happens when there's a crowd out there."

"It's always better," I say. "And I'm really proud of you." It feels so geeky out of my mouth, but I *am*. He's come way further than anyone else.

"Thanks, Dev." He kisses my cheek, which I am not not not expecting. It happens too quickly to fully enjoy it. "See you at places."

I rush into the girls' dressing room and change out of the boring navy dress that unfortunately is my costume for "Now You Know," and into the yellow dress that's way more flattering and more my style for the beginning of Act II. Mr. Deans told us the costumes are more about establishing the backward-moving timeline than anything else, which makes sense, but it's tough being obsessed with style and then getting forced into boring, unflattering clothes.

"You sounded so great," Mira says, making her way over to me. "Is it scary? Closing the act like that?"

"I know it should be, but . . . " I grin and shrug. "It's totally not. Just amazing. You were great, too. You actually got laughs during 'Franklin Shepard, Inc.,' which is usually totally impossible because Sai's part's so flaily and scene-stealing."

"Yeah, that was my goal," she says. "If I could get attention off of him even once, I figured I did my job."

I still feel like thinking about it too much might jinx it, but I wonder if maybe we could end up actual friends. Who knows why I even want to—Mira can be so terrifying. But that's the weird thing about L.A. Almost everyone who matters is terrifying somehow.

The second act is pretty much seamless, with no missed lines or lighting cues or lyrics. Every time I'm waiting in the wings, Mr. Deans is chewing his fingernails and sweating like it isn't the most air-conditioned backstage I've ever been in. I want to say something about how well it's going or how it's seriously a nearly perfect show and also maybe how lucky I feel to land at this school with a teacher who completely gets it. But I'll say something later. Right now it seems kinder to let him keep chewing.

"Our Time" is the last song, and for some reason I think it's the hardest. Not, like, musically, but even though I love this show maybe more than any other, it's a super cheesy song, and sometimes during rehearsals we sounded so so so fake and lame that either Aaron or I would laugh, and the other would follow, and soon even Sai—who takes everything more seriously than we do—would fall apart, too.

We've gotten better and haven't done that in ages, but I still find myself searching desperately for the right emotions, so I don't sound too innocent and unrealistic. And I still don't think I'm as good as I could have been, but tonight I feel myself hit a bunch of right notes, musically *and* emotionally.

So many people are so good at so many things. Right now I'm lucky we're supposed to smile during the curtain call, because I'm so happy this is the thing I'm good at.

Backstage, Mr. Deans congratulates us before rushing into the lobby, which I guess I'm not expecting, but I tell myself I can live without more praise and head to the dressing room to change. Mira is somehow already in jeans and a *Spring Awakening* T-shirt and heading out.

"Good show," she calls.

"You, too." Normally I would have taken my time changing, stepped aside for all the people who were rushing out to see their parents or whoever else. Dad came to some of my shows, of course, but he didn't seem to grasp any of the rituals. Like, I never got flowers from him. And I guess he never knew what to say. "Good job" was what usually came out, which sounds nice, but we both knew he couldn't understand why this meant so much to me and I couldn't understand why he couldn't.

But tonight is something new. There were so many people in that auditorium (sold-out crowd!) and, amazingly, four of them were here just for me.

So I do what lots of kids do. I run right into the hallway in costume.

I spot my mother and Brad as soon as I walk out, and for once I'm not nervous. I'm just glad they're here.

"Holy shit," my mother greets me. "You are fucking incredible."

"You can't talk like that in a school," Brad says, which makes my mother and me laugh really hard.

"Seriously." She hugs me really really really tightly. "A-*ma*-zing. I'd say I was proud but that doesn't even begin to sum it up."

"Thank you," I say, but into her hair because she's still holding on. "I'm so glad you came."

"Devan!" Kate dashes around the corner, followed by Vaughn, who's carrying a huge bouquet of bright flowers. "Sorry we weren't here when you came out, sweetie, but the flowers looked dangerously dry, so we were searching for a water fountain."

"Oh my God, thank you," I say, as Vaughn hands them to me and kisses my cheek. "No one's ever gotten me flowers before."

"You were absolutely amazing." Kate crushes me in a forceful hug. "I'm so impressed with you. Though now that I know this is what you're capable of, I'm pushing you much harder whenever we work together."

"C'mon, Katie, let her enjoy it," Vaughn says. "Great show, kid."

My head is buzzing from the attention and the compliments and the sweet scent of the flowers. I could totally get used to this.

"Are we going out?" Kate asks. "If you guys don't mind driving over the hill, there's a great little—"

"I think we're sticking closer to home," my mother

says. "It's late and Devan has school as early as always tomorrow."

"Hint taken." Kate hugs me again. "Call me when you've got free time, sweetie. We'll grab dinner and chat."

Once Kate and Vaughn have left, my mother apologizes. "They're just not always good at making things about other people. Or at least keeping them that way."

"And who wants to drive over the hill just for food?" Brad asks.

"Well, sometimes it's worth it." My mother laughs and slings her arm around Brad's waist. "Oh—give her the thing."

"Yes." Brad digs around in his pocket and takes out a key. "Your mother is demanding I get a new car—"

"It's a long story," my mother says. "And I wouldn't say *demanding*."

"But, as it were, we thought you might like the old one." He hands the key over to me. "I'm sorry it isn't red and more fashionable."

"Oh my God." I stare at the key. "Seriously?"

"Like, totally seriously." My mother grins at me. "You said cheap. This one's basically free. So I hope we're all happy with this solution."

"Thank you *so much*." I tuck the key into the pocket of my pajama pants so I can put it on my red key chain later. "It's seriously okay? I mean, I can't even drive yet."

"We'll make sure you learn," Brad says. "Well, I will. And, yes, we're both fine with this. You've earned it, with all of your hard work in school and this show."

I don't know how to tell them how much it matters to me that they even noticed.

"Oh, hey." Sai exits backstage into the hallway. "Figured everyone would have taken off already."

I recognize his technique. It's too crappy to find yourself in the midst of everyone getting hugged and congratulated when no one would be doing the same for you. Waiting it out is really the best option.

"Excellent show, Sai," Brad tells him.

"Thanks, man," he says. "Dev's awesome, though, right?"

"Totally awesome," my mother says with a smile. "And you didn't suck."

"Good to hear. Dev, I'll see you tomorrow."

"We're getting Mexican," my mother says. "If you want to join us."

Sai nods. "If you guys are okay with that."

"We're okay with that," my mother says. "Devan, go with him and we'll meet at Mexicali."

"I'll mind your flowers." Brad swoops them out of my arms and gives me no choice but to run backstage and change before leaving with Sai.

Not that it's a problem.

"Your parents are awesome," he says as we walk out to his Audi. "So it's good? That you met them recently and all?"

I shrug, because it is, mostly, but sometimes it creeps into my worries that it might be like I'm looking at one tiny beautiful part of a painting, and when the rest is revealed I'll realize it wasn't at all what I thought. But also it's still weird taking compliments where my mother is concerned. And it feels mean being so happy when Sai has none of it.

But our super late dinner is great, crowded around a table on the chilly patio, talking about our favorite moments from the show (both as written and as performed tonight), and laughing so much, and knowing we're staying out way too late, and feeling secure, suddenly, about my place here. Not just L.A., but everything else, too: theatre and school and maybe even *this*.

My mother and Brad walk into the kitchen as soon as we get back to the house to unload the dishwasher and get the coffeemaker ready for the next morning and whatever else grownups do in the kitchen at night. I, on the other hand, am being weird and staring at my mother's bag, because there's something I caught out of the corner of my eye earlier while Brad and Sai were quoting Shakespearean sonnets (nerds). I heard the rustle of my mother reaching into her purse, saw her open a pill bottle and pop one into her mouth. Which I guess isn't that odd? Except that it is.

And even though I know my investigation is basically over—since my Reece Malcolm List was about figuring out who she is, so that I could solve how she could have left me—I can't deny I have a weird feeling right now. Reece Malcolm still has secrets.

So I take a big chance, because I rarely snoop when she's home. But how else will I get a chance to look in her purse? She never leaves the house without it. I reach in, and my hand closes right around the prescription bottle. I feel dumb immediately, because there are a lot of things people take that aren't big deals. Right? What am I going to add to the list, *Reece Malcolm is on a mild dose of antibiotics?*

And, okay, actually. These are just vitamins. Except—

Oh my God.

There's a word preceding *vitamins.* A word I never never never expected to be used in conjunction with Reece Malcolm again. I'm so sure it's a mistake that I read it four times, but it reads the same each and every one of those times.

And I know some people take this kind of vitamin to make their hair or nails better, but this is Reece Malcolm. Reece Malcolm wears the same pair of Chuck Taylors almost every day and sometimes—I'm pretty sure—has the same barely brushed ponytail from the day before.

I shove the bottle back into her bag, walk away from it like I haven't been riffling through its contents. Which is hard because I'm shaking like I did the day I found out I was coming here—maybe worse, because at least back in September I didn't feel like I was expected to act normal. November Devan has a higher set of expectations upon her.

"Hey!" My mother walks into the room with a goofy smile on her face. Reece Malcolm doesn't do goofy. Sixty seconds ago I would have found it adorable, but now I wonder if it's because of the pills, of what the pills mean, of this huge huge huge thing she hasn't told me. "You should probably head to bed."

She hugs me, but I just stand there because it's like I forgot how to hug back. I can't even savor it, like I was served my favorite meal but have a terrible stomachache. Why hasn't she told me? Doesn't that mean something? Maybe she didn't have to tell everyone, but she should have told me, of all people. Right?

"I like the boy, you know."

I shrug. "Me, too. But it's pointless."

"I wouldn't call it that." She grins again. "I'll see you tomorrow."

It's a couple hours later than I usually go to bed, but it still takes forever to fall asleep.

Chapter Twenty-One

Things I know about Reece Malcolm:

38. *She's pregnant.*
39. *She didn't tell me.*

Our show is good, if not quite as fresh-out-of-the-gate, on Friday night. Once I'm onstage it's easy to forget about my mother and the baby, though I'd be lying if I said they don't take up 90 percent of my thoughts up until showtime.

I go out afterward with Travis, Mira, Brian, Liz, Jasmine, and Lissa and Elijah, who came to see the show. Nicole did, too. I saw her in the hallway waiting for Sai with a couple of her friends. And I still want to hate her (and, okay, maybe I do?) but it's good Sai has someone who's there only for him. I try to dwell on that instead of on how much more fun I'd be having if he were out with us, too. It's easier to believe that lie than it is to pretend I'm not thinking about the baby Reece Malcolm is having. The baby who won't be me. The baby she won't run away from until the law demands otherwise.

(Pretend to myself, though, is what I mean, because I'm great at faking it with everyone else.)

Saturday night is our best show yet: no mistakes from anyone, louder laughs than ever before during *all* of the funny moments but especially all the lines I deliver like I'm drunk during "That Frank," and practically deafening applause at curtain call. If I wasn't so mad at my mother—wait, am I *mad*?—I'd be sad she and Brad missed it.

We go out afterward again, and this time Sai comes along, too. Travis, for some bizarre reason, suggests bowling, so we end up at the place behind Jerry's Deli where the lanes are lit up with black lights like it's a disco and not freaking *bowling*.

"You're just mad because you can't wear your cute shoes," Travis tells me as we wait for Sai to set up the scoreboard.

"Shut up." I feel stupid that he isn't entirely wrong. Weird red rented shoes don't look nearly as good with my outfit as my silver flats do. But mainly I'm annoyed that we're doing something stupid, and I hate that I saw my mother in the morning and between shows, two good opportunities, and she still hasn't said anything.

"Your boyfriend looks cute up there." He nods at Sai, who's very engrossed in keying in our names for the scoreboard. "So serious."

"Please don't call him that," I say. "If he hears you I'll die."

"Like, literally? That would be a dramatic medical episode."

I elbow Travis. "I hate you."

Mira sits down on my other side. "Why do you hate him this time?"

"I can't believe we're *bowling*," I say. "It's so Midwestern."

"It's *Rock 'n' Bowl*." Mira points to the signs that pronounce it as such. "What's lame about that?"

We laugh as Sai heads over with his arms in the air.

"Victory," he says in a big boomy voice. "Dev, you're up."

"He put your name in first," Travis whispers to me. "If that isn't love I don't know what is."

I elbow him again, harder, before getting up to bowl a gutterball.

"Devvie, this is *pathetic*." Travis runs over to me. "Come on, you need a coach."

He demonstrates the right way to release the ball down the lane. I try again and knock one pin down, which feels pretty impressive, considering. Travis is up next, so I sit down in the seat he vacated, considering Sai is where I was sitting.

"Nice work," he says to me with a grin. "Good knowing you aren't perfect at everything."

"I'm totally not perfect at *anything*," I say. "But thanks?"

We laugh and watch as Travis bowls a strike.

"Who knew Kennedy had secret bowling talents?" Sai asks. "Man, not me."

"Right?" I lean against him a little, because he's there,

because he smells really nice, because sometimes my brain gets carried away with itself and urges me to do things I shouldn't, because I need badly to feel safe with someone. We're friends, though. It's okay to lean against friends.

(Okay, maybe it isn't okay to lean against friends while wondering what it would be like to kiss them.)

"You want to do this the rest of your life?" Sai asks, right into my ear. Basically the whole cast is here but it's a private conversation suddenly, just for us.

"Bowl?" I somehow manage not to jump as his hand rests on top of mine. It's possible I just want this to be true, but it—combined with his voice soft in my ear—doesn't feel like a friend gesture. "No, um, yeah. I've wanted theatre to be my whole life for a long time."

"You're lucky to know what you want," he says.

I never know how to tell Sai I'm not nearly as lucky as he makes me out to be.

"You could do it your whole life, too," I tell him. With his hand still on mine.

"Maybe. Maybe I don't even want to. Got a lot to figure out first." He leaps to his feet, and my hand is suddenly freezing without his covering it. "My turn up there. I'm gonna demolish Kennedy, wait for it."

Mira leans over and raises her eyebrows with a glance in Sai's direction. It makes me feel sane because I must not be imagining things if Mira sees them, too. But what does that actually change? So I shrug and watch as Sai bowls under the disco lights.

❁ ❁ ❁

As much as I love basically everything about theatre, it's always at least a little bit of a relief when days off roll around. I spend most of my free time making sure I'm caught up on homework, and then a little time studying the California Drivers Handbook. It's a terrifying read. I don't know how anyone keeps track of all these numbers and rules. And unlike getting a problem wrong on a math test, getting this wrong means maybe you'll crash a car or kill someone or even die. And yet it feels like in L.A. alone billions of people drive every single day like it's no big deal at all.

Maybe I'm as bad as my mother because I'm totally pretending I don't know anything about the baby, either. Yeah, partly because I can't say what I know without admitting I've gone through her purse, but things are *better*. We make conversation constantly and she wants nightly details of my performances and if I forget about the vitamins life is maybe the best it's ever been.

And I should enjoy that while I still have it. That much I know. There's no way this isn't changing everything.

My phone beeps with a text on Wednesday night, and I sort of jump when I see that it's from Sai. Normally he just calls. *Can I come over? Bad night. Need to talk.* "Um," I say aloud, causing my mother to look up from her computer. "Is it okay if Sai comes over?"

"Of course," she says, her eyes immediately back to her screen. If she still thinks something's up with Sai and me, at least she's shut up about it. Maybe she's shutting up about a lot now.

Sai is there in record time. He must have texted while driving, which according to the California Driver Handbook is a huge and deadly risk. His eyes are red-rimmed and he's quiet, which shakes through me. I hate seeing him like this.

He walks ahead of me to my room. "Sorry. Man, just a bad night."

"It's okay." I wait to see where he sits down (the bed) before sitting down next to him. Safe amount of space between us, of course. "Is it Nicole?"

Why why why did I ask that?

"It's not," he says. "Why'd you ask that?"

"No, I just— Since you're here. If it was something else I thought you'd—"

"Right." He nods. His hair looks like it's wilting. "Just—my dad and I got into it, nothing new. Well, worse than usual. Last time it was bad I called Nic, but she was kind of . . . I dunno. Freaked? Just that I was so upset. I know it's lame."

"It's not lame to be upset," I say. And the rest comes out before I can stop it. "And I don't think I'd want to go out with anyone who couldn't handle it if I wasn't happy all the time. Especially since it's not like you guys seem to have anything else in common." Hopefully it's fair to not include their shared hotness.

"Man, you're *my friend*," he says in a perfectly nice way, but no one wants to hear the F word from the person they ~~love~~ like. "I needed to talk to someone. And you don't know her. She's smart and funny, even if she's not into show choir and everything else."

"I'm *sorry*," I say. (I'm not.) "Anyway. Do you want to talk?"

"I don't know." He leans forward, drops his head into

his hands. "Was it bad when you lived with your dad? You guys fight a lot?"

"No," I say. "He would have had to talk to me more to fight with me, so . . ."

"That sucks," Sai says. "But I'd take it over getting yelled at every goddamn day."

"Yeah." I rub his shoulder with my hand. It feels like the right thing to do and not just an excuse to touch him. "I'm sorry you have to go through it."

"Dev, thanks." He looks up at me, leans in kind of close, gets closer. I'm totally no expert on kissing, but it feels a lot like it's about to happen. I lean in, too, smell his Sai smell (hair product and Altoids). It's weird. We just pause there with eyes locked like someone hit a button on a remote control.

I know it's kind of taking advantage, too. He's emotional and in my room. Okay, fine, I'm not *kind of* taking advantage. I am *totally* taking advantage. Wrapping my hand around the back of his neck, leaning in.

"Hey, uh." He's suddenly in motion again. Ducking away from me. "Sorry, I didn't mean—"

"No, it was totally me, I—"

"You know why my parents got divorced?" he asks. "Because my dad was cheating on my mom and I caught him."

"Did you tell her?"

He nods. "Now she says she can't look at me without thinking about it. Which is why I'm stuck here with him. Like it's *my* fault. And of course he hates me for it."

"You did the right thing," I say. "Even if they're being stupid about it."

He covers his face with his hands. "I just keep thinking it'll start sucking less. And it doesn't."

I think back to living with Dad and Tracie, and how anyone telling me it would be okay wouldn't have mattered at all. So I stay quiet, just reach over and touch his hair. (It feels as nice as I hoped this whole time.)

I should mention I'm pretty mad at the side of me using Sai's total meltdown as an excuse to touch his hair and smell him and be sitting so so so close to him. Still, come on, of course that side is winning. That side is frustrated. I owe it something.

He lays his head in my lap. Now it seems practically obligatory to run my fingers through his hair. I try to keep it from wilting completely.

"Do you really think that about Nic?" he asks. "We don't have anything in common?"

I shrug because now it feels like kicking him while he's down. "I don't even really know her. I shouldn't have said it. It's just that—"

"Yeah?"

Shut up, Devan, shut up. "N—nothing."

"No, whatever you're thinking, say it."

"Just that—I don't know. You call me like every night and—I mean, you're over here now." With your *head* in my *lap.* "And sometimes—"

"Sometimes what?"

"Sometimes the way you act around me . . ." Oh my God, what am I saying? "You know what I mean."

"We're *friends*," he says again, but I believe him less this time. (It still stings.) "I don't know why you're saying this shit."

"Really? You have no idea?"

He jumps up, paces the length of my room a couple more times before walking to the door. "Thanks a lot."

"Sai, don't go, I—"

But he's gone. And then my words echo through me, and I think about accusing him of *liking* me, of me being better for him than Nicole, or a lot of things *of course* I think about all the time. You don't just *say* that stuff, though.

"Devan?" My mother leans into the room. "Everything all right? Sai took off without saying *awesome, Ms. Malcolm* five times, so . . ."

I burst into tears and shake my head. "I'm so stupid."

"I doubt that, kid." She pulls me into her arms, hugs me tightly. *Tell me*, I pray. For all that I don't want to deal with the changes it'll bring, at least I'll feel like someone Reece Malcolm thinks worthy of the truth. "Want to talk?"

"Not really," I say, and not just because I don't want some big emotional talk over the thing I can't say.

She wraps me into another hug, which is kind of weird. "Ooh, let's go get milkshakes. All of a sudden I'm craving a milkshake. And guy drama always goes well with milkshakes, I've found."

"Okay," I said, even though I feel all prickly at the mention of a *craving*. "Do you think it's bad to tell someone the truth, even if maybe you shouldn't say it out loud?" I mean Sai, but I guess I don't not mean her, too.

"I don't know." She pulls me down the stairs after her. I

really hope we're going to a drive-through, because my face is bright red and tear-stained. "Sometimes honesty is by far the honorable choice, but I believe people lie to protect each other all the time. And I don't think there's anything inherently wrong with that."

"Then I think I messed up," I say while wondering if she's protecting me right now. And if the baby means I need to be protected, is that bad news? Is it everything that eats at me when I stop to think about it for more than a moment?

"We all mess up," she says as we walk into the garage. "Don't make it more than it is. I mess up more with the people I care about than anyone else, and luckily they tend to forgive me."

I bite my lip hard not to say anything.

The garage door opens, and Brad's Jetta pulls in. (He hasn't gotten a new—presumably baby-friendlier—car yet.) I know technically Brad isn't anything to me. Not my stepdad, definitely not my father. But I keep thinking of how he's going to be *someone's* dad and that someone is never going to have to wonder if his or her dad will someday forget how to talk to his own kid.

"Hey," my mother greets him. "We're getting milkshakes. Are you in?"

Brad glances at me, probably appraising my post-cry face. "We could stay in and I could make milkshakes."

"No, I want a milkshake I pay for, ordered from a drive-through speaker." She grins at him and holds out her hand. "Come on."

They're always so polite about romantic stuff in front

of me but it's not like I can't see the way they look at each other. Normally it makes me really happy to see, not just that they're in love but that love like that is possible.

Right now, though, I just kind of want to throw water on them.

Chapter Twenty-Two

Things I know about Reece Malcolm:

40. *She still hasn't told me.*
41. *She's had chances.*

Sai doesn't speak to me the next day during school, which I guess is expected, but as we gather backstage before the show, he still refuses to make eye contact. Almost all my scenes are with him, but once I'm onstage, I'm not really myself, so it's a safe time for anything to go wrong in a part of my life that isn't the show. And—no matter how much I maybe want to—I can't hate Sai. I can't even really dislike him. When he sings I still hold my breath hoping he'll get everything right.

I'm not sure if that makes me mature or pathetic.

If anyone else notices, they don't mention it. Not even Travis, who seems to follow us like a soap opera. It's not our best, but it's still a good show. And so is Friday's, and so is the Saturday matinee. But I don't want to close out our whole run with just a good show. I want it bigger and better and so full of energy you're convinced it might burst. As easy as it is to put everything out of my head during a performance, I don't want to, especially with the cast party looming afterward. The first cast party I feel completely wanted at. Spending it avoiding Sai sounds more awful than worrying if I should be there or not.

I go home between our matinee and evening shows mainly as an excuse to get Sai advice, but also because my mother offered to order in Thai. She isn't my favorite person right now, but I can't deny that she understands boys.

"So, um," I say while she chomps on a spring roll, "Sai still totally hates me."

"He'll get over it."

"I just don't want to spend another show knowing how mad he is at me—"

"Unfortunately, that's life," she says with a little shrug. Not what I want to hear.

"Sai's not just—" I cut myself off because it takes a moment to figure out how to say it. "He's not just some boy I want to kiss."

"I'm running to the bathroom." She gets up and heads out of the room. "And I know how many spring rolls are left, and I will count when I get back."

I shoot a glare at her as she walks away. Her acting like spring rolls are more important than something big in my life probably shouldn't surprise me—considering she's been pretending something big in hers isn't going on at all—but it still pisses me off.

Her laptop is lying open on the coffee table, and I swivel it around to see how many of her emails I can get through before she's back. I lost a lot of chances to investigate thanks to the show—and to thinking things were fine—and, seriously, now is more important than ever.

The most recent emails are from Kate and Vaughn and unimportant, but then I strike gold, because she and Brad apparently never shut up about the baby in their emails these days. I can't believe I let the hunt get away from me like this. I would have known so much sooner if only I hadn't gotten so complacent.

"What are you doing?"

My mother is out of the bathroom and practically in the living room. I was way too focused on the screen to realize she was walking up behind me. Crap crap crap.

"What the hell are you doing in my email?" she asks, as I close out of it really really really quickly. "In what world is that all right?"

"I'm sorry, I—"

"You're *sorry*?" She shakes her head. "I asked you a question. Several, actually. I'd like an answer."

I try to explain, but nothing comes out.

"This is my fucking house," she says. "And I'd like to think at least here I have some modicum of privacy. Thanks for absolutely destroying that."

Somehow, this is worse than anything I could have imagined.

"Is this what you do?" she asks. "Go through my things when I'm not around?"

I don't know what to say because that is *exactly* what I did. "I'm—I'm really sorry."

"No, this is the thing," she says. "There is no fucking way you could have thought going through my private emails was all right. So don't give me that. Don't tell me you're sorry for something that was never, ever acceptable. You know better than that."

I start to apologize again. I start to say that I guess I did know better. But something dawns on me in a big bright flash: I don't want to be quiet mousy Devan. The last thing I want to do is apologize over and over. "Not that it's okay I snooped, but maybe you should have told me."

"Told you what?"

"That you're *pregnant.*" I say it like it's a curse word. "It's a totally crappy thing to keep secret. Especially from me."

Saying it aloud somehow makes it feel like that's even truer than it already was.

"Like, I can't believe you would totally abandon me my whole life, until they forced you *by law* to take me in, and now that you feel like it, you're going to be a mom to someone. Just not me."

"That's such bullshit," she says.

"It totally isn't," I say, because it's *not.* And calling out Reece Malcolm feels *good.* "I mean, you don't tell me *anything.*"

There's a burst of realization in this moment that I could stop. I don't have to keep talking. I can apologize again and beg her not to be mad at me. I can go back to not realizing I even feel all of this stuff. But I don't.

"I still don't know why I'm here at all, if you didn't want me why you even had me, if you ever asked Dad about me to make sure I was okay, if you're totally going to forget about me now that you're having a baby you actually *want*, why you dedicated your stupid book to me when you could have just been around for me instead."

It's the strangest sensation to realize as you're saying things that you believed them for a really long time. You would think finally letting go would be a weight lifted, but everything is still pulling at me.

"Like, I think you're a terrible person for that," I say. "And I hate you for getting a second chance. You totally do not deserve one."

I'm crying at this point so who knows if any of what I'm saying even sounds like words and not just unintelligible ranting. Who even cares.

"Is that all?" she asks. Utterly emotionless by now. I wonder if I *did* think she was a terrible person all along. I wonder if I hated her as much as I do right in this moment.

"I hate you." I say it haltingly to test how true it seems on my lips. It doesn't taste like a lie, but it doesn't exactly ring true, either. Still, I think I've wanted to say it for a long long long time now, way before I even met her or knew who she was. "You couldn't even come and *get me*. My dad died and you just sent your stupid lawyer. And he shouldn't have brought me here because you don't want me anyway."

She's staring straight down at the floor by now. I assume she's hoping I'll shut up soon so she can get back to everything else. Everything that doesn't involve me. She finally has an excuse—a few, even—to send me on my way. "Maybe they shouldn't have."

"I—I, um." I point to my wrist even though I'm not wearing a watch. "I should probably— I have my show."

"Can you get a ride?" She walks down the hallway and slams shut her office door.

I get out my phone to call Travis. He agrees to pick me up, so I wait on the front porch, my heart pounding in my throat and ears and fingertips. Probably it's dumb to even attempt going to the show tonight, but it's our final performance, after all. I'll get through it, and maybe it'll be the last good thing that happens to me. Theatre has always carried me through before. There is no reason it won't tonight.

When I get there, I touch up my face with a ton of powder and fake being in a good mood so I don't have to explain anything to anyone. By the time I'm onstage and singing my part of the first "Merrily We Roll Along," I'm Mary Flynn and not Devan Mitchell. Definitely not Devan Malcolm. Theatre is saving me yet again.

It's a good show, too. Sai is totally *on* during "Franklin Shepard, Inc.," and I feel all fiery and barely restrained at the end of Act I. During intermission while we're dashing around changing into our costumes for "It's a Hit," Sai even glances my way and gives me a little nod. "Nice one."

"You, too." But that's it. We're back to not knowing each other. I wonder if after tonight we'll ever speak again. I mean, who even knows where I'll end up?

The second act is as solid as the first, and during the closing number, "Our Time," I link arms—in character—with

Aaron and Sai, and tell myself to hold on hold on hold on to this moment. If everything changes, I still have all of this. Next life change, next new school, I won't be a timid mouse, and I definitely won't *ever* be a wild squirrel.

Maybe I'll be okay after all.

Mr. Deans tries to keep us after our curtain call (many solid minutes of crazy applause) to give us a speech about how much we've learned and grown and accomplished, but the cast party is planned at Liz's place, since her parents are out of town, and everyone is inching toward the door and not paying attention. So he cuts us loose, and I run to the dressing room to switch the pajamas for a newish red dress, my red flats (while trying not to think about my mother buying them for me), and a black cardigan, before meeting up with Travis and Mira in the lobby so we can take off.

"Your mom," Travis says to me, "is so cute."

"Why are you talking about my mom?" I snap, instead of responding in any number of normal ways.

He rolls his eyes. "Because she just walked by!"

"Trust me, she didn't," I say. "Someone who looked like her did. Can we go?"

Mira nudges me as we walk out to Travis's car. "You okay?"

"I'm fine."

"Right." She nudges me again. "Let me know if you're not, seriously."

"Thanks." I won't be spilling anything to Mira but the offer is still nice. Justine pushed me so hard to reveal my deepest thoughts but never even seemed to notice when I just needed her to *be there* for me. It's kind of weird how Mira can read me so well. It's even weirder that she knows to ask and then let it go.

Liz's place is already pretty packed when we get there, clearly not limited to just cast and crew. Travis dashes off, probably to solve the Aaron Finley Sexuality Conundrum, but I hang near the front room. And despite Sai, and despite my afternoon and what I fear waits for me at my mother's house, one thing I feel right now is wanted.

"I'm getting something to drink," Mira says. "You want anything?"

"I'm fine. Thanks."

People keep coming up to let me know how great I was, how much they liked the show or liked working with me. So I get drawn in. And that's how I stumble upon Sai, even though I've been doing my best not to (and assuming he won't be here anyway).

"Oh, sorry," I say, because somehow we're the only two in the little darkened hallway between the kitchen and the rest of the house at the moment. (I was looking for the bathroom . . . maybe he was doing the same?)

"Sorry?" He grins like the last few days didn't happen. "You didn't even run into me."

"Shut up," I say. "Just—"

"Just what?" He leans in close close close. Our foreheads almost touch. "Good show tonight, Dev. Maybe your best."

"You, too. I hate it that I seem to get my best right before the show closes."

"Yeah, you started off pretty strong, though." He leans

in closer, slides his arms around me like we're going to hug, but instead I close the remaining space between us.

And our lips meet.

Sai's fingertips press into the small of my back. I wrap my arms around his shoulders like I'll float away without his leverage. We kiss again, though to be very honest it's tough knowing where one leaves off and the next begins. His hands trail up my back, cup around my face, pull me closer because somehow that's possible. We're still kissing. Again again again. It's everything I've ever heard about kissing, too—not like kissing Elijah. Which was perfectly nice but. This is heat and hands and teeth and forgetting to breathe and deciding who needs to breathe anyway? Everything I taste see feel is Sai.

"Shit," is what he finally says. Not exactly the first thing you want to hear after the best kisses of your life from the boy you're maybe in ~~love~~ like with.

"What?"

"Just—" He steps back from me, rubbing his mouth with the back of his hand. And I start to cry. "Dev—no. It's not you. I'm just . . . I'm no better than my dad."

"Nicole," I say.

"She's my girlfriend. And I just screwed up big. I said I'd never be like him and I am *exactly* like him."

Normally I would comfort him. Normally I would say how obvious it is that kissing someone while dating someone else isn't exactly on par with cheating on your wife. But I am not not not in the mood to comfort Sai, and I'm not sure I ever will be again.

"I'm going." He stomps past me, and I spin around

before I can stop myself. I think about my role in the show and how Mary Flynn's life ended up crappy mainly because she could never speak up and admit how she actually felt to the people who mattered. No timid mouse, no wild squirrel, and definitely no Mary Flynn.

Saying every bit of truth to Reece Malcolm might have changed everything for me. It might have even *ruined* a lot of things. But even if I could go back to this afternoon, I'd never change that it happened.

"You're such a jerk to blame me," I say. "You didn't *have* to kiss me. You didn't have to kiss me *multiple times*. Go ahead and hate yourself if you want, but—"

"You know I could never hate you, Dev," he says. "You're my—"

"I'm your *what*?" I ask instead of letting him finish. "I'm not your friend because friends don't lead friends on or blame them when they're mad at themselves. And I'm definitely nothing more to you. I am going back to the party. You can do whatever you want."

But of course that's just an excuse to sound tough. In reality I find an empty room to slip off to. Maybe I can cry this all out and get back to life before anyone notices. I might not be a timid mouse or wild squirrel but I'm still *me*. My heart's not heavy with unsaid words but, well, it's still *heavy*.

Also I wish there were a way to forget how kissing Sai felt.

"Devan?"

Holy crap, I have to get better at looking out for people. Somehow Mira is already in here. "Oh my God, I thought I was alone."

She laughs, but this snuffly laugh. Like she's been crying, too. "Are you okay? If you say you're fine I'll hit you."

"No, I am totally *not* fine," I say. "Are you?"

"Nope. Lissa's making out with Aaron Finley."

"What? What about Elijah?"

Mira, unsurprisingly, can still roll her eyes when they're teary. "*Right*? She only wants him when she can't have him, I guess."

It did at least solve the Aaron Finley Conundrum. "So Travis is pissed? And was mean to you?"

"No . . ."

"Oh. Do you like Aaron or something? I didn't even—"

"Devan!" She smacks me, but not hard. "Have you seriously not figured out how pathetically in love with my best friend I am?"

"Totally not. Clearly." But suddenly a lot of things click. "Does she know?"

"Hopefully not," Mira says. "That's the only thing that would make it more pathetic."

"If it makes you feel better, I just kissed Sai. A lot."

"Uh, that doesn't make me feel better at all. Why does everyone get to kiss someone tonight except for me?"

"Afterward he *wiped off his mouth*," I say, and Mira cringes. "And freaked because he's still going out with Nicole. So I think I win."

"Yeah, maybe you do." She buries her head in her hands. "I'm such an idiot. I really kept thinking because she couldn't actually get things to work with E that maybe . . . there was this chance. But if she's making out with Aaron, it's not about not being completely okay with guys, it's Elijah-specific. Which means this was always hopeless."

"I'm sorry," I tell her. "But it's easy to get hung up on the wrong person. I'm like the biggest example of that ever."

"I should have told you sooner." Mira's expression is soft for once. "Not that I was pining over Liss, just that I'm . . . I figured you're from the Midwest, and—"

"Yeah, but I'm friends with Travis," I say. "And I'm nice to the other guys in—"

"No, but, a lot of girls are like that with gay boys, but then they find out a girl's gay, and they freak. But, still. You're pretty much nice to *everyone*, and I should have given you the benefit of the doubt."

"Yes," I say. "You should have. But I get how it is to have this part of you that seems like no one could handle it if they knew."

"If you ever want to talk about whatever that is," she says, "you can. No judgment."

"Ha!" I smack her this time. "You're totally full of judgment."

"You know what I mean." She sighs and wraps her arms around her knees. "I always want parties to be fun, but I usually end up in some room crying about some girl."

"Let's go be social, then," I say. "It's less pathetic, and maybe we can try to forget how much tonight sucks."

"You go be social," she says. "I need to be pathetic for a while longer. But get a full report on Travis's reaction to Lissa and Aaron, okay? It'll make me feel better."

"Hey, um." I get up and hover in the doorway. "Do you

think I could maybe spend the night at your house tonight? My mother and I had this huge fight, and, maybe—"

"Definitely. Let me know when you want to go. We can try to catch a ride or call my dad to pick us up."

So I stay a while longer, even though I want to be pathetic, too. I sing at the top of my lungs along with everyone else, I sample the punch someone dumped a flask into, and I manage to let full minutes pass without thinking about Sai. Or my mother.

It's a bad night. But in a lot of ways it's a really good one, too.

Chapter Twenty-Three

Things I know about Reece Malcolm:

42. *Maybe I was right about her all along.*

We sleep in late the next morning, rare for me after performing *and* with so much on my mind. But it isn't until Mira's mom knocks on the door letting us know breakfast is ready that I open my eyes. Sleeping on the floor left me feeling a little broken, but at least it matches my mood. I hate easy mornings after awful nights. They're such lies.

"I, um, I guess maybe I should go home?" I say to Mira after breakfast. It isn't that I want to face my mother, but I can't avoid her forever. Getting it over with seems the smartest option, and I want to know what's next for me, the stuff I can't control at least. "Is that okay?"

Mira asks to borrow her dad's car, and her parents agree. So we take off for the house, and I know that later I'll need to call her and explain a lot. It's funny how safe Mira seems now.

When she drops me off, I wave and make my way as slowly as possible up to the front door. And I'm hoping to hide out in my room for a while, but as I walk in, my mother looks up from the living room sofa.

"Hey," she says.

"Hi." I take a deep breath, like I'm launching into a monologue or something. In really bad form. "So, um. I guess I should know where you want me to go, or if you need to call your lawyer or whatever."

"You idiot." She leaps to her feet and bolts across the room. And hugs me. I'm way too confused to react. "I mean—blah, blah, something comforting and nice."

Somehow that actually makes me laugh.

"We had a *fight*," she says. "A long overdue one."

"You said maybe they shouldn't have sent me here."

"Yeah, and so did you." She taps my nose with her fingertip. "You're right; I am in no way a good mother to you. Which is exactly why I worry constantly I shouldn't have told them to send you to me. It feels so goddamn selfish. I wasn't ready to be a mother then, and—even though I'm aware that I'm not now—I want to be."

"Right," I say. With a glance to her still very flat stomach.

"Stupid," she says. Somehow nicely. "God, sorry. Just—I don't mean the kid. I mean you."

"Seriously?"

"Totally seriously," she says in the voice she uses

whenever she makes fun of something I say. It's really good to hear. "It was such a relief having you here when I found out I was pregnant. Brad and I kept saying, *Well, Devan's amazing so the kid should probably turn out fine.*"

"Really?"

"I guess you didn't get that far back in my email." She sits down on the couch again. "Stay out of my stuff, all right? I don't like this snooping side of you."

"I just . . . I had to find out." Suddenly the truth seems smarter than any excuse I could come up with. "Why you left me. I wanted to make sure you wouldn't do it again, so—"

"Devan," she says in this waterlogged voice. I'm really not prepared to see Reece Malcolm cry. "Oh, God, kid. There isn't some big mystery. I was fifteen when I got pregnant, sixteen when you were born. *Your age.* Could you take care of a baby now?"

I shake my head.

"That's *it*," she says. "It's no more complicated than that."

"But—that didn't mean you had to, like, walk away completely."

"It, well . . . it sort of did," she says. "The agreement I thought I was signing—"

"You *thought* you were signing?"

"My mother thought I'd regret giving up custody of you," she says. "So it turns out the papers never made their way back to the lawyer. But I was under the impression I had to stay out of your life, which I thought was for the best. I can barely function with people my own age, as you've seen. I had no business being around you."

"That's totally not true," I say. "All Dad did was ignore me—at least it seemed like it—and Tracie was awful, and he never stopped her, and you would have been better, I know it."

"Maybe," she says. "I had a lot of growing up to do. Anyway, I can't fix the past. If I had some magical way to give you an instant happy childhood, I'd do it in a heartbeat. But all we have is now and everything after."

"So if you'd actually signed those papers, I wouldn't have been sent here," I say as it dawns on me. "When Dad died. That's how you found out your mom didn't give them to the lawyer? So you could have told them that. That your mom interfered or whatever the legal word is, and you didn't know you had custody of me."

"I could have," she says. "But I figured I wouldn't have gotten the call if you didn't need me. I offered to work something out with your stepmother so you could stay, if that was what everyone wanted, but—"

"Oh my God," I say. "That would have been awful."

She laughs. "Worse than this?"

"Shut up," I say. "I actually totally love it here."

"Except for worrying I was looking for a way to get rid of you?" she asks. "You should have talked to me."

"Don't act like that," I say. "Like you're easy to talk to! You are like the absolute opposite. Ask anyone."

I'm just responding, not lashing out, truly, but she sniffs really hard and I realize I hit her hard with that. I don't feel all that guilty, though.

"I know you're right," she says. "I wish you weren't."

"I'm sorry I went through your stuff," I say. Maybe it's

dumb, but I didn't think about how I was invading her privacy until now, just taking care of myself. "I didn't mean—"

"You're forgiven," she says. "And I'm truly sorry for what I said. I was just . . ."

"Mad?"

"Quite. But everything else, too, you know. Worried about you. Worried about this kid. Worried about my fucking relationship. Worried all the goddamn time, about all the people I could potentially fuck up. Sometimes I think you'd be better off with anyone but me." She stares at her hands in her lap before glancing up at me. "And this isn't how I wanted you to find out."

I'm not entirely sure what she means, since a lot has come out in the past twenty-four hours. So I stay quiet.

"I know if my mom had turned up pregnant when I was sixteen—"

"We aren't you and your mom." I don't want her pretending it's the same when they had a whole life together. We've only had September and everything after.

"Trust me, this I know." She makes really direct eye contact with me. "Mom and I have never been that close. I was hoping we'd be more than that."

"Seriously?"

She laughs really hard. "Yeah, seriously!"

I decide to take advantage of this very truthful afternoon. "I, um, you . . . you said once that getting pregnant with me ruined your life." I hear it echo in my head for only the millionth time and shiver a little. "If that's how you feel—"

"Well, yeah. It *is* how I feel. But you are an amazing

person, Devan, and I love you more than I have the capacity to express. Would my life have been easier if I hadn't gotten knocked up at fifteen, though? Of course."

"That's not my fault," I say.

"No, it isn't," she says. "I never should have said that, either. And I apologize."

"It's okay," I say, because the apology is nice, and the thing about loving me is maybe the best thing I've ever heard. No, not maybe. It just is. And not just because I guess we're sorted out, me and Reece Malcolm, or because the mystery isn't a mystery and therefore doesn't need solving, or because I feel it now in my heart, how safe I am here in this house. In *my* house.

"We'll figure this out," she says. "Last night I heard myself yelling at you and was horrified. I have to stop treating good people the way I do. Which includes you and Brad."

"Brad'll be a really good dad."

She nods many many many times. "Yes. Thank God one of us is nurturing."

I laugh even though I guess that's mean. Luckily she joins in. "Maybe you can try?" I say.

"You can be my guinea pig. Sure."

"Are you getting married?" I ask.

"I've never really wanted to," she says. "Which is a hard thing to explain. But I love what I have with Brad. We're good as we are, I think. Well—I'm buying him a TV and he's promised to enjoy going to concerts without me. So we're getting there. He's around for good."

The doorbell rings, which makes us exchange Raised Eyebrow Glances. I like it when we're mirrors of each other.

"I hate people who don't call first," she mutters, jumping up to glance out the window before opening the door. "Hey there."

Her tone has shifted entirely, and I lean over to see who could have earned such a 180. *Oh my God.*

"This isn't a good time," I say, running to the door. It all comes out in a lump, *thisisn'tagoodtime*. But Sai is normal Sai again. He just grins with a slight shrug of his shoulders.

"I knew you'd say that. It's why I didn't call first."

"I admire your tactics," my mother says to him, which makes his full smile break out. Too bad there isn't a vaccination against its effects.

"I'll be right back," I say to my mother. Then I walk past Sai and close the door behind me. "What?"

"I wanted to give you something." He reaches into his pocket and pulls out a key. "I remembered what you told me about your old choir room and . . . I thought . . ."

I take it from him, wondering what this means, wondering if we can call our fight over so soon after what happened last night, wondering if we don't have to keep avoiding each other, wondering if after hours in New City's choir room would be as healing as—"Hey!"

"Yeah?" he asks with his stupid cocky gorgeous grin.

"This is, like, a blank key." I hold it out at him. "It won't open anything."

He's still grinning. "Yeah, it was a nice move, though, right?"

"You came all the way over here to give me a stupid blank key?"

"I, uh, I actually came over here to tell you I, uh . . . "

He runs his hand through his hair, shuffles his feet, steps back from me a little. Is Sai *nervous*? That seems physically impossible. "I broke up with Nic."

"Oh, I'm—I'm sorry?"

"Hoping you wouldn't be." He crosses his arms across his chest. "Or maybe you hate me now, dunno, maybe I deserve it."

"I don't hate you," I say. "But you do deserve it."

"Man, yeah," he says. "Everything you said last night was true."

"It's not okay," I say. "How you've been. And I don't know when it will be."

He nods, looking down at our feet. "Dev, I'm sorry."

"Except." I step closer to him and place my hand on his arm. "I don't care if we don't wait for things to be totally okay."

I kiss him so hard the wind is knocked out of me. Or maybe my heart and lungs stop for other reasons entirely. It seems brave but I know it isn't. Boys don't show up with worthless keys and breakup stories for nothing. I've barely caught my breath when he kisses me back.

"You have to stop," I tell him once I can breathe again. His face falls, and I let him be panicked a few seconds before continuing. "We're in clear view through that window and, trust me, my mother is spying on us."

He laughs and pulls me farther from the window before kissing me again. I've imagined kissing Sai more times than I would admit to anyone (even myself), but now that this is real, it isn't anything like that at all. Obviously it's better than what my mostly inexperienced brain conjured up, but also it's *actually happening.* There are so many small things, not just his lips against mine, but how electric his fingertips are against my face, how natural it feels sliding my arms around him and pulling him closer, how his hands keep moving: my face to my hair, the small of my back, my face again. Also—and maybe this is stupid—he's still Sai. He is still a boy I like talking to who cares about things and isn't afraid to be himself and gets really excited about books and who, I know, is there for me.

"You wanna go somewhere?" Sai takes my hand and pulls me to him, grins the whole time. The truth is he's such a dork, too. "Take a drive? Hunt down a key? Get pizza? Oh, man, I heard there was some crazy show at some theatre down in—"

"I think I'm staying in," I tell him. "My mom"—it comes out just that naturally—"and I have a lot to talk about, and I think we're just going to hang here."

"Maybe later?" he asks.

"Maybe, yeah," I say. "I mean—you're okay and everything, right? Your dad—"

"I'm okay," he says. "Call me later? If you're free."

I rise to my tiptoes to hug my arms around him. "I'm glad you came over."

He kisses my cheek. "Me, too, Dev."

It hits me that he's one of my best friends, wrapped up in something else, too. I want to tell him that, but we have a lot of other things to talk about first. I'm still a little mad at him—he hasn't done everything like he should have. Not to me, not to Nicole. But I'm okay working on that later and being with him now.

I can say I go right back in to hang out with my mother, but that would be a big lie. Sai pushes me up against the side of the house, and I truly truly truly lose track of how long we stand there kissing. My lips are sore when I finally detangle myself, so it might have been a while. We say good-bye again, successfully this time, and I head inside. My mother looks up from her laptop, not even concealing her smirk.

"Stop."

"Stop what?" she asks in what isn't close to an innocent tone. "How's that going, by the way? Better?"

"Um." I feel my face flush as I take my red key chain out from my purse and slide on the blank key. "Yeah. I mean—it's actually going."

"It's about time." She laughs and closes her laptop. "What do you think about Lysander?"

"What *about* Lysander?"

"For the kid's name."

I make a face. "He'd get beat up every day for having a name like that."

"It's not that weird," she says. "It's Shakespearean! And it's *Los Angeles*. Though Brad agrees with you."

"Maybe it's good Dad named me," I say, throwing his name around like we talk normally about him all the time.

"Oh, your father did *not* name you," she says. "Did he tell you that?"

"No, I just—I assumed."

"They had some terrible name picked out for you—"

"Lysander?"

"You're hilarious. I liked the name Devan. Who knows,

I probably read it in a book the week before. I told Mom to demand, and they agreed."

"I've always liked my name," I say. "Especially now that I know it could have been Lysander."

"You're dead to me," she says. "Hey—on that subject?"

"Me being dead?"

"You being dead, sure." She picks up a *Merrily* program from the coffee table. "I noticed at Parents' Night you're using my name, and I'm assuming it's some clerical error New City made."

"Did you go to my show last night?" I ask, not only to change the subject, but because I remember something Travis said.

"I did. I figured with the way we'd left things you might have a better show if you didn't know I was out there."

"I'm really glad you were," I say, and she grins.

"Me, too."

"It, um, did start as a clerical error or whatever," I say. "I should have told you. I just—I know it sounds stupid, but it seemed good being Devan Malcolm instead. Dad never . . . "

She watches me for a few moments as I fade out. "Your father—"

"What about him?" I ask, but it comes out in another lump.

"He was a good guy," she says. "He tried to do a good thing. He genuinely believed I was the eighteen-year-old I pretended to be, and I know he wanted to be a good father to you. He wasn't an asshole running around taking advantage of young girls or whatever you've decided."

"He was an asshole running around cheating on Tracie, though," I say, thinking about Sai and his dad.

"Yeah, but I think hooking up with someone who sneaked into a college party's a more forgivable offense," she says. "Anyway. I have no idea what he's told you and what he hasn't. But I guess it's more than time we talked."

"He didn't tell me anything. Just . . . I was reading *Destruction*, and I noticed the dedication, and—I guess it sounds dumb—but it did make me wonder if you were my mother. I mean, back then I thought *everyone* was. I was desperate to figure it out. But Tracie saw it."

"I always wondered if you'd see the dedication," she says. "I'm not sure why I did it. Just—to put something out in the world, in some ways it reminded me of you."

I have no idea why *that* is the thing that makes me burst into tears.

"Come here," she says, and I obey, letting her wrap her arms around me. She stays quiet as I continue to cry. It's as if a book opened, one I shoved onto a shelf so I could get through each day since Dad died, since I came here in constant fear this time was somehow limited. For the first time ever, it actually feels good to cry.

"Do you miss him?" she asks me softly.

I shrug. "I miss that it can't ever be okay. I kept thinking, like, one day we'd figure out how to relate to each other or he'd understand the things that were important to me. It was bad enough I didn't have a mom, but . . . not having a dad when he's living in the same house as me totally sucked."

She strokes my hair, still holding me close to her. I've wanted a moment like this since I was little. "I have something," she says.

"Something what?"

She jumps up and pulls me to my feet, leading me upstairs to her room. I sit on the bed while she digs around in the bottom dresser drawer, a place I never thought to look. Good thing I'm done with the spying thing. I'm freaking *awful* at it.

"You can open this." My mother flops down next to me and hands over an envelope. "If you want." It's unopened but yellowed with age, and it's addressed to Reece Malcolm at East 77th Street in New York. And even though I don't recognize the return address, the handwriting is like a ghost.

"Dad," I don't mean to, but say aloud. The envelope is thick, like there are photos inside of it. "Why didn't you ever open this?"

"I know what you're thinking," she says really quickly. "You have to believe it's not that I didn't care. It was so goddamn hard, kid. I didn't see a reason to torture myself."

I open the envelope, even though the act feels like walking into a museum and smashing something. The photos slide out right away, and I stare at them, because we weren't exactly the type of family who hung baby pictures all over. Also, to be fair, when you move a lot, photos are a huge pain because frames are fragile, and you get sick of putting stuff up on walls just to take it down.

Reece,
I hope you're doing okay and that by now you got into NYU like you hoped. I don't know if you wanted to hear from me or not but I thought maybe you'd like to hear how Devan is. She's great, and you can see from the pictures that she's the cutest kid I've ever seen. I think she looks a lot like you.

Good luck with everything, but I don't think you'll need it.

—Jeff

I blink back tears, because I don't want to cry over this. My mother's right. Despite everything, Dad was a good person. And I'd rather dwell on that than the sad parts I can't change.

"I used to be way cuter," I say so my mother will know I'm not up for another serious moment.

"Weren't we all." She takes the photos from me. "If you didn't peak as a child as far as cuteness goes, there's something wrong with you."

She walks back to her dresser and riffles through the box in the bottom drawer again. Finally she lugs it over to the bed and pulls out a few photos, which I realize are of her as a baby. "Bad news for you how alike we looked."

"Totally not bad news." I hold a couple of pictures side by side. "Can I keep these?"

"Of course."

"Can I keep the letter, too?"

She kisses my forehead. "Absolutely."

It's then that I notice two new photos on her nightstand. One is of Brad looking serious as he tends to the stove, and the other is of me. I'm in my *Merrily* costume—the stupid pajamas—and I must have been talking to someone because I look caught up in a moment of happiness.

I like how being happy looks on me. (Way more than I like the pajamas.)

"I, um, I have something to show you, too," I say to her, and race to my room to retrieve my notebook before I can stop myself. My mother sits down on my bed with it. Probably I should be terrified or embarrassed or some kind of hybrid combo but I just sit down right next to her.

"I'm impressed," she says. "I'm hard to Google."

"Tell me about it."

"Next time you want to know something," she says, leaning over to my desk and grabbing a pen, "just ask. I promise I'll tell you, whatever it is. Deal?"

"Deal." I laugh as she starts scribbling onto the list. "What are you doing?"

"Don't worry," she says with a grin. "I'm making it better."

Things I know about Reece Malcolm

A list originally by Devan Malcolm, updated by Reece Malcolm

1. She graduated from New York University ten years ago with a GPA marred only by a B in Algebra. Who expects writers to take math anyway?

2. She lives in ~~or near Los Angeles (even the Internet can't confirm)~~ Studio City, California, with her vaguely irritating boyfriend and hardly irritating at all excepting the amount of time it takes her to get ready to go anywhere daughter.

3. ~~Since her first novel (Destruction) was released nine years ago she's always had at least one book on the New York Times bestseller list.~~ Her latest book will be dedicated to the same person as her first. And this time, that person will get to see it right away.

4. She likes strong coffee and bourbon, the only personal details she gave in a rare interview with The Daily Beast. A fact that will make the next several months excruciating for her and all around her.

5. She's my mother. And one day will even be amazing at it.

Acknowledgments

My editor, Stacy Cantor Abrams, understood the book I was trying to write better than I thought another person could. Thank you for your hard work helping me get it to where it needed to be.

Thanks also to amazing assistant editor Alycia Tornetta for your insight and enthusiasm, publicity dream team Heather Riccio and Misa Ramirez for your tireless work, and everyone at Entangled.

Thank you to my agent, Kate Schafer Testerman, for believing in this story for a very, very long time.

A huge and hearty thank you to Meghan Deans, friend and critique partner extraordinaire. This book couldn't have become what it is without your support.

Thank you times one billion to early *early* readers: Sharon Gorman, Chelsea Jupin, Liz Kies, and Christie Baugher. Remember when we discussed this book on LiveJournal? (No, me neither. Never.)

Thank you to Rochelle Hartson for distracting me with *America's Next Top Model*, to Sarah Skilton for unstoppable optimism, to Courtney Summers for the best use of Twitter DMs, to Brandy Colbert for keeping me sane, to Sara Zarr for your infinite wisdom, to Stephanie Perkins for the phone pep talks, and to Nick Weber for knowing—when I was at my lowest—to ask me *What Would Leslie Knope Do?*

Thank you to Hope Larson for general awesomeness, for ice cream, and especially for hosting Writing Night, which kept me on track on a weekly basis (even when I didn't think I could be).

Thank you to cheerleaders and note-givers and support squad: Kristen Kittscher, Trish Doller, Kayla Cagan, Carrie Harris, Jasmine Guillory, Kevin Fanning, Siobhan Vivian, Lindsay Ribar, Andrea Robinson, Sara Beitia.

Despite my geekiness where it's concerned, I needed help with some *Merrily We Roll Along* specifics, so thank you: Sylvia Stoddard for infinite knowledge and opinions; the cast and crew of The Chance Theater's production, especially director Oanh Nguyen and killer Mary Flynn, Amie Bjorklund; and the person who taped the 2002 Kennedy Center production—you are a true hero.

Thank you to my cover team: photographer Jessie Weinberg, model Cassandra Morris, P.A. Connie Shin, and designer Emmett Kenny.

And, lastly, thank you to my parents for never discouraging me from being weird.

Get tangled up in our Entangled Teen titles...

***My Super Sweet Sixteenth Century* by Rachel Harris**

The last thing Cat Crawford wants for her sixteenth birthday is an extravagant trip to Florence, Italy. But when her curiosity leads her to a gypsy tent, she exits . . . right into Renaissance Firenze. Cat joins up with her ancestors and soon falls for the gorgeous Lorenzo. Can she find her way back to modern times before her Italian adventure turns into an Italian forever?

***Conjure* by Lea Nolan**

Sixteen-year-old twins Emma and Jack Guthrie hope for a little summer adventure when they find an eighteenth-century message in a bottle revealing a hidden pirate treasure. Will they be able to set things right before it's too late?

***Pretty Amy* by Lisa Burstein**

When their dates stand them up for prom, Amy, along with the beautiful Lila and uber-cool Cassie, take matters into their own hands—earning them a night in jail. With Lila and Cassie parentally banned, Amy feels like she has nothing—like she *is* nothing. Navigating unlikely alliances and two very different boys, Amy finds that maybe getting a life only happens once you think your life is over.